THE RELUCTANT ASSASSIN

BOOK ONE
OF
THE RELUCTANT ASSASSIN
A HUNDRED HALLS NOVEL

THOMAS K. CARPENTER

The Reluctant Assassin

Book One of The Reluctant Assassin

A Hundred Halls Novel

by Thomas K. Carpenter

Published by Black Moon Books

Cover design by Ravven
www.ravven.com

Discover other titles by this author on:
www.thomaskcarpenter.com

ISBN-13: 978-1727065930
ISBN-10: 172706593X

Other Hundred Halls Novels

This book is dedicated to Rachel

THE
RELUCTANT
ASSASSIN

Chapter One
Tenth Ward, September 2013
He wasn't a commando

After spending three days surviving the Merlin Trials—the grueling entrance exams to the Hundred Halls—Zayn Carter was ready for anything the Academy of the Subtle Arts could throw at him: disarming magical traps, sneaking through minefields, or escaping from murderous manticores—even a mage duel using only the Five Elements. Zayn was ready for anything...anything except what actually happened.

Zayn and twenty-nine of his fellow first years—including his cousin Keelan—stood in two uneven rows in an empty Wizard's Coffee while Carron Allgood paced before them in his heavy brown duster, slamming his claw-ended staff on the tile floor every other step for emphasis.

The mage was not an unfamiliar figure to Zayn, as he'd been coming to his hometown of Varna, Alabama, for as long as he could remember to recruit mages for the Hundred Halls, the only magical university in the world. What was unfamiliar was the level of anger directed at them.

"Let me ask again," said Allgood in a growling tone, "who the idiot was that used faez when I explicitly told you that there will be no magic today. Period."

Everyone glanced around, hoping that someone might admit it, and release the tension from the room. Faez was the raw stuff of magic that mages molded into spells. Any mage with the ability to get into the Halls could sense its nearby use. A slight metallic scent tickled the back of Zayn's tongue. It hadn't been a lot, but it'd been enough to get Allgood's notice.

"If no one's going to fess up, then I'll have to pick whoever I think it might be," said Allgood, glowering at them. His face had more nicks and scars than a blind man's cane.

As he walked by, hot breath steaming from his nose, Zayn sucked in his gut, hoping to avoid his attention. The instructor walked past, and a sense of relief flooded into Zayn. He wasn't sure who'd used magic, but he knew it hadn't been him.

Allgood stopped at a spot on the end of the line to Zayn's right and shoved his finger into someone's chest. "You're the maggot that can't listen, aren't you?"

Zayn leaned forward, only to see that it was his cousin, Keelan, whom Allgood had picked. Zayn and his cousin looked a lot alike, same tight Afro, same wide smile, except Keelan's skin was a little lighter, more cocoa than black coffee.

Before Zayn could control his mouth, he blurted out, "It wasn't him."

Allgood was in Zayn's face so fast, it felt like he'd teleported.

"Did I ask anyone to tell me who they thought it was? No. Because I don't care. I wanted to hear one thing and one thing only, for someone to admit that they listen like a log," said Allgood.

Zayn's gut twisted and his heartbeat pounded in his ears as Allgood focused his attention on him. He could sense him making a decision, and he didn't think it would be good.

"So tell me...Zayn."

Zayn nodded.

"Why do you think you're so smart that you know it wasn't him?" asked Allgood.

"Because that's my cousin, and I know what his faez smells like," said Zayn.

Allgood snorted. "Knows what his faez smells like. Doesn't that sound like a load of bull. I think it was *you* that did it, and you just felt bad when it was your own flesh and blood that got blamed."

He put his calloused hand on Zayn's shoulder. It felt like a truck backing onto him. "Everyone, this is Zayn. Zayn doesn't know how to listen. Don't be like Zayn." He patted his shoulder twice. "Is that right?"

Zayn responded, "Yes, Professor."

This set Allgood off again. "Professor? I'm not a damn professor. I do not profess. And I do not teach. I mold and shape. So you'd better learn to be malleable. But since I'm not a total monster, and so you assholes don't start calling me Mr. Allgood, or some crap like that, you can call me Instructor, or Instructor Allgood. Got it? Good."

He surveyed the room before pointing at Zayn again. "Since you think you know better than everyone else, I'm going to make this a little harder on you." He snapped his fingers. "Remove your clothes, everything but your underwear, assuming you're wearing any."

"Wha...?" Zayn started to say before he remembered what talking out of turn got him.

"It appears Mr. Carter is learning," said Instructor Allgood.

The other first years glanced at him, while keeping their eyes generally faced forward.

"Did I not enunciate enough for you?" asked Instructor Allgood, pointing his claw-ended staff at him.

Zayn pulled his shirt off and tossed it onto the nearest table. He caught a glimpse of his reflection in the window as he unbuttoned his jeans and shimmied out of them. His chest had never filled in like it had for Keelan, who could have played football in high school, so he felt ridiculous standing in the middle of a Wizard's Coffee in his boxers surrounded by his fellow first years.

He heard a few snorts of laughter, which judging by the instructor's expression was encouraged. It took all Zayn's self-control not to cross his arms. He tried to tell himself that this was no different than going swimming with the other kids behind the Castlewood trailer park, but his face betrayed him, growing so warm with embarrassment that it was hard to pay attention.

"Today we're going to learn a little something about each of you," said Instructor Allgood, taking up position at the front of the room. "Passing the Merlin Trials was quite an achievement, one that earned you a place in this hall. But magic is a tool. Even the student with the highest capacity for faez will not last long unless he learns to use this." He tapped on the side of his head while giving Zayn a side-eye. "So today, you're going to scurry out these doors on a mission. This is the tenth ward in Invictus, a moderately prosperous section of the city. A proper member of the Academy of the Subtle Arts can turn any difficult situation into a boon. So that's what I'm asking today. I want you to go out into the city and *bring back something of value.*

"Remember your challenge is that you cannot use magic. Not one iota. If I find out you even used a simple back scratching spell, you're going to wish you were back home with mommy and daddy."

Instructor Allgood glared at them for a long moment before pointing to a stack of papers on the table.

"These are the locations in the ward that you will stick to. So you're not teaming up, or falling all over each other, everyone gets their own area. So on your way out the door, grab one. Be back here at five p.m., and don't be late!"

There was a general push towards the stack of papers, while trying to stay as far away from Instructor Allgood as possible. Zayn lingered near the back, delaying the journey outside in his boxers for as long as possible.

The last few first years glanced back at him with smirks on their lips, except for a shorter Latino girl who looked on him with pity.

He hesitated at the door, with the sheet of paper in his fist. When he looked back at the instructor, he was studying him as if he were trying to read his mind.

"Go on," said the instructor, motioning towards the door.

He glanced back at his clothes draped over a chair.

"Don't worry. No one wants your clothes. We've got the shop all day. They'll be here when you get back, unless you'd like to give up now," said Instructor Allgood.

Zayn took a deep breath, opened the door, and wearing nothing but his boxers—and under explicit instructions not to use magic—walked into the city of sorcery.

Chapter Two
Tenth Ward, September 2013
The subtle arts of streaking

Zayn's sudden appearance brought the gaze of every passerby. He quickly checked his paper to find his destination only a few blocks away. He moved in that direction, swinging his arms in exaggeration, hoping it made him look like a speed-walker rather than a streaker, but it didn't help. He could feel every eye upon him, and it was almost like he wasn't wearing gray cotton boxers at all. He'd never really had that "accidentally went to school naked dream," but now he understood the terror of it.

When he stubbed his barefoot toe on the curb as he hurried across the street, it was almost a relief to feel pain. He'd practically run for two blocks. Zayn stopped on the corner, running his hand across his Afro as he took in his surroundings. There were a lot of places he'd expected to be on his first morning of training, but standing on the corner of Fifth and Morgana in his boxers was not one of them. Even his time working for the Goon back in Varna—an experience that came with big perks and bigger dangers—hadn't prepared him.

A woman in a blue tracksuit ran past giving him a

questioning stare and nearly collided with a businessman checking his messages. Zayn took a deep breath and rubbed his hands together.

"Let's take stock of our inventory," said Zayn as he patted his bare stomach. "We've got, let's see, one set of boxers, and... yeah, that's about it."

A kid on a bicycle gave him a funny look, but Zayn ignored him and focused on what he could control. And things could have been worse: it wasn't winter, or raining.

The buildings on the street made him feel small. The tallest building in Varna besides the water tower was the Lady's mansion, and no one went there unless they had to. Having spent the entirety of his seventeen years in a small town in Alabama without expectations that he would ever get to leave left him a little bewildered about what was available in the middle of a major city.

He didn't even know the proper etiquette for crossing the street, though it became clear pretty quickly that the only rule was "don't get run over," and even that was sketchy, as he watched an old woman with a cane smack a Ford Festival that got too close when she was on the crosswalk.

Across from him was a local park, the only thing remotely resembling a location from his home. He saw runners and people walking their pets, including an older lady with a long-haired cat on a leash.

Further out, he had a good sight line on the Spire at the center of the city. Zayn wasn't sure if he was twenty or fifty miles away, since the Spire could be seen from everywhere as it was twice as tall as the highest skyscraper. It was the central hub of the city, and in a way, of the Hundred Halls. While the Spire was the most important landmark in the city, Invictus was the most important city in the world, because it was the only one that taught people how to use magic.

Gondolas slid through the sky on invisible wires. Seeing one reminded him of his first day in Invictus, when he rode one with Keelan on their way to the Merlin trials. He'd stood in the exact center of the gondola so he wasn't forced to look out the window at the cavernous expanse beneath them.

But nothing about coming to the Hundred Halls had been normal. He was still a little surprised that he'd made it this far, given that so many aspiring mages failed, even ones that came from Varna.

Zayn knew that he was more prepared than most, since he'd been able to use magic without the danger of faez madness for his entire life. While faez was the raw stuff of magic, it was also inherently dangerous to humans unless they'd built up a tolerance or psychically connected themselves to a more experienced mage. This was how the Hundred Halls was set up, with each student pledging themselves to the patron of their hall, to teach and protect them from faez madness until they were older and experienced enough to operate on their own. Zayn's patron was Priyanka Sai, who ran the Academy of the Subtle Arts, the hall commonly called the Assassin's Guild.

Ever since he realized the only way to save his town—and his family—was to join the Hundred Halls, he'd dedicated himself to learning anything that might help him, including any spells that he could find, a difficult task in the middle of Alabama.

All that preparation wouldn't help him now, since he wasn't allowed to use magic to solve the problem. But he did have one thing that would help: growing up poor. If there was one thing his family knew how to do, it was how to repurpose junk into something useful.

Feeling less naked than he had a few minutes ago, Zayn went into the nearest alleyway and dumpster dived, producing a smorgasbord of potential answers. Standing in the middle of an oily puddle, Zayn reviewed his newly acquired belongings.

"Let's see, we have a couple of unread newspapers, the *Herald of the Halls*, whatever that is, a table leg, a traffic cone that looks like it's been chewed on by a bear, half a can of gold paint, a pair of sunglasses with no lenses, a roll of leftover green tape, and a plastic mop bucket with a crack running through the side. Great," he said, scratching the back of his head, "this should be easier than eating corn on the cob with chopsticks."

Zayn placed the items in a row. He moved them around like letters on a Scrabble bench, trying to conjure ideas from them. He had a lot of practice repurposing back in Varna, since their home was a couple of shipping containers stacked on top of each other. His family lovingly called it the Stack.

When an idea came to him, Zayn got right to work. He made an origami crown from the newspaper, something he'd learned from his younger siblings, the twins: Izzy and Max. Then he painted his dark skin, his boxers, the newspaper crown, and the table leg with the gold paint. Covering his face without damaging his eyes was the hard part, but he put tape over the lensless glasses to make them an eye guard as he sprayed.

He found a good spot in the park near a mermaid fountain. He set the bucket on the ground and made himself into the Statue of Liberty, holding the gold table leg like the torch.

Within a few minutes, a handful of change had been thrown into the bucket.

"Thank you," he said after the man, then remembered that he was supposed to be silent, and gave him a wink for good measure. A little later, an old woman wearing too much perfume with a gray cat on a leash threw a few coins at his feet. The hefty feline had long gray fur and marched like a bulldog.

The first few hours were relatively easy. Zayn was able to

keep his muscles absolutely still and the change came quickly, but as the day wore on, so did his muscles. By the afternoon, he could barely keep his arm up and had to switch hands frequently before the shaking hit.

Zayn was so lost in trying to tame his muscles, he didn't notice the ratty brown terrier until the hot stream of urine hit his leg.

"No! Bad dog!"

The terrier hurried away, but it was too late. Zayn moved to the fountain, splashing water on his leg to clean off the dog urine.

"I didn't realize those living statue assholes were allowed to move," said a rough voice from behind him.

"That must mean he's not one of them, which means this pretty little blue bucket is fair game," said a second voice.

Zayn glanced over his shoulder to find four young men around his age standing near his bucket. The second speaker, the one who'd put a claim on his money, had a patchy beard and was scrawny pale, as if he'd spent the last three years in his parents' basement. The other three were variations on the same, but they clearly thought of the fourth as their leader as they watched him squat down and rattle his hand around in the bucket as if he were fishing for minnows in a pond.

But Patchy was watching Zayn, waiting for a reaction. There was something about the guy that bothered Zayn, and not because he was about to rob him. He had the look of someone who was holding back a dangerous secret, one that he would gladly reveal if Zayn was willing to push back. Given that it was the city of sorcery, and that it had the highest concentration of supernatural creatures and mages in the world, Zayn felt it would be unwise to assume he was a normal human.

Not that four guys couldn't knock the crap out of him

with ease anyway, as he wasn't supposed to use magic for the challenge. But he couldn't stand giving up the money he'd earned and would need for whatever test this was, and he wouldn't put it past the Academy to be the ones behind this gang.

Letting his southern accent thicken his words, as there was no use hiding where he was from, Zayn said, "Maybe it's the paint I've been sniffing all day, but you boys look dumb enough to drown in a desert."

Within half a breath, they'd surrounded him. He heard the telltale click of a switchblade opening.

The guy with the patchy beard put his finger against Zayn's chest. "You might want to rethink your words, country boy."

The blade pressed against his side, leaving no doubt about the danger. There were a lot of things he could do in the situation, but running wasn't one of them because he'd come to the Hundred Halls to save his family from the Lady of Varna. But he had to do a lot of things before he could confront the Lady: the first thing on his task list was to convince a couple of fuzz-faced gang members not to put a switchblade deep into his guts.

Despite the precariousness of his situation, he wasn't "knocked a hornet's nest off a branch" kind of worried, maybe just the "big fat horsefly perched on his arm" kind. He'd been in worse situations. His Uncle Jesse's funeral came to mind, and in a way, the best part of that day were the bruises and the cracked ribs.

Chapter Three
Varna, October 2007
Even a bad day can always get worse

Zayn had never wanted to have his ribs kicked in by the Clovis brothers, but sometimes these things had a way of happening, especially when his cousin Keelan was involved. It didn't help that Keelan had just lost his dad, and while Uncle Jesse was a garbage person, you only got one father, and you had to make do with what you had.

His parents had sent him after Keelan when he disappeared from the trailer. Zayn was relieved it wasn't the middle of summer, since he was tromping through the Alabama forest.

The sound of a rock hitting metal echoed through the vine-choked trees, which meant that Keelan was nearby, but Zayn wasn't about to call out and chance him running again. It was bad enough that they were supposed to be at Uncle Jesse's funeral in an hour.

The woods, which stretched from the trailer park to the old plantation road, was the place people dumped their old junk to rot in the Alabama heat. Which meant that Keelan could be throwing rocks against just about anything. A couple of years ago they'd found an old wood-paneled station wagon with the windows still intact. They'd planned to come back the next day with slingshots and knock the windows out, but they could never find it again.

Luck was on his side today, and Zayn found Keelan in a patch of sunlight, side-arming rocks against a cluster of old metal barrels. The way the barrels absorbed some of the impact suggested they were half full of oil or some other waste material. Probably from the Varnation Garage.

Zayn watched his cousin for a moment before speaking. Keelan was a year younger, but already taller and wider in the shoulders. The high school football coach was already trying to recruit Keelan as a running back. People often confused them for brothers, though Keelan's skin was lighter like his father's. Jesse liked to say they were like two bullets in a chamber, firing off one after another, causing trouble.

But as close as they were, both socially and physically, Zayn knew they were different inside. And he knew that one day that might come between them.

"You pitch like a drunk falling over," said Zayn, leaning against a tree at the edge of the clearing.

Keelan turned around in his brown suit that Aunt Lydia had bought him with the donation from the Lady. It wasn't a Goodwill suit like Zayn's. They'd gone into Selma and picked it up from a store in the mall.

His eyes were puffy and red. Keelan could barely stand, making little correction steps and shaking his head as if he were having an argument.

"And you look like an ice zombie banged your mother," said Keelan, and though it was a joke he'd told a hundred times about Zayn's ice-blue eye color, this time it came out with a streak of meanness.

"Everyone's at the trailer," said Zayn. "And Doc said he can't wait forever to take us to the funeral home and back.

He's got a junk pickup at three."

"Tell them to leave without me," said Keelan, launching another rock. It went straight over the barrels, crashing into the trees.

"That would break your momma's heart, you know that," said Zayn. "And things are tough enough after her surgery."

With fists at his sides, Keelan said, "I don't know why we gotta go to his funeral. He got himself killed and now we gotta pay the price."

Keelan wiped his nose with the back of his coat jacket, which hung disheveled on his broad frame. His cousin looked like a person ripped apart and then put back together with safety pins and glue.

"I can go back and tell them I couldn't find you if that's what you want," said Zayn. "But you really want that on you? You know Aunt Lydia holds a grudge like a banker does gold. You know when she's making you pancakes, she'll pour you syrup and be all like, here's some syrup, son, you know I love you even though you didn't come to your daddy's funeral."

"But his body ain't in the damn casket," said Keelan, a thread of desperation in his voice. "We're gonna say our respects over an empty hole."

Zayn gave him the side eye. "You think that's gonna stop her?"

Keelan shook his head exhaustedly. "No. You're right. If I don't go, it'll be a lifetime of hearing about it. I don't think I could take that."

They walked back towards the trailer park. Keelan was quiet, and Zayn let him be that way. They passed a giant tangled web stretched between two trees with a purple-veined spider crouched at the top. They gave the web and spider a wide berth.

"I hate this damn place," said Keelan, glaring at the spider.

"Someday I'll leave it."

Zayn hushed his cousin. "Don't be stupid, you never know if she's listening."

Keelan raised his voice towards the spider. "What does it matter? *She* knows we all hate this place."

He raised his arm to throw the rock in his fist, but Zayn grabbed him around the wrist. "We got trouble enough for one day."

When they were far enough away from the web, Keelan muttered, "I do wanna leave."

"So do I," said Zayn, taking a speculative glance behind him. "But that ain't the way it works. Not unless you want to work for her, and then, you're even less free than you were before."

There was a strangled realization in Keelan's brown eyes, a little loose and off, as if he were a rat drowning at the bottom of a well, claws scraping at the smooth stone walls.

They came out of the woods near Route N, a quarter mile down from the trailer park, behind the Varnation Garage. Across the lonely road was the Clovis Diner. There were three trucks and five motorcycles in the gravel parking lot.

Keelan threw the stone in his hand against the brick wall of the garage. The impact made hardly any noise, but suddenly three of the Clovis boys were there.

The town of Varna was like any other town in Alabama. It had the Haves, the Have-Nots, and the ones trying to move from the second group to the first. The Clovis family were members of the last group, as the father was a deputy in the local police force. The Clovis boys had names, but nobody called them by those. He was thankful that Big Clovis wasn't there, but Mean, Rock, and Wheezer would be trouble enough. Mean was only a freshman running back at Varna High, but playing on the varsity squad.

"You two fairy lovers holding a dinner party in the woods?" asked Mean.

Zayn put his hand on Keelan's arm. "We're heading to his dad's funeral."

He hoped that was enough to defuse the situation, but Wheezer spat out a mouthful of brown tobacco juice and said, "Shit, son. You mean the Lady letting him have one after all that ruckus?"

"Shut up, Wheezer," said Mean. "If it's your daddy's funeral, why you out in the woods? What you hiding, fairy boys?"

"We ain't lying," said Zayn. "Just letting off a little steam, and we got lost on the way back."

Mean's forehead knotted. He glanced at his brothers. "I think you two are bullshitting me. And you know what they say about bullshitters."

Under his breath so only Keelan could hear, Zayn said, "You like to eat what we speak."

Normally this would have gotten a reaction out of Keelan—a smirk or a light snort—but he kept staring straight ahead at Mean as if he were waiting for the firing squad to get it over with.

"You got something to say?" Mean asked Zayn, to which he shook his head. "Anyway, as I was saying, you can't bullshit a bullshitter. Now, I don't know why you all dressed up in the middle of the forest, but I know you lying to me. The Lady don't give funerals to traitors. But since I don't know what you been up to, I think we should tell the Goon about that dumb bastard Keelan throwing a rock against his garage. The Goon probably not like that. And since the Goon is one of the Lady's favorites, maybe we gotta teach you a lesson for him."

Zayn checked with his cousin, who was dangerously quiet.

"Mean, please. I'm not lying. You can come with us.

Everyone's waiting at my Aunt Lydia's trailer."

As soon as he mentioned his Aunt Lydia, Mean's eyes lit up like a searchlight. He had a leering grin.

"That one-armed bitch? She was hot before the Lady took her arm, but I'd love to get a piece of that action now," said Mean.

For a brief moment, Zayn thought that Keelan wasn't going to react. He went calm, his body completely relaxing as if he were lying on a bed of soft grass. This confused the Clovis brothers too, as if they'd expected Keelan to act right away. But then Keelan shot out like an arrow at Mean. He caught him with a right hook under the chin, and the bigger kid went down.

Zayn didn't hesitate, throwing himself at Rock before he could get to his cousin. His fist connected with Rock's elbow, and then he lost track of the comings and goings of the fight, as he was outweighed and outnumbered.

When Zayn looked over next, Mean was on top of Keelan, pounding away at his face with two hammer-like fists. This sight was brief, as Wheezer kicked Zayn right in the gut, exploding the air from his lungs like a bellows.

Completely defenseless on the ground, Zayn thought things were going to get worse until he heard another voice. The Clovis brothers climbed off them and disappeared. Keelan ran off too, back into the woods, as Zayn wiped blood and gravel dust from his eyes.

He found himself looking into the face of the Goon, who was leaning against his garage in a straw cowboy hat. He was one of those people that either looked fifteen or fifty, never in between, and had stayed that way for as long as anyone had known him.

"That cousin of yours is gonna get you killed," said the Goon.

"His dad's dead," said Zayn, trying to rub the life back into his lower jaw.

"And his momma had her arm taken, all because they were stupid. The Lady is not cruel, but she does not brook with traitors," said the Goon. "And what the hell is picking a fight with boys that can whoop you gonna do about a dead father?"

"I don't know, I didn't start the fight," said Zayn.

"But you got yourself in the middle of it, just the same. Like I said, he's gonna get you killed. I've seen boys like that, and deep down inside they know there's only one end for them, and they be rushing headlong to get there," said the Goon.

"What should I have done then?" asked Zayn, realizing that his good pants were ripped at the seams on his right leg, and his good shirt had blood all over it.

"That's for you to figure out, but everybody wants something. Your cousin, he got what he wanted. So did the Clovis boys. What did you get out of it? A dumbassed beating?" asked the Goon.

"Why do you care?" asked Zayn.

"Because you're a smart boy, Zayn Carter," said the Goon.

"Keelan's smart too. He gets straight A's," said Zayn, a little bewildered that the Goon knew his name. It was like opening up a history book and finding your picture inside.

"I always liked your parents. Maceo and Sela. Smart in ways most people don't get." The Goon glanced over his shoulder as if he had somewhere to be. "If you ever want to work some odd jobs, make some extra money for your family—I know you could use it—come see me."

"I appreciate the offer, but no thank you," said Zayn.

"If you change your mind, the offer stands," said the Goon, who tipped his straw hat, and headed across the street towards the diner.

With Keelan fled back into the woods, Zayn dusted himself off and started the lonely walk back to the trailer park where his Aunt Lydia lived. He prepared a story about falling down the culvert when he was out looking for his cousin. He knew the adults wouldn't believe it, but they wouldn't say anything either. Zayn was busy thinking about what the Goon had said about the fight, and how everyone had gotten something out of it but him.

He hated when someone pointed something out to him that he hadn't already figured out himself. But he wasn't too proud not to take his advice to heart, especially in Varna, where to be too stubborn was to court death herself.

Chapter Four
Tenth Ward, September 2013
How not to make friends and still influence people

The key to a good con was to make sure the mark was focused on anything but what you really wanted. This wasn't the best of circumstances for Zayn—painted gold and wearing nothing but his boxers—and he hadn't a lick of planning, but the Goon had told him more than once that he'd taken to improvisation like Coltrane did to jazz.

The tip of the switchblade pierced Zayn's side, letting a bead of blood form against his gold skin. Having survived a few beatings in his younger years, Zayn was acquainted with the looks one received before they started, and this gang of young men, only slightly older than him, would not hesitate to leave him bleeding against the mermaid fountain.

When Zayn opened his mouth again, he spoke to them as if they were acquaintances working out a business deal.

"I take it you fine gentlemen have never been noodling," he said.

Patchy frowned, eyes creasing with the decision: do we stab this guy or let him talk? His friends seemed more curious than angry, but they weren't the ones he had to convince.

"What the hell you talking about, country boy?" asked Patchy.

"Noodling is when you dive down into cool river waters, searching for a nice hole to shove your hand in," said Zayn, holding his hand up as a fist. This display brought tension but no action, yet.

When no one stabbed or punched him, he continued, "The goal to this seemingly inexplicable action is that sometimes, big river fish like to hide in these holes, waiting with their wide mouths for little fish to come rest, and when that moment comes, they snap down"—Zayn squeezed his fist for effect—"and that little fish joins the bones in the big fish's belly."

"Where you going with this, country boy? You think you're the big fish and we're the little fish?" asked Patchy.

"No," said Zayn, imbuing that word with warmth and support. "No, you are neither the big fish or the little fish. Like I said at the beginning, when you dive down to the bottom of the river, holding your breath like the world gonna end, and shove your fist into a hole, you're hoping there's a big fish in that hole and that you shove your fist right down its gullet."

Zayn wiggled his arm upward, and they all looked a little mortified by this idea.

"Once the fish is safely ensconced on your arm, you drag it out and swim up to your boat, throwing the fish inside. It's the fastest way to catch a big fish," said Zayn.

"What the hell does this have to do with anything? If you think this is going to keep us from taking your money, you got another thing coming," said Patchy.

Despite his insides tumbling over themselves, Zayn kept a calm face. His fist still hung in the air, and Patchy gave it a tentative glance, expecting something to happen.

"But sometimes," said Zayn, letting the amusement in his voice dry out as if it'd been baked for a hundred days in the summer sun, "when the noodler shoves his fist into one of them hidey-holes, he finds a big ol' Hoss. The kind of fish that a noodler likes to tell stories about. And this Hoss, he's got himself burrowed into the bottom of that river like a tick on a terrier, and he clamps down on that fist as if his life depends on it, 'cause it does. That's when the real battle starts, because once the noodler knows he got a Hoss, he tries to pull his arm out, but the fish don't care. He holds on." Zayn shook his arm as if the battle were happening before their eyes, transfixing them. "If the fisherman gets his arm out, he lives. If he don't, and the air runs out, well, shouldn't have been sticking his fist in random holes."

It took all of a three count for Patchy to make the connection. Zayn was sure he could have counted it out from the moment he finished to when Patchy's eyes widened with anger.

"You think you can scare me with your stupid story," said Patchy as he marched back to the blue bucket and dumped the money on the ground. While keeping his eyes on Zayn, Patchy told his guys, "Pick this up. At first, I was just planning on taking a toll for you working in the Glaucos Sixers territory without permission, but now I'm taking the whole thing. And if you ever come back...don't."

As Patchy marched away, one of the other gang members collected the dollar bills and change on the ground. Then the last one smashed the blue plastic bucket with his boot until it was in pieces.

The cut on Zayn's side was still bleeding, so he washed it off in the fountain before picking up the broken bucket and throwing it and the gold table leg in a trash can. A scrolling ticker feed on a building across from the park showed it was nearly five o'clock, which meant he had to head back to the Wizard's Coffee with the rest of the first years.

Zayn started walking back, stripped down to his boxers and painted gold, but no one gave him more than an idle glance this time as if this were less unusual than his earlier streaking.

Without everyone focused on him, he thought back to something the Goon had said to him many years ago about how everyone wants something. Patchy and his gang had wanted his money, and if they'd taken it right away, they'd have left him without a thin dime to bring back to the Academy.

But Zayn had wanted something too. He'd wanted them to come closer and not pay attention to what his left hand had been doing.

Content that no one was watching, Zayn covertly opened his left hand, revealing a small plastic baggie containing a sparkly powder. The baggie looked like it'd once had a sticker on the side, but it'd been peeled off.

Bring back something of value, Zayn quietly mused to himself. Everyone got what they wanted, and maybe even some got what they deserved.

Chapter Five
Tenth Ward, September 2013
After a relaxing day in the park

Zayn was nearly the first to return to the closed Wizard's Coffee. His father the former high school teacher liked to say on time was late, as it showed a careless attitude with deadlines. But Zayn had learned that early was the best when there was information to be gleaned.

Despite what Instructor Allgood had said, his clothes were nowhere to be found, which didn't seem so bad considering he was covered in gold paint anyway. Zayn might have asked the instructor, but he wasn't around, and neither was Keelan, so he stayed in the corner and watched his fellow first years.

He studied them carefully, examining the items they'd collected, or how they were dressed and moved. A massive guy with broad shoulders and a guffaw of a laugh held a couple of dog-eared romance novels it looked like he'd swiped from a used bookstore. Despite his size, he moved with an efficient grace, and he spoke to the other first years with a cheerful expression that would have made a politician proud.

The Latino girl who'd looked at him with pity stayed mostly to herself and spoke Spanish back to anyone that tried to engage with her.

Around the time Keelan showed up, so did the instructor, who quickly organized them in a line.

"Now that everyone is here we can head to the Hold. Keep whatever you found in the ward—we'll take a look at it later, and find out what you're made of." He slapped his staff against the ground again. "No talking. Pay attention. Keep up."

Before anyone could move a muscle, he went into the back of the coffee shop. They followed behind him like a trail of lost ducklings until they reached a basement door that went below the store.

Rather than lead into the basement, the stairs kept going into the darkness. At first the walls were concrete, stained with leaking water, and then they turned to bedrock.

They marched downward for an hour until they came out into a cavern lit only by a floating ball of light above Instructor Allgood's head.

"The trail gets rougher as we go from here," he said, throwing a pair of sneakers to Zayn and another to a girl with silky black hair wearing crimson stiletto heels. She made no move towards the more functional shoes, staring back at him with a pleasant smile on her face.

The instructor shrugged. "Skylar Chu, right?" She nodded. "Not my problem if you break an ankle."

Zayn was intrigued by her silent defiance as he slipped the shoes on. They were uncomfortable to wear without socks, but better than walking across the rough cavern stone barefoot.

Vin, the big guy with the booming laugh, raised his hand until Carron noticed.

"What in Hades' hole? Did I give the impression that it was question time?" asked the instructor. "This is looking to be the worst incoming class of all time. Fine. What's your question? You look like the kind of asshole who won't be able to handle not having your hand held at every moment."

"Instructor, is this the Undercity?"

The instructor tilted his head as if he couldn't believe that was his question.

"What is your name?"

"Vincent Moretti, but I go by Vin."

Instructor Allgood ambled towards him, cracking the ball of his staff on the stone as he walked. Despite his size, Vin seemed to shrink until he was smaller than their instructor. He rested the claw end of the staff on Vin's chest.

"Well, Vincent. It takes a real genius to figure out that after walking down stairs for the last hour that we're in the Undercity." Allgood turned to the rest of them. "I swear to god, if the rest of you are this dumb, I'll slit all your throats in your sleep."

The journey continued in absolute silence, which at first didn't seem odd until Zayn remembered Skylar's four-inch heels. Her shoes were a minor miracle for two reasons: the first was that the stone floor was jaggedly uneven and filled with ankle-breaking scree, and the second was that the heels made no noise on the stone.

She strode across the stone as if it were a ballroom floor, unless someone was near her; then she would artfully stumble, requiring a steadying hand from a fellow student. She picked at least three pockets during that time.

They stopped before a stone wall with a runed archway cut into it. Instructor Allgood addressed them as they stood in a semicircle, his earlier anger tucked beneath a gruff mask.

"This is the only time you'll take this path into the Academy. We use this route to ensure the secrecy of our hall. Now that you are sworn to our patron, the other pathways will be available to you in the future," he said.

He tapped on the runes with his clawed staff, awakening

the archway until a swirling darkness appeared.

"In you go," he said.

One after another, the students in front of Zayn stepped into the archway, disappearing in a flash as if they'd been sucked into a black hole.

When it was his turn, Zayn hesitated.

"Hurry up," said Instructor Allgood.

When his foot touched the blackness, the world spun around him. Zayn had never ridden a rollercoaster, but he imagined it was like being strapped to one and forced to ride it for hours, even though the journey lasted a blink of an eye.

He landed on his knees. A pair of hands helped him up and pushed him towards a long trough that the other first years were bent over. He didn't have to wonder long what the trough was for, as the meager contents of his stomach hurled up, splattering into the stainless steel.

Older students wearing black robes loosely around their shoulders with street clothes beneath directed them into a large hall with vaulted ceilings. Tables had been pushed against the walls, clearing a spot in the center, where Zayn and his fellow first years were herded.

"Alright, maggots," said Instructor Allgood. "Make three equal lines. Now!"

In the ensuing chaos, Zayn ran into at least three people before he found a spot. Then it appeared they'd made four jagged lines, so everyone started talking over each other trying to condense it back to three. When they were finished, their instructor looked ready to break his staff in half and leave.

"I don't know how any of you idiots can expect to follow a spell book if you can't figure out simple instructions like *make three equal lines*," said Instructor Allgood.

He glowered at them and was revving himself into another volley of insults when a slight woman with smoky brown skin strolled into the room and put her hand on Carron's shoulder. He bottled his anger and respectfully moved to the side.

Zayn was intrigued. She moved like an elegant dancer approaching the stage, even though she was only wearing jeans and a skintight black shirt. She radiated danger, and when she spoke, he understood why.

"I am Priyanka Sai, your patron. It is within my hall that you shall train for the next five years." She glanced back towards Carron with a mischievous grin. "Assuming you can survive the first year of instruction. The Academy of the Subtle Arts. Some call us spies and diplomats. Others name us assassins. These are not unjust names, and inside these halls, wear them proudly. But from this day forward, you must become inscrutable to the world, a mystery without a key. Answer nothing about your time here, or I will hear about it, and that is the last thing you'll ever say.

"I have little more to speak with you about, because at this point in your training you are nothing. You don't have a clue of how the world works, or what we're trying to accomplish here. That will be the purview of Carron Allgood, your keeper and blacksmith, who, with the proper dedication on your part, will forge you into a proper tool, or discard you if he cannot.

"Before I swear you to my patronage, I have but one question, a question that you will need to answer before this year is out. If at this time, you do not think you can, then you will be given the opportunity to leave right now and never come back. But if you stay, know that this question will come, and you'd better be ready to answer it."

She paused, looking to each of them, studying them as if she could see inside their souls. When her gaze passed across Zayn, he felt naked, but something in him kept him from looking away, and before she moved on to the next student, he swore he detected the minutest twitch of her lip.

When she was finished surveying the group, she asked, "What will you do when you have to kill?

"If you cannot answer this question," she said, "leave the line, and one of the fifth years will take you back to the surface."

After a long minute, in which no one moved, Priyanka smiled. "Good. At least you've got that much spine. You're going to need it."

Chapter Six
The Hold, September 2013
To find a diamond in the rough you need a lot of coal

The Hold, they learned as the fifth years led them to another area in the complex, was the place the first-year students in the Academy of the Subtle Arts would call home during their first year. It was named as such because it resembled the belly of a great ship. A kitchen and dining area sat in the middle, with a separate classroom space on either side. The one side had blue sparring mats like Zayn had seen in the Varna martial arts studio, with Instructor Allgood's apartment right off that. The other side looked like a dance studio with mirrors and a massive closet. Zayn had seen no sign of the rooms in which they would be staying, but there were two sets of stairs heading up off the dining area.

The first years were organized in a long line, then one by one, each went into the dojo, where they showed what they'd found to Instructor Allgood and Patron Sai. He noted the items they carried, especially a few of the students that had returned with items of little or no value, which seemed odd until he thought about it, and since he had an inkling of what was to come, he formulated a plan based on that knowledge.

When it was finally his turn, the other twenty-nine first years waited in a long line with their hands behind their backs. A table along the wall held the treasures they had acquired during their challenge: bills held together with paperclips, stacks of change, a pink bicycle with a horn, a bowie knife, a bowling ball, and other assorted items.

As soon as he walked in, Instructor Allgood said, "You know, you look like somebody screwed an Oscar statue."

A round of snickers broke out. Already they saw him as a joke. He'd been foolish enough to speak up, and earned a trip into the city without his clothes. Now he had to show what he'd found, and he could see by their eyes, they expected nothing special.

The fifth year that had brought him in pushed Zayn towards Instructor Allgood, who was on the far end in his gray duster, leaning on a clawed staff. Priyanka Sai was standing near him, but watching the proceedings intently.

"Tell me, Zayn, why the hell did you paint yourself gold? Are you not taking this seriously?"

"I made myself into a gold version of the Statue of Liberty." He looked at his hands. "I left my crown and torch in the park."

A round of laughter, this time more sympathetic, traveled through his fellow first years. He caught a creasing of Priyanka's eyes, before her expression disappeared behind a mask.

"Well then, come here and show me what you got; otherwise, your clever idea wasn't worth shit," said Instructor Allgood.

As Zayn approached, he noticed one of the fifth years standing at a wipe board behind Instructor Allgood. Everyone's name was written on it with a number beside each name between one and ten. He took a quick glance at the numbers, cringing at some of the results, but guessing the reason for their lowness, which solidified his plan. He reached into his boxers for the baggie, receiving an audible gasp from the other students. He dumped the baggie into Instructor Allgood's calloused hand.

"What's this?" he asked.

"Drugs," said Zayn.

"Drugs?" Instructor Allgood asked, turning towards the students. "I didn't ask you to buy drugs. I asked you to bring back something of value. Are you dumber than a slug in a salt factory?"

It felt like he'd been shoved under a microscope and a millions eyes turned upon him.

"I got robbed," Zayn started, and he hesitated, expecting Instructor Allgood to interrupt, but he stared at Zayn as if he could read his thoughts. "When they took the money, I lifted this off them. They're a part of the Glaucos Sixers gang."

Instructor Allgood reached out and touched the dried blood on his side. "Got them close enough to take it?"

"Told them a dumb story, but they pricked me just the same," said Zayn, trying not to smile, but he couldn't help but let the corners of his lips curl up with pride.

Instructor Allgood opened the baggie and waved it in front of his nose. His focus went inward, but then he shook his head.

"This is a first," said Instructor Allgood, throwing the baggie to Priyanka. She gave him a narrow glance and waved the baggie before her nose, repeating the same inward focus.

"I didn't know this was possible." Zayn didn't know if she meant him or the drugs. The dangerous woman turned to him. "You lifted this from a couple of gang members in the tenth ward?"

"Yes, ma'am," he replied.

The corner of her exquisite mouth twitched with mirth. "I suppose I need to keep my eye on you." Priyanka nodded towards Instructor Allgood. "What do you think?"

The instructor ambled over to the fifth year and whispered in his ear, producing a wide-eyed response. The fifth year found the name Zayn Carter on the board and next to it wrote a "10." Zayn felt his heart hop around in his chest as he realized the next highest score was an "8," which had been Keelan's score.

"Alright, it appears we have our team captains. Zayn, Charla, Eddie, Keelan, Chen, Marcelo. Up front with me," said Instructor Allgood.

Zayn wished he could have maneuvered his cousin onto his team, but there was no way to coordinate their scores during the contest.

When the other captains didn't move fast enough, Instructor Allgood yelled, "When I say move, you move."

The other five students joined Zayn.

"Welcome to the Academy of the Subtle Arts, maggots," said Instructor Allgood. "But before you learn to be subtle, you have to learn to be crude. Except for some language and etiquette lessons with Instructor Pennywhistle, I will be your sole teacher, which means it is my word that passes you, and I will not tolerate mediocrity. If you cannot excel in every task that I give to you, then you will not be a member of this hall.

"Point two," he said, thrusting his finger into the air. "During the year, there will be a box of coins in my office. On each of these coins is one of your stupid names. By the end of the year, you have to retrieve the coin with your name on it, or you will not pass, point-blank, no matter how well you do otherwise. You may not take anyone else's coins, and you are free to attempt it at any time, even if I am not in the building."

Heads turned and eyes creased at the corners. There was a sense of anticipation about this challenge, but Zayn didn't think it'd be as easy as people thought, especially when he checked the faces of the fifth years, who smirked quietly in the back.

"Point three. You will be placed in teams. While the term assassin conjures the image of a lone specialist wreaking havoc upon their target, the truth is more complicated. If you are talented enough to graduate from the Academy, you will find that surviving the challenges of the real world takes a team. If you cannot learn to work in a team in your first year, then there is no hope for you and you will not graduate. Also, whoever the last-place team is at the moment will serve the other teams during all mealtimes, and clean up afterwards. If you don't want to be a kitchen steward, pay attention and excel.

"I'm not going to ask if you understand. It is up to you to figure it out, so learn to pay attention, it may save your life someday.

"Alright, Mr. Ten," said Instructor Allgood, "you get first pick. Each of you will get four choices."

A sea of eager faces looked back at him. The other captains were looking at the board, but Zayn watched the other first years. He already knew who he was going to pick and had an inkling of how poorly it was going to be received.

Zayn called out, "Portia Rodriguez."

One of the other captains to his right spoke, Eddie perhaps. "But she's only a four."

There were more than a few disdainful glares in his direction from the other first years. Many of them had expected to be picked first. He hoped this wouldn't make things more difficult during the school year, but he also didn't care.

When Zayn made no move to change his mind, the fifth year at the wipe board wrote her name beneath his. Portia joined him at the front while the others made their picks.

Portia had a plump figure that made her look fourteen. She looked bewildered at being picked first and mumbled a *gracias* in a thick Mexican accent before taking her position behind him.

When it came back to him, Zayn called out, "Vin Moretti."

"A damn three," said Eddie, shaking his head. "I love this guy."

Vin lumbered over to them. Like Portia, he looked a bit unsure of why he was chosen. Keelan gave him a hands spread questioning stare, but Zayn shook him off.

While the other picks were being made, Instructor Allgood pulled him aside. "You are aware that it's customary to pick the top scores for your team. In fact, it's more than customary, it's a wise choice, because this first test is usually a good measure of how a student will do. You're not trying to sabotage this, are you? I am aware of your initial reluctance at coming here and the constraints of being from Varna."

"I'm not sabotaging anything," said Zayn earnestly. "And I'm not reluctantly here."

"If so, then act like it," he said.

When it came time to make his fourth pick, he grimaced because he knew the reception it would receive.

"Skylar Chu."

"A two, he picked a damn two. Wonders will never cease," said Eddie.

As the other students shook their heads, Skylar Chu tiptoed over and joined them. She was on the verge of tears.

She whispered, "Thank you?"

The last pick came quickly, but before Zayn could say a name, Instructor Allgood stepped forward and said, "Since you're not taking this seriously, you don't get a last pick. One of the other teams can have an extra."

Zayn faced Instructor Allgood. "I *am* taking this seriously.

I should get a last pick since I had the top score."

"The evidence shows otherwise by your complete lack of judgment or common sense," said Instructor Allgood, gripping his staff so hard his knuckles cracked. "To me it looks like you're trying to throw this, and if that's what you want to do, I'll help you out. You and your team can have the storage room next to the kitchens to sleep rather than a real room."

Zayn stepped towards the instructor. "You asked me to bring back something of value and I did. Then you asked me to pick a team without stating the criteria that you thought I should be picking by. Now that I have, you're taking my last pick and giving us a storage closet to sleep in. This isn't right."

As soon as he said the last words, he knew he'd gone too far. The claw-ended staff hit Zayn around the midsection, throwing him across the room.

Though it seemed impossible that he could have moved that fast, Instructor Allgood was glowering over him as he slid into the wall. Zayn remained as still as possible, hoping to avoid further beatings.

Instructor Allgood addressed the group, "Let this be a lesson to everyone. I don't give a crap what you think. You're here to learn, not to have an opinion. On the rare occasions that your opinion matters, I will let you know, but until that point, *keep it to your damn self.*"

After the instructor dismissed the others and then promptly left, Zayn was alone in the dojo. He stared at the chalkboard for a while, especially at the low scores of his teammates, hoping he'd made the right evaluations about who he thought they were. If he was wrong, it was going to be a long year.

Chapter Seven
The Hold, September 2013
Realizing that gold paint covers bruises well

Carrying out a plan was one thing. Convincing the others involved that it made sense was a whole other thing.

Zayn limped to his new quarters, cringing every time he put his right foot down. He found the rest of his team staring into a storage room jammed with old tables, chairs, and kitchen equipment. The three sets of eyes regarded him with less than enthusiasm.

"You're probably wondering why I picked you," said Zayn, holding his side.

Vin stepped forward. "No, I'm wondering why you screwed us. If you'd let us be picked normally, we'd have been picked last, but we'd have been on a team with a chance. With only four, we're totally up a creek without a barn door."

Zayn blinked a few times, trying to process if Vin had meant to mix up his metaphors, before responding, "We would have been fine if Instructor Allgood hadn't taken our last pick."

"Don't be a *cabeza gruesa*," said Portia, her thick accent barely making her understood as she faced off with Vin. "He got highest score possible and he pick you, and now you ungrateful?"

"You're damn right I'm ungrateful. You heard Instructor Allgood, he doesn't want to be here, or something like that," said Vin.

Portia turned to Zayn. "Do you want to be here?"

"Yes," said Zayn.

She threw her arm in his direction while addressing Vin. "See! He said he wants to be here. I do not care what that instructor said. He picked us for his team, so I am on his side."

"That's because he picked you first!" said Vin.

Skylar crossed her arms. "Why did you pick us? Tell us, because nothing makes sense otherwise."

"I'll tell you if you answer why you brought back a handful of change when I saw you lift the wallets of at least three other students," said Zayn. "You could have brought back anything, but you purposely sandbagged."

Skylar blushed, put a hand to her chin. "I wouldn't do that, and I didn't steal anything."

"Same with you, Vin. You purposely antagonized Instructor Allgood, so he'd give you a low score. Plus you brought back a bunch of used books you can get for the change that Skylar stole."

Vin made a face, shaking his head.

"And I saw the way you talked to everyone, glad handling them like an experienced politician. If you can do that to your fellow students, you should have been able to navigate Allgood," said Zayn.

"What about her?" asked Vin, gesturing towards Portia. "She hasn't done anything." His forehead wrinkled. "And I didn't even know she spoke English until now."

Zayn held his hands out. "Exactly. She was playing on everyone's expectations. No one wants a teammate you can't talk to."

Portia glanced to the side with a sly grin, confirming what he'd just said.

"But you still haven't explained why we would do that," said Skylar.

"You did it so you'd get on a better team. If everyone gets judged correctly, then no one really has an advantage between the teams. But let's say your last pick is really a seven or eight, rather than the two they want you to think they are. Wouldn't that make a team stronger?" He paused. "Unless someone saw through the ruse and picked you anyway. The way I saw it, I was getting all the top students, until Instructor Allgood ruined it."

Vin glanced cagily at the others. "I'm not sure about that. Seems like a risky strategy, especially on the first day in the Hall."

Skylar opened her mouth to answer, then her head whipped to the right, looking into the cluttered storage room.

She said, "Does anyone know how to perform an exorcism?"

"What?" said everyone else.

Skylar pointed into the back of the room, where something luminous was hiding behind the clutter. It had the vague appearance of a human being, but something about the shape was off.

"Exorcism? That's for people possessed by demons. I think that's a ghost, which means you want a banishing," said Vin.

"That's not a ghost," said Portia. "We had one that haunted my father's restaurant. They don't put off light like that."

Everyone looked to Zayn. He held his hands up. "Don't look at me, we didn't have anything like that in Varna. It's just a boring piece of backwater Alabama."

That wasn't true by any means, but Zayn didn't want

any more questions about his past or why he'd come to the Hundred Halls. Portia gave him the side eye, as if she knew better, but she was kind enough not to call him out.

"It's gone," said Skylar.

"Yeah, I don't see it either," said Vin.

"We should really get this cleaned out," said Zayn. "I don't think any of us have slept in days, and we won't until we finish this."

"What about the glowy thing in the room?" asked Skylar.

"If it were dangerous, they wouldn't put us in here," said Zayn.

"Are you sure about that?" asked Vin.

"No," said Zayn, "but I'm not about to march up to Instructor Allgood and demand a new room now."

The threat of the instructor's wrath seemed to outweigh the threat of the thing in the room, so everyone got to work moving the old furniture out. Zayn's sore ribs made it hard to breathe and lifting anything heavy made him nauseous from the pain, but he'd caused his teammates enough problems, so he kept his mouth shut.

It took hours to empty the storage room. When they were done, they acquired cleaning supplies from the kitchen and scrubbed down every grimy surface. The back and forth motion was worse than lifting heavy desks. It felt like someone had left a half-dozen rusty staples in his side where Instructor Allgood had hit him with the staff.

By the time they finished it was late into the night. Instructor Allgood had promised them an early morning, so everyone collapsed on their beds. Skylar was asleep first, and snored like a chainsaw.

Try as he might, Zayn couldn't fall asleep. He tossed and turned for hours, trying to find a different position that would help him doze, but he'd been thinking about the Hundred Halls for years, and now that he was here, his thoughts and dreams were swirling in his head like a fretful whirlwind. He had so much to learn, so many things to do, and he was dying to get started.

Chapter Eight
The Hold, October 2013
Learning how to foul up his words

Classes for the first few months were relentless. Zayn and his fellow first years stumbled from lesson to lesson, trying to keep up with everything the instructors were throwing at them. They had kickboxing lessons for three hours every morning, a list of spells they had to memorize and demonstrate each afternoon, and other assorted tasks given by Instructor Allgood with the kind of glee reserved for sadistic headsmen. All this Zayn and his team had to do while keeping up with the chores they'd earned from being the bottom team. But despite the pace, Zayn loved it.

When they found out they'd be skipping kickboxing with Instructor Allgood that morning and getting another lesson from Instructor Pennywhistle, everyone was excited. Not only because their legs were so tight they could be used to launch rocks like a catapult, but because everyone loved classes with Instructor Pennywhistle.

When Pennywhistle sauntered in the room everyone put away their phones and sat up. She dressed and moved like a 1950s movie star with a tight black skirt and kitten-soft aqua sweater. Her skin was like pale milk and appeared so supple that she would bruise merely from being touched. The way everyone stopped what they were doing to stare at her entrance each time they had class had started the rumor that she had succubus genes.

"Good evening," she said with a grin, exposing perfect, pearly white teeth. "While you still serve and eat dinner like a bunch of savages, we're moving on to a new lesson. Tonight we shall work on those disgusting accents that are fouling up your words."

"But I don't have an accent where I'm from," said Charla, leaning into her Southern twang and winking at the class.

Instructor Pennywhistle approached Charla's table. There was a sparkle in her eye that always made Zayn feel like she was the wolf dressed up like the grandmother in Red Riding Hood.

"My dear Charla," said Instructor Pennywhistle, "you don't have an accent. You have a sign around your neck every time you speak that says 'I'm an uncultured buffoon who shouldn't be trusted to pour water and is probably racist.'"

The class burst into laughter. Charla's face grew bright red.

"I wouldn't laugh. The rest of you are no better," said Instructor Pennywhistle, wandering to another table. "When our dear Eddie Lynn speaks, what do you all think?"

Someone shouted from the back, "He's an asshole."

True to form, he started to rise from his chair as if he were going to start a fight, but Instructor Pennywhistle placed her hand on his shoulder, keeping him seated.

Next she placed her hand over Portia's head.

"Zayn. What do you think of Portia's accent? What does it tell you?"

His mouth went dry. "I don't know."

"Of course you do," she replied, then turned her head towards the class. "If we cannot be honest with each other, no matter how much it hurts, we cannot improve. So, Mister Carter, what does Portia's accent say to you, a young man from the South."

The way Portia was looking at him made him feel about two inches tall.

He closed his eyes as he said, "That's she's probably a part of a gang or something."

"And what if it were more Spanish sounding?" she asked.

"Sexier," said Zayn, peeking with one eye.

"I'm not here to change society's opinion of what *your* accent means to them. Neither should you care, because those accents, in time, will become a tool. But before you can use them as a tool, you must build up the muscles in your mouth. Your whole life, you've been speaking one way, and your mouth, tongue, and lips are trained to that way. Tonight we're going to start working on the muscles that you're not using with some articulation exercises. I want you to start by touching the bottoms and tops of your teeth with the tip of your tongue like this."

Instructor Pennywhistle extended her neck and ran her tongue along her top and bottom teeth.

"Instructor Pennywhistle," said Marla, a dark-haired girl from Keelan's team. "Isn't there a spell that can do this? Make us talk without an accent, or in another language?"

"There *are* spells that can quickly give you the knowledge necessary to communicate in another language," she said. "But what you must learn is how to convince someone that you are *from* that country, and not only that country, but a specific region, maybe even a particular town and class level. For example, since we have three students from the South, can you hear the differences between them?"

"Yeah," said Eddie. "Charla's the rich girl and the other two are poor as pisswater."

"Thank you, Eddie, for once again proving the point about your accent," said Instructor Pennywhistle.

The corners of his eyes creased as he tried to figure out if he'd been insulted while the rest of the class chuckled behind their cupped hands. He opened his mouth to say something, but hunched his head instead. A word from Instructor Pennywhistle, and Eddie would be breathing from a straw during the next lesson in the dojo.

The class settled into mouth muscle exercises. Instructor Pennywhistle gave them a list of them to practice three times a day for at least an hour. Zayn didn't know where they were going to manufacture this time, except by cutting out more sleep.

It was nearing the end of class when a piercing scream froze everyone in their tracks. Everyone's head turned towards the door to Instructor Allgood's room, which was now open. The screams were coming from inside.

The class hurried towards the door, but no one went in. Adrian Parker, a guy from Charla's team, was lying on the ground with his eyes wide open. The screams were not coming from him, but an owl figurine on the table next to the box of named coins.

"Oh, god," said Marla, pointing at Adrian. "His skin looks like it's boiling."

"Back away, everyone," said Instructor Pennywhistle.

She made a few rapid gestures, so quick and precise like a surgeon, completely antithetical to her demeanor, that Zayn realized the calm persona of Instructor Pennywhistle was merely a front.

Sparks exploded around the doorframe when she finished the spell, eliciting cries of surprise from everyone.

"Hand me a staff," she said, snapping her fingers.

Someone grabbed a staff from the rack of weapons. She hooked the fallen student's leg and dragged him out of the room. It took her three spells to get his skin to stop boiling. When she was finished, she pulled a whistle from her pocket and blew it. No sound came out.

A minute later, a couple of fifth years appeared with a stretcher. Instructor Pennywhistle helped them load Adrian onto it, and then they headed towards the portal.

When they were gone, Instructor Pennywhistle turned towards them, a somber expression on her face.

"If you were wondering why we have taught you few spells so far, this should be your answer. Knowing a spell and knowing how and when to use it are two different things. That stupid fool tried to put an undetectable charm on himself, thinking that would be enough to bypass Instructor Allgood's traps. Despite the reputation of our hall, we pride ourselves on not wasting our students carelessly like the other majors."

Charla looked almost gray as she held a hand to her mouth. "Will Adrian be okay?"

"No. We'll never see him again. The only thing that kept him from dying in there was that I was here to pull him out. If he's lucky he might live a somewhat normal life, though I suspect he'll never have the same sense of touch he had before. Pity for his love life." She frowned. "Everyone back to your chairs. I have one more thing for you, before you can return to your rooms and practice your articulation exercises."

Instructor Pennywhistle handed out books to everyone. Each was a different shape and size.

Zayn's said Jamaican Patois.

"You wanted a spell that will help you speak a language," said Instructor Pennywhistle. "Well, here it is. These were made by Arcanium Hall. They are not easy to come by, nor are they cheap."

The inside of the book had no words, only arcane scribbles and symbols.

"How do we cast the spell?" asked Keelan.

"You don't cast it. You eat it. *Bon appétit.*"

"Brazilian Portuguese," said Eddie in a raised voice. "What the hell is this shit?"

Portia had a look of quiet victory on her face.

Vin was the first to eat his book, shoving the edge of the binding into his mouth. Miraculously, the book morphed as he crammed it past his teeth.

When he was finished, confusion passed across his face like a storm cloud until he said, "*Neurobil nič?*" He slapped his hand on the table. "I guess it worked."

The rest of the room devoured their books, laughing and speaking in a variety of languages, while Zayn couldn't get the image of Adrian's skin boiling out of his head. No one else seemed bothered by the fact that one of their fellow students had nearly died. It wasn't that Zayn hadn't expected it. People died in the Hundred Halls all the time. Magic was dangerous. But seeing it nearly happen reminded him of the stakes.

"Is something wrong, Mr. Carter?" said Instructor Pennywhistle.

He looked around, finding himself nearly alone. His face flushed from her nearness.

"Nothing wrong," he said. "Just a little daydreaming, I guess. Between Academy work and keeping up with the kitchen duties, I'm not getting much time for sleep."

"You're not learning anything while you're sleeping," she said.

"I'm not learning anything in the kitchen either," he said, catching himself when she raised an eyebrow. "I'm sorry. That was inappropriate."

She placed a hand on his arm. If he thought his face had been warm before, now it was a raging fire. It was hard to piece together two consecutive thoughts without veering off into wild fantasies.

"If you feel it's too much here, you can always return to Varna," she said.

The heady attraction he was experiencing blew out of his mind the moment she made her suggestion. "I'm not leaving. I came here to succeed."

"Are you absolutely sure? Because the circumstances of your coming here leaves a lot of questions." She sighed, glancing towards the door. "Look, all instructors are fully aware of the peculiar aspects of Varna. We were all briefed about what happened during the Ceremony and how you were chosen."

"I know what it looks like," he said, "but I swear I want to be here."

"Part of me wants to believe that. While your class work has been exemplary, the incident during the team choosing still lingers in everyone's mind. You are a contradiction, Mr. Carter. But know that if you are not fully committed to the Academy, it will not go well for you."

"I understand," he said.

"Good," she said, though her eyes said otherwise as she slipped away.

Zayn rubbed the binding of his book and thought about his family. It'd only been two months and already it was hard to picture them in his head. While he was happy about coming to the Academy, and all he was learning, he missed them and wondered what they were doing right then. He could almost hear Imani laughing as she tormented the twins in her lion costume, and the sounds of Neveah's pots clattering across the stove. He missed listening to the patient scribble of Sela's pencil across architectural drawings, or the smell of paint from Maceo's brush.

He hoped his family would one day understand why he'd chosen the path he had. He couldn't ever tell them—it would put them in too much danger—but he wished things were different, especially after what had happened at the Ceremony.

Chapter Nine
The Lady's Mansion, August 2013
Ceremony night

On a rise at the center of Varna, a plantation house stood tall and strong, a white building at the end of two rows of towering oaks. Zayn hated the Lady's plantation. He hated the way it welcomed them in like a greedy mouth, gobbling up the town in its vast belly. Sure, it spit them out at the end, but he always felt a little more different at the end of Ceremony, like he was losing part of himself each time. It was safer to hate the house, rather than those that resided within, because the alternative led down roads he wasn't ready to walk. But he hated it just the same.

He found Keelan sitting on the steps leading up to the house. Keelan was smiling and greeting people as they went by, but Zayn saw the tension in him. He looked like a bowstring pulled taut.

"You missed a delicious dessert," said Keelan with a smile on his lips as his knees bounced. "Man, Neveah can cook."

Zayn moved close and spoke under his breath. "You're going to do it, aren't you?"

Keelan looked away. "What are you talking about?"

"I saw your spell books," said Zayn. "You want to get picked."

Keelan rubbed the top of his knees with both hands, rocking as he did. "You've got your family, your art school. I've got nothing."

"We're your family. You don't want this. This"—he motioned with his eyes—"isn't what you want, you know that."

"Easy for you to say," said Keelan, his face screwing up with anger. "I'm stuck here, in this prison. I'll go mad if I don't have something to do, some purpose."

Zayn whispered as loud as he dared, "A prison is right, and if you do this, you'll be one of the guards."

"Better than a prisoner," said Keelan, defiantly.

Zayn threw himself onto the step next to his cousin and leaned his head close. "If you want, we can get out of town for a while. If we save the substance, stretch it out, we can spend a few months elsewhere. Or we can get some from the Goon, he keeps extra around for trade. Others have done it. It's not forbidden. Come on, Keelan, don't do this."

"Then come with me," said Keelan. "If she knew what you could do, she'd pick you in a heartbeat."

"It's not that easy, Keelan. People die all the time. The last two years both students didn't come back. What would that do to your mom?" asked Zayn.

"She supports me," said Keelan, lips squeezed tight. "And I know it's risky, but so is living here. You can't tell me that you never wanted to join the Hundred Halls?"

Zayn shoved his hands between his knees. "That's not the point. It'll change you."

"I'm sorry, Zayn. You've been like my brother, but I have to do this," he said.

Before Zayn could reply, a Watcher appeared before them. Zayn was suddenly aware the lawn was empty, and they were the last to enter the antebellum plantation house.

"It's time," said the Watcher.

There was something creepy about the way she spoke, as if an alien being were using her voice, making it vibrate slightly, like the tremor of a fly landing on a silken strand.

Zayn scurried up the steps with Keelan right behind. Inside, a grand staircase covered in red carpet swept towards the second floor. Zayn had heard from his mother that the Lady had patterned the interior of her home on the Palace of Versailles in France, and though it was not as large of a structure, the amount of gilding and white marble was astounding.

He was going to say something to his cousin as he entered, but another Watcher directed them towards the side of the room. Before they'd turned seventeen, they'd always attended the Ceremony with the rest of their family, but since they were eligible for the Hundred Halls, they were given a special spot near the front.

The Ceremony was held in the Grand Ballroom. Not everyone in town had to attend—some like the Goon had special arrangements and those that were older were given permission to miss—but a majority of Varna was seated on white metal folding chairs. A silence not even found at Sunday services prevailed; even the babies were unnaturally quiet.

All young men and women between the ages of seventeen and nineteen stood in rows before the dais. Zayn knew everyone there, since the entire graduating class of Varna high school for the last three years was in attendance.

Craning his neck, Zayn found where his family was sitting, all the way in back by the doors. He couldn't find Aunt Lydia, though he knew she had to be somewhere in the room.

A single bell tone announced the beginning of the Ceremony.

The Speaker, an older blonde woman wearing a white pantsuit, whose name had been swallowed by time in her role for the Lady, stepped onto the dais. Her wrinkles had been smoothed away by sorcery.

"Evening, Varna," said the Speaker in a cultured Southern accent. "Her Ladyship bids you a warm greeting, and good fortune on Ceremony night. As always, it is a time for coming together and for community. There is nothing better in this world than spending time with your friends and family. But her Ladyship also knows that in this day and age, everyone is busy, so we will, as has been customary these last few years, get right to the doing."

A low chuckle came from the older folks, the ones in her favor who sat in the front rows. In the past, the Ceremony had been full of pomp and circumstance, and had gone on through the night until dawn.

The Speaker pulled out a cell phone and read from her screen.

"First, we would like to acknowledge the blessed unions that have occurred this year, and offer a gift. Would Mister and Missus Davis please come up."

The newlyweds, Wesley and Vivian Davis, marched up hand in hand and accepted an ornate wooden box from a Watcher who'd come up from the back. The Davises babbled their thanks to the Speaker, before scurrying back to their spots with anxious expressions.

The Speaker lifted her chin to speak again, but a child in back, no older than two or three, started bawling, pulling away from her mother. Zayn didn't know the family, but had seen them at the Ceremony before. The child made a demand for a Mr. Charlie, which Zayn assumed was a favorite toy, but the parents pleaded desperately for Sissy to be quiet. Everyone in the room waited on knife edge. Some glanced covertly at the offending family, but Zayn watched the Speaker, whose exterior slowly hardened as the interruption went on.

A pair of Watchers collected the father while the mother was trying unsuccessfully to muffle the child with her hand. The father, a puffy middle-aged guy who ran the local hardware store, was led into a side room. The high-pitched scream that followed was like nails on a chalkboard. Zayn had no idea what they were doing to the poor man, but his mind filled in the details, suggesting lashes with barbed wire, or stabs from an electric prod.

A few moments later the father stumbled into the Grand Ballroom, shaking, his jacket missing and his blue button-down shirt soaked with sweat. He yanked the child into his arms and put his hand firmly over her mouth—not one person made a motion to condemn.

As the Speaker resumed her announcements, Zayn tried hard not to think about the child gasping for breath against her father's hand. He looked around him to see his fellow "aspirants" with their heads down, trying hard not to notice what had just transpired. It was a farce. A carefully constructed illusion of civility. Anger threaded through Zayn's limbs, building steam until he was digging his fingers into his legs to keep from saying something. But he knew he wouldn't for the same reasons no one else did. Because whatever he did would come back tenfold on his family, just like it had for his Uncle Jesse and Aunt Lydia.

This continued for an hour, as the Speaker gave gifts for weddings and births, expressed condolences for those that had passed away, and mentioned significant business deals or promotions around town. There was little that avoided the Lady's network. This display was a reminder that nothing in the town happened without her permission.

Zayn eyed his cousin during the proceedings, but Keelan

was internally focused. It was like his cousin hadn't even noticed what had happened before.

While the Speaker was announcing the new alderman in Varna, a thick man in a heavy gray duster ambled onto the dais from the back with a slight bowlegged limp. Zayn elbowed his cousin.

Carron Allgood. Representative from the Academy of the Subtle Arts, trainer of the first years, scourge of young men and women in the place most called the Assassin's guild, the only Hall anyone from Varna was ever allowed to join. If he'd ever heard Carron's name without a string of profanities either before or after, then he'd never heard the name at all.

Carron Allgood leaned on a wooden staff with a claw on the top. Unlike the Speaker, who hid her age with sorcery, Carron wore his scars and wrinkles proudly. His gaze roamed the line of potential apprentices, and when it fell upon Zayn, it felt like the gaze of Zeus was upon him, so he looked at his shoes.

Sensing that the man from the Halls had usurped her prominence, the Speaker cleared her throat. "Before we move to the final announcements of the evening, we shall begin the receiving of communion."

A knot of Watchers filed into the Grand Ballroom and stood before the dais with large copper stemless cups in their hands. The privileged front row stood first, ambled to the dais in their Sunday best, received their substance, and returned to their seats. Row by row, the town followed. His family gave him nods as they went past, except for the twins, who covertly stuck their tongues out at him.

Noisy foot scuffs and the rattle of metal chairs provided enough cover for Zayn to lean over and say to his cousin, "Do you think she's watching right now?"

There was no need to explain who the *she* was in this

context, as everyone said it with a special emphasis. Keelan tapped a spot beneath his eyes, indicating the sunglasses the Watchers wore. It'd long been his theory that she could see through their eyes. Zayn disagreed, though he had no way to disprove it.

When it was his turn, Zayn took a large mouthful of the bitter yellowish drink. It had a sweet aftertaste that hung in the back of the throat, but otherwise Zayn disliked it. But there was no point in dying when an alternative was offered. The Lady's poison would sustain him for another few months, and as long as he kept up with the regular doses, he'd never have to worry about anything.

"Now with great..." began the Speaker, but the low clatter absorbed her voice.

Carron banged the black ball at the end of his staff on the dais, silencing the congregation.

The Speaker nodded towards him. "Thank you, Carron." Before turning to the crowd. "Now, with great pleasure, we choose the two young men and women who will represent our fair city of Varna at the Hundred Halls. No other town in the world has so many of its kin as alumni, and we should thank her Ladyship for bestowing this grace upon us."

A tense silence intruded as everyone remembered that the kids they'd sent the last two years to the Hundred Halls hadn't come back. A loud sniff from Kellyanne's mother—one of the parents who'd lost her child—punctuated the moment, a reminder of the price.

"Now, if any aspirants would like to demonstrate their worthiness before the choosing, please step forward."

For a moment, Zayn thought that Keelan had changed his mind, but then he gave him a guilty glance and stepped through the line towards the dais. Other kids followed, and while there were parents who hid their concern in handkerchiefs or cupped hands, most had proud grins.

When the rearranging was done, seventeen young men and women stood before Carron Allgood. He let the claw-end of his staff drift towards the end of the line.

"You, Blonde, show me what you got."

Gretchen Sandalwood was the head cheerleader and resident mean girl of the high school. Her blonde hair had been dutifully hardened into place with enough hairspray to make her look like a cobra. It was not at all surprising to anyone who'd had the displeasure of interacting with her that she had stepped forward.

As much as Zayn hated this spectacle, he couldn't help but watch as Gretchen launched into an intricate spell involving seductive hip wiggles and complex fingering. When she was finished, Zayn thought the spell had fizzled, because nothing happened, but then the young man three down from her, Buford Ash, dropped to his knees and began kissing her designer pumps, bringing a spate of much-needed laughter to the room.

The only reaction that Zayn detected from Carron was a slight grumble of distaste, followed by a swift sweep of his staff, after which, Buford came to his senses and returned, bewildered, to his spot in line.

Gretchen gave a neat curtsey before the next person, Billy Ray Upchurch, stepped forward. His demonstration was brief, mostly because he fumbled his words and a blast of flame blew up in his face. He returned to his spot with his head down and the scent of burnt hair drifting into the room.

One by one, they performed for Carron. When it was Mean Clovis' turn, he stumbled before the dais, looking like he was going to throw up. It took him two tries to get started. He had to wipe his palms on his pants, and then his forehead with the back of his forearm.

Based on his trembling hands, Zayn was expecting spectacular failure, but when Mean finished the spell, he flew at Carron. He moved in a blur, throwing three punches and two kicks before Zayn even registered that he'd moved.

Carron was not surprised, and blocked them, but Zayn had never seen anyone come that close to hitting the Hall teacher. He gave Mean a slight bow of the head, which brought a collective groan from the remaining students.

At that point, there was no doubt in Zayn's mind that Gretchen and Mean would represent Varna at the Halls. Their demonstrations had been better than anyone else in the past five years.

But when his cousin started his spell, Zayn knew he would take one of the positions. There was a crispness to his spellwork that upstaged the others. It explained where Keelan was when he wasn't doing chores or hanging out with Zayn. He must have been practicing all this time.

When Keelan finished the spell, a second illusionary version of himself stepped to the side, bringing an "ohhhh" from those assembled. Keelan continued to impress by advancing both himself and his illusion towards Carron Allgood in a threatening manner. Carron kicked his staff towards the original Keelan, only to find that was the illusionary version. A scattering of applause filled the room. When he was finished, Keelan took his spot in line.

"Thank you for your demonstrations," said Carron. "I will not require a second round. The choices are clear. Roy Clovis and Keelan Walker." He looked to the Speaker. "I am finished."

The rest of the Ceremony concluded without Zayn remembering a bit of it. Keelan, on the other hand, looked radiant in his excitement.

When it was time to file out of the Grand Ballroom, Keelan

reached out and squeezed Zayn's hand. It was a bit of an apology, and a farewell.

As Zayn marched out, he glanced back to see Keelan standing before Carron, along with Mean Clovis.

The line exiting the plantation was long. Around the time Zayn was about to leave and join his family beneath the wide oaks, a Watcher approached.

"Zayn Carter. You're requested back inside."

"What? What did I do?"

The Watcher nodded back towards the center of the house. When he stepped inside the Grand Ballroom, he saw Mean Clovis lying on the hardwood floor, twitching and foaming at the mouth. Two Watchers stood over him, casting spells, but he didn't seem to be responding.

"Don't you worry about him," said Carron from the dais when everyone lingered, banging his staff to get them to hurry. "I still want to make the overnight train, so this is gonna be quick."

Zayn was hanging back, checking on Mean Clovis, when a booming voice rattled his ears.

"I said forget the damn kid and get over here, or do you currently have shit for brains?" said Carron, who clearly was letting his true self shine without their families around.

When Zayn reached the others, Allgood was staring him down. Zayn moved to the back and tried to move out of sight. Carron paced across the dais, mumbling and cursing under his breath. He looked like an angry bulldog who'd missed out on biting the mailman.

"Everyone from before, get back in line," said Carron gruffly, sweeping his staff along the ground, indicating where he wanted them to stand. The fourteen who didn't get picked the first time hurried to their spots and stood as stiff as boards.

The first-year trainer prowled back and forth, sometimes

stopping before one person, then shaking his head as if he couldn't believe he was even thinking of picking them. When it seemed like he'd settled on picking Billy Ray, getting as close as extending his staff in his direction, the Watcher from outside tapped Carron on the shoulder.

The pair moved away from the edge of the dais, and spoke in hushed voices.

"Who the hell is Zayn Carter?"

Everyone turned and looked at him, and his stomach dropped twenty feet.

"Shit for brains?"

Zayn stepped forward. "I'm Zayn Carter."

"It seems you've been picked. Congratulations," he said with as much warmth as a blizzard.

Zayn looked at his classmates, the other kids he'd spent his whole life with at school. They were staring at him with absolute confusion at why he'd been picked. He'd never demonstrated any magical skill, or even indicated that he wanted to join the Hundred Halls, which was exactly the point. He and the Goon had cooked up this scheme so the Lady wouldn't suspect anything about either of their intentions. Of course, Zayn hadn't revealed his plans to the Goon, but it was enough that their goals aligned for now.

"But I didn't step forward," said Zayn. "I wasn't in line. I didn't even show you anything."

"Clearly you showed somebody," said Carron. "Now come with me, I don't want to miss that train."

"I have to tell my parents," he said.

"There's no time," said Carron, and he marched into the darkness, expecting Zayn to follow.

He felt an invisible umbilical tug him forward. A whirlwind of thoughts careened through his head.   Sometimes when young men and women left for the Hundred Halls, they never returned.   And other times, when they did, everyone wished they hadn't. But no one returned without being changed, and even if he managed to avoid that, at the end of his five years, he would serve the Lady for the rest of his days.

Chapter Ten
The Hold, October 2013
A side quest for peculiar treasure

After a couple of months at the Academy, the routine, while exhausting, had become predictable. Hurry from class to class, trying to keep up with the breakneck pace of learning, while working in the kitchen morning, noon, and night as punishment for being the team in last place.

That predictable schedule took a turn one evening when a scream of frustration startled Zayn from his studies. He was sitting on his bed with his back against the wall with the tome *Modern Enchantments* resting on his knees. He'd just gotten settled after they finished cleaning up the Hold kitchen. Vin was shaving in front of the wall mirror, while Portia was bobbing her head, listening to the music in her ear buds. The screamer had been Skylar, who stared into her clothing drawer as if a flame-spitting dragon was about to come flying out.

Zayn closed his thumb into the tome, saving his place. A keen sense of frustration settled into his shoulders. The other teams had apartments with private rooms. Their living arrangement made privacy impossible. Only Portia seemed unfazed by it, as she would change clothes in the room without hesitation, while the rest of them used the bathrooms.

"Everything okay over there?" asked Zayn, hoping this was just a minor blowup, not a full-fledged meltdown like she'd had a few nights before over a bottle of spilled nail polish.

"No," said Skylar, making a tiny foot stomp that shook her silky black hair.

She blushed with a mixture of rage and embarrassment. "There are *things* missing."

Zayn caught Vin's eye roll reflected in the mirror.

"I'm not sure how you can tell, you've got half the storage space in the room," said Vin.

Grabbing a hairbrush off the dresser, Skylar pointed it at Vin as if it were a wand. "Did *you* take my stuff?"

"No," said Vin, elongating his cheek as he scraped the razor across it. "What's missing, anyway?"

Skylar's blush deepened. "That's not important. What matters is that it's missing. Which means we have a thief."

Portia, who until that moment had been in her private world of music, popped out an ear bud. "You missing stuff too?"

Wild-eyed victory lit up Skylar's face. "See! I'm not crazy."

"No one ever said you were, Skylar," said Zayn.

But she sent an angry glare in Vin's direction. Despite the aching desire for sleep, and the need to get caught up on his studies, Zayn sensed an opportunity. So far, his team had as much toxic chemistry as a meth lab. He set his tome down.

"We should all check our stuff," said Zayn. "Even you, Vin. Let's see what's going on."

Vin shrugged, threw the razor in his dopp kit, and started searching through his gear.

After a complete review, they determined they were missing two bottles of perfume, one of cologne, a pair of red stiletto high heels, a gold chain, and a few unspecific items that Skylar refused to elaborate on.

"I don't see the connection," said Zayn. "Anyone seen anything strange going on? Anyone near our room?"

"How could we?" said Vin. "When we're not in class or in the kitchen, I'm passed out, trying to get a few hours of shut-eye before the next day."

Portia nodded along. "I agree with Vin. I have seen no one near our room, and when we work in the kitchen, we can see if anyone goes to our door." Then she got a weird look. Her forehead scrunched. "Do any of you see that weird glowy light in our room at night?"

Zayn recalled waking up to light, thinking one of the others had turned on a lamp. "Yeah, I think. I just thought someone had to use the bathroom."

"I've seen it too," said Skylar. "I think it's that thing we saw on the first day. Maybe it's stealing our stuff. But what is it?"

No one had an answer, so Zayn suggested, "Let's keep watch for it tonight. Maybe we can trap it, or follow it. Get our stuff back."

The eagerness of their gazes told Zayn he was onto something. They'd have to give up some sleep to catch the thief, but everyone seemed to think it was worth it.

"It's settled then," said Zayn. "We should all lie down like we're going to bed. Keep your clothes on so we can follow it."

Vin mentioned their ploy as a scene from a magical heist movie he'd watched called *The Perfect Game*. Everyone rolled their eyes, since magical heists were Vin's favorite subject.

With the lights out, the room lay in near pitch darkness. The LED from Skylar's smart watch provided the only faint light in the room. Zayn held himself as still as possible, listening for sounds of intrusion, but after an hour, he had to fight the urge to sleep. A snort-snore from Vin only made it harder as Zayn wanted to succumb to glorious slumber.

When he didn't think he could stay awake much longer, a pale luminosity slipped through the door, which Zayn hadn't heard open. Through half-closed eyes, Zayn watched as the creature moved through the room. It kept its light dim, but Zayn sensed that it couldn't make itself completely dark. It had a vaguely humanoid shape, but not enough definition to know if it was somehow related to humans. It could have been the ghost of an alien being for all Zayn knew.

The creature hovered over Skylar's stuff. A couple of clinks announced that it was picking through her gear.

Zayn craned his neck to see that the others were watching. He held up his hand and counted down, using his fingers. When he hit three, they all popped up. Portia slapped the light on.

"Gotcha, you freak," said Skylar.

The luminous creature dropped whatever it was holding and fled from the room. Vin and Portia tried getting in its way, but it blew between them and slipped out the cracked door.

The thing was fast, because by the time they got out of the room, it was across the dining area. The four of them dashed across, dodging between the tables, bumping some of them along the way.

"It went to the portal room," said Zayn.

The portal was a stone archway with runes along the curve. They arrived just in time to see a grouping of runes glowing with purpose and the whirling darkness of the portal activated.

Without concern for where the portal might take them, they threw themselves through it before it ended. Traveling by portal was always a little terrifying. The four of them landed on rough stone in darkness, the runes from the other side of the portal fading fast. A glowy shape moved through the darkness ahead, but then winked out.

No one moved, but there was a lot of heavy breathing from their short sprint.

"Does anyone know where we are?" asked Vin.

"It looks like a big cavern," said Zayn. "I think this is the Undercity. Probably the way we came in that first night."

"Sí," said Portia. "It is."

"Which means we can't get back into the Hold," said Zayn. "Unless someone knows the activation runes from this portal."

Everyone shook their head.

"Well," said Zayn. "Let's find our thief first, and then worry about how we get back."

"But this is the Undercity," said Skylar. "First years aren't supposed to be here because it's too dangerous."

Zayn faced her. "Do you have another idea?"

"I guess not," Skylar said despondently.

"Don't worry," said Zayn. "There's four of us. What could go wrong? Now where did our thief go?"

Portia knew the spell for glow lights and took the lead as they walked. A pair of bobbing balls of light hovered along with them as they headed off in the direction they'd last seen the creature. When they reached the last area they'd seen it, they paused, as the tunnel branched into a series of smaller caverns.

"Which one?" asked Zayn.

Portia walked into the next tunnel, disappearing for a minute. When she came back, she said, "The passages split further up. It is practically a maze."

"Ideas?" asked Zayn.

Skylar had her arms crossed and a frown on her lips. "I know a spell. But it might not work if it's too far away."

"Great," said Zayn. "What does it do?"

The earlier blush returned. "Does it matter if it gets us

there?"

Skylar made gestures with her fingers, then she shoved them into her mouth and sucked on them. Zayn wasn't sure if it was a spell until he caught the faint smell of faez. Skylar pulled her fingers from her mouth and stared into the darkness.

"What did it do?" asked Vin.

"Hush and listen."

Zayn stilled himself, listening with his whole body. At first he could only hear his beating heart. But after a few minutes, he heard a faint buzzing noise.

In a whisper, Skylar said, "This way."

They followed her forward. At each new split in the passage, they listened until they could hear the buzzing again. She had to repeat the spell a few times, but eventually, they found the correct cavern.

The glowy creature hovered over the spot the buzzing emanated from. It fled as soon as they entered the cavern.

Much to Zayn's surprise, Skylar sprinted across the uneven stone, oblivious to potential dangers. The rest of them followed close behind.

Before they reached the spot where they assumed their stuff would be found, Skylar turned around and put her hands out. "Stop. Please."

"Why?" asked Portia. "What's wrong?"

"Can I get my stuff before everyone sees it?" asked Skylar, lips flat with worry.

"It's okay, Skylar. Whatever it is, we don't care," said Zayn.

"Sí," said Portia. "We on same team. Everything is good."

Zayn looked to Vin to add his encouragement, but he'd crept forward, peering into a small depression in the stone that the buzzing had come from.

"Holy sex dungeon," said Vin, mouth agape.

His exclamation drew them forward. As the light hit the objects piled on the cavern floor, breaths of incredulity followed.

In a space a bit larger than a dinner table were piles of condom packets, dildos, vibrators, bottles of perfume, whips, leather underwear, and anything else found in a sex shop. There were other objects that didn't quite fit, like wooden spoons, an empty bottle of shampoo, and hair clamps, but Zayn got the idea right away.

"It's a sex-geist," said Portia with a tone of authority, and when everyone looked to her, she added with a shrug, "There was one in my neighborhood in Mexico City. They're harmless."

Skylar squeaked and lunged forward to snatch a pink object from the stone, then shoved it into her backpack.

"You have nothing to be embarrassed about," said Portia as she strolled forward and grabbed a black dildo from the pile, waving it like a wand.

Vin coughed into his cupped hand and lifted the leather underwear from the pile, adding with a shrug, "I like the way they feel."

Zayn grabbed a tube of lotion and waggled it before slipping it into his pocket. "This is one way to get to know your teammates."

There was a moment where everyone held their breath and glanced to Skylar. She'd spent the majority of their little adventure looking like she was ready to explode into flames from embarrassment.

When she opened her mouth, Zayn feared they were going to get a lecture, but laughter came out like a flood. As soon as she laughed, the rest of them followed, until they were bent over, sides bursting.

When it finally subsided, everyone was wiping tears from

their eyes.

"What was that spell you used?" asked Portia, when they could finally speak again.

With her hand on her chest to catch her breath, Skylar said, "It's a magical vibrator. The spell makes it operate."

"Ohmygod," said Portia. "But the buzzing was so loud?"

Skylar winced. "I think it activated more than mine."

"What do we do now?" asked Vin.

"About the sex-geist?" asked Zayn.

"No. Getting out of here," said Vin, "but I guess we have to deal with the sex-geist as well."

"I can find a spell to ward our room," said Portia.

"If we make our way back to the portal, we should be able to get out, following the path we took on our first night," said Zayn. "Once we're above ground we can take the trains back to our regular portal."

"That was a long hike," said Skylar.

"I'm open to ideas, but I don't think we have much choice," said Zayn.

Before they left, Vin grabbed a packet of condoms. They decided to leave the rest where they'd found it, as no one wanted to go through it for sanitary reasons. Also, they didn't know how long the geist had been thieving from the Hold. Based on the size of the pile, and assuming it only stole from the Academy, it'd been operating for quite some time.

The journey was long, but not as arduous as Zayn would have expected. Portia made them all laugh when she marched at the front, using her dildo like a baton. When she flipped it into the air and caught it behind her back, they applauded her.

Before they reached the surface, Skylar, as she nervously tucked strands of hair behind her ear, asked, "So...what are we going to do about our room?"

"What do you mean?" asked Zayn.

Skylar blushed. "About privacy. Since we don't have separate rooms like the others."

"We could get some privacy screens," said Portia. "They can be very beautiful."

"That's good," said Skylar, but based on the way she hunched forward, Zayn knew that wasn't everything.

"Are you worried about?" he asked, nodding towards her backpack.

"Yeah," she said, scrunching up her face.

"We can make a schedule," said Zayn. "If you want a little me-time, then you can sign up. Doesn't even have to be for... you know."

Skylar let out a relieved chuckle. "I can't believe we're making a schedule. I mean, I'm glad, but it's not what I expected from the Academy."

"They're training us to be spies and diplomats and assassins," said Portia. "Like Instructor Pennywhistle said in our accent class, we need to learn how to be honest with each other."

"She's got a point," said Zayn. "I'll try to be more honest."

Everyone added their promises, and then Skylar added, "Since we're being honest, am I the only one with a mad crush on Instructor Pennywhistle?"

"How could you not," said Vin, shaking his head incredulously. "But I think that's the point."

"I'm honestly tired of marching through the Undercity," said Portia, drawing noises of agreement from the others.

"Me too," said Zayn, "but at least we can say The Great Dildo Recovery Operation was a rousing success."

"Rousing?" laughed Skylar. "That's a groaner."

"Or a moaner!" added Vin.

"You guys are all wet," said Portia with a sly grin.

"This is *hard*ly the time," added Zayn.

"I can't wait to thrust myself beneath my covers," said Skylar.

Zayn put out his hand and rocked it back and forth. "That one was passable."

They kept the sex-related puns up until they reached the surface. By the time they made the Red Line train that would take them back to the hidden portal, it was nearly five in the morning. The four of them collapsed on a bench as the train rumbled towards their destination. Without a word, they hooked arms and leaned against each other. Though he was exhausted, he was also contented. For the first time since he'd come to the Academy, they were a team.

Chapter Eleven
Ninth Ward, November 2013
What happens in the bodega stays in the bodega

A cold and wet Atlantic wind blew in from the coast, forcing Zayn's hands into his pockets as he walked beside Instructor Allgood. The instructor had an elements charm, keeping the worst of the November weather off him, but he'd forbidden Zayn from doing the same, even though it was a spell that he actually knew.

Before they'd left the Hold, Instructor Allgood had given him a shirt with the colors of the Jamaican flag to wear. Zayn didn't bother asking questions, since he knew the explanation would come in time, and questions only invited insults.

When they stopped inside a bodega on a corner in the ninth ward with Bob Marley playing in the background, Zayn thought the instructor needed a bite to eat, until an old guy with graying dreads, wrinkles like deep valleys, and a full beard greeted them.

"Larice," said Instructor Allgood with a rare spot of warmth in his voice, reaching across the cluttered counter to clasp hands. The easy manner made the instructor almost unrecognizable.

"Carron, man, it's good to see you," said Larice in a heavy Jamaican accent. He looked past the instructor with his clouded eyes. "Ya, man. You the new kid? He's a good lookin' boy. He make a fine helper. What's your name?"

"Zayn."

Larice winked at Instructor Allgood, who was staring intently. "No, man. What's your *name*?"

"Zayn," he said, but this time with the Jamaican accent he'd been practicing for weeks.

"*Wah bout yuh patwah*?" asked Larice.

"*It like mi did baan inna Kingston*," replied Zayn.

"Good man," said Larice. "He have that Kingston vibe. You be my brother's son who live in Kingston. I give you the family tree later."

Instructor Allgood put his hand on Zayn's shoulder. It felt like a bear had leaned on him. "Listen to Larice. No magic. Keep your eyes and ears open, you got it?"

"Yes, sir."

Instructor Allgood wrinkled his nose.

"I mean, ya man."

"Better. Don't forget, eyes and ears."

He left, leaving Zayn with his "Uncle" Larice, who showed him the ins and outs of the store. The bodega was smaller than his group room back in the Hold, packed with shelves with barely enough room between to move.

A woman with greenish-blue hair in a messy Mohawk entered not long after they'd settled behind the counter. She wore a white lab coat over a Garbage Kings T-shirt with the sleeves cut off. She had a cute face with a button nose, and a frenetic energy about her, as if she'd never stopped moving in her life.

"Hey, Katie. How you be doin' today?" asked Larice.

"Excellent, Larice. Excellent. We got a gig at the High

Dragon, most def, most def," she said, sharing a complicated handshake with Larice. "Who's your boy?"

"This is Zayn, he's my brother's boy from Kingston," said Larice. "And this is Katie Crescent."

Katie reached across for a fist bump, which he returned. "Irie."

"So what'dya come here for?" asked Katie as she was tapping her fingers on the counter in an up-tempo rhythm.

Zayn's mouth went dry. They hadn't talked about his back story yet, but the words came easily. "A bit of trouble back home, so my dad sent me here."

"Sorry to hear, but I know your Uncle Larice could use the help," she said, then her face brightened like a supernova. "Hey! You should come see us play at the High Dragon. We're totally gonna rock it."

"Katie's the drummer for her band," said Larice.

She tugged on her white coat. "Lab tech by day, rock god by night. Or at least, wannabe rock god. Our band is pretty new."

"What kind?" asked Zayn.

"Retro jazz-hop," she said. "We're called the Sticky Wickets. Our lyricist is sick. So you in?"

Buoyed by her enthusiasm, Zayn nearly said yes. "Sorry, man. I'm not even twenty-one, and I promised my da that I'd stay out of trouble. Respect."

"That's cool. Oh shit, I've got to get to practice. Hamal hates it when I'm late," said Katie as she ran out of the bodega without buying anything, throwing a "Bye!" over her shoulder as she left like an unruly but cute whirlwind.

Uncle Larice let him run the counter for an hour, introducing him to the locals, giving him their backstory in between.

"Okay, man. I gotta go. You do alright. I'll be back at

five after my treatments." He snapped his fingers. "One thing, there's an orange tabby that likes to wander into the store. Don't let him in, he's trouble that one."

Uncle Larice gave him a shoulder-hug before disappearing out the front.

The weather turned wet, and customers came rushing in. He sold a lot of cold medicine and lotto tickets.

By the afternoon, he had the hang of the cash register and his back story, since anyone that was a local stayed and chatted, forcing him to repeat it. The bodega served a mix of neighborhoods. There were some expensive flats north of the bodega. He met an older well-dressed black woman who worked nearby that lived in one with her wife. A couple of rent-controlled apartments to the south contained a lot of families, while lower-cost flats to the east tended to have young professionals and artists like Katie. On the west side was an office building for D'Agastine-branded products. The side of the brick building had a giant mural of Celesse D'Agastine with a giant alien moon behind her. Zayn didn't know much about the Hundred Halls, but even he knew who Celesse D'Agastine, the patron of the Alchemists Hall, was.

When the sun came out, his customers dried up. Zayn was resting his chin in his hands with his elbows on the counter when he heard the bell on the door rattle, but the door didn't fully open. When he didn't see anyone in the bodega, he let his eyes drift closed.

His eyes flashed open when he heard the soft click of cardboard tumbling together. He looked over the counter, examining the aisles, but found no one in the store.

"Hello? Anyone here, man?"

Zayn heard a crunching sound, directly on the other side of the counter. He leaned all the way over, looking straight down at a large orange tabby cat with little raccoon-like hands gobbling down a chocolate bar. The area in front of the counter was littered with wrappers.

The tabby turned its head until its green eyes were staring up into Zayn's face. Its eyes went wide, then it darted towards the door, somehow slipping its fingers beneath the bottom and pulling it open enough to squeeze out before Zayn could reach it.

He got outside in time to see the tabby scurrying across the street, weaving into the pedestrian traffic on the other side. A half-hearted, "man," slipped out before he returned inside to survey the damage.

He was scooping up the wrappers, there had to be at least twenty, when the bell clattered behind him, and he heard, "Dammit, man, I told you not to let the tabby in the store."

Zayn's stomach sunk three feet. Uncle Larice was standing behind him with his hands on his hips.

"I'm sorry," said Zayn. "I didn't see it come in, and how does a cat have hands?"

Uncle Larice used the counter to crouch down with him, helping him collect the wrappers. "Must be fifty dollars of sales lost, right here, man. You got to keep your eyes open. Were you sleepin'?" He gave a soul-worn sigh. "I'll let this one go and not tell Carron, but that's it. No more mistakes. And yeah, man, the cat have hands because it not a cat, it's a callolo."

"What's a callolo?"

"A right bastard is what it is, that's all I know," said Larice, shaking his head. "You best ask Carron. Anyway, now you know. You can head back now, I take over from here."

On the way back, Zayn mulled over the encounter with the callolo and how he could have done better. He was cutting through a street construction area with orange cones, passing a closed deli, when he heard a strange noise from across the street, behind a scrap trailer piled with old concrete.

A guy in sweatpants and a ratty black T-shirt was holding his chest as if he were having a heart attack. He was sweaty and shaking. His bright red forehead looked like he was a volcano about to erupt.

"Are you okay, man?" asked Zayn, stepping off the curb.

"I'm alive. I'm alive," he said feverishly.

"You don't look so good."

The guy held a hand before his face as if he were seeing it for the first time. Then the skin on his hand turned crystalline, the many facets catching the sunlight and gleaming like the crown jewels.

"Ha! See," said the man breathlessly.

"That's a nice trick, but you still don't look so good," said Zayn. "You should get to a hospital. I'd bet this city has a good one."

Zayn checked the street. He was the only other person on it.

"I can do this," said the guy as he held both his arms before his face, straining as if he were trying to pass a kidney stone.

Zayn took a few more steps, deciding whether or not the guy was dangerous. Before he could make his final decision, the crystalline substance that had transformed the man's hand spread to both his arms.

"I did it!"

But the crystalline skin didn't stop spreading, and the man's face quickly turned to horror as it moved to his chest and down his torso, taking over his legs and even the clothes around him. As it went up his neck and transformed his head, he mouthed the word, "Help," before his mouth was swallowed by it.

The crystalline man staggered on his feet, unbalanced

by his newfound weight. He took a step off the curb and plummeted forward.

Zayn moved to catch him, but he fell too fast. The crystalline man shattered into a million tiny pieces as he hit the concrete.

Zayn stood amidst the dust. *What just happened?*

Moments later, a taxi came flying up the street, and Zayn hurried back to the sidewalk. The speeding vehicle swirled the dust, turning the air glittery. It took him a bit to regain his senses. There was no one on the street to share his experience with, and it seemed so incredible and horrifying that he wasn't sure he'd tell anyone either.

Before he'd come to the city of sorcery, he'd heard wild tales that he hadn't believed, but after watching a man turn to crystal and explode into dust, he recalibrated those stories in his head. Zayn checked the street for passing cars, then headed back towards the Academy.

Chapter Twelve
Twelfth Ward, November 2013
What if 4H Club educated assassins?

For the first three months of their education, they'd been taught exclusively by Instructors Allgood and Pennywhistle, and the majority of the classes had been with the former. While Zayn had come to enjoy their yin-yang personalities, it'd also grown a little stale being screamed at, and then politely lectured, by the same two people. It was like waking up in an ice cave, then wandering out into the desert, only to get shoved back into the cold each night.

When they learned that the day's lessons would be taught by Instructor O'Keefe, there was general excitement among the first years. They'd traveled to another location in the city on the Blue Line, arriving at an empty factory with the windows blocked off and cleared of equipment.

They were told that O'Keefe taught the upperclassman, was one of Priyanka's longest serving instructors, and could be quite peculiar.

The cluster of first years stood in the back of the empty factory, on smooth concrete that bore scorch marks further out. A series of tables with coverings on them waited to their left. The place had a chemical smell like formaldehyde, and it made his nose burn a little when he inhaled too deeply.

"Anyone heard anything about O'Keefe?" asked Skylar.

"Not a word," said Zayn, looking around the empty factory. "If those tables weren't over there, I'd think we were in the wrong place."

"Maybe she's going to teach us how to take a nap," said Vin, raising his arms in a stretch. "I can't remember the last time I slept more than three hours."

"I like it when you sleep less," said Portia, playfully punching Vin in the arm. "Because you snore like two chupacabras having sex."

Vin turned immediately. "You've heard a chupa—"

An explosion at the center of the factory, like a miniature supernova, startled them into silence. Zayn was used to flashy spells, and even the Five Elements could make grand gestures, but this was a raw, primal display of magic that he felt in his gut.

A woman's thick Scottish accent cut through the silence as the black smoke at the center of the factory rolled towards the high ceiling.

"I hope I got your attention there. Nothing like a good explosion to wake you up and wet my panties."

The class turned to find a woman with steel-gray hair bound into a long braid that hung over her shoulder. She looked like an older, wiser version of Lara Croft in a tank top and cargo shorts.

Instructor O'Keefe walked right up to Vin, who was her same height, poked him in the chest with her finger, and said, "You're a fine slab of meat that in my youth I might have torn into like a pride of lions."

Vin looked more stunned by her comment than he had by the explosion. He stammered out a collection of syllables that barely resembled a word.

Instructor O'Keefe moved back to the front of the class and held her hand up. "If you haven't figured it out yet, I'm Instructor O'Keefe. I'm in charge of giving you the right tools to survive your future missions, assuming you survive that right bastard Carron's maltreatment."

She gave them a big wink, eliciting laughter from the group. Zayn found himself liking her right away.

"First I'm gonna show you a few things, give you an idea of what yer capable of. And if you survive yer first few years and join me in class, you'll get to learn more. Alright now, who's the resident arsehole of this here class?"

Before even a word could be spoken, someone shoved Eddie forward. He stumbled next to Instructor O'Keefe, who had him by inches and pounds. She put a hand on his shoulder.

"Nice to meet you..."

"Eddie. I, uhm, nice to meet you," he replied.

She winked at the class. "You won't be saying that for very long. You're going to help me demonstrate what's possible in this Hall."

Eddie swallowed as he glanced back at the place where the explosion had happened minutes before. He looked like he was going to be sick.

"So Carron has been drilling it into your wee heads that you've got to be ready, got to be prepared for anything. I'm sure you've been up late cramming with your papers, trying to eat it all like a python with a puppy." Everyone made an "eww" noise. "But you can't be prepared for everything, and spells take time, time you may not have. So Priyanka wants me to show you a few things, little tricks."

Instructor O'Keefe wandered over to a table and yanked its covering off with the flair of a magician, revealing a scattering of items that Zayn couldn't make out from the back of the class. But he didn't have to wait long, as Instructor O'Keefe grabbed a bottle of whiskey and two shot glasses. With the bottle cradled in her arm, she brought them back to Eddie, gave the shot glasses to him, and poured two generous shots of amber liquid.

She clinked her glass against his, spilling whiskey on her fingers, and lifted it in salute. Eddie looked at it suspiciously.

"Trust me, kid. This is to loosen you up, you're tighter than a pair of gym shorts." She threw the whiskey into the back of her throat, shoved the glass into a pocket on her shorts, and proceeded to lick her fingers while she waited for Eddie to drink his shot.

Reluctantly, Eddie took a tentative sip, then shook his head slightly before finishing the shot.

"That wasn't so bad, was it?" she asked, taking the shot glass from him and putting it in the other side of her cargo shorts.

"No," said Eddie.

"Good," said Instructor O'Keefe, smiling like a cat who'd just convinced a family of mice to join it for dinner. "One of the ways you can bypass a target's defenses is to enchant something that they drink or eat. But"—she held up the bottle of whiskey—"a worthy target will have their food or drink tested. This whiskey is as it looks, just whiskey."

She wandered back to the table, set the bottle down. Then pulled the shot glasses from her pockets.

"But these, specifically this one," she said, holding up the glass that Eddie had drank from, "is enchanted to imbue whatever liquid is placed within with a mild suggestive." She looked to Eddie, whose forehead was tightening with increased concern. "Eddie, would you please demonstrate what a chicken does in its yard."

Eddie's expression turned to horror with the realization that he was going to follow her command. He held his elbows out at his side, crouched a bit, and started moving his head back and forth on his neck.

"Cluck, cluck, cluck," said Eddie, looking like a man trapped in his own body.

Laughter exploded from the class, growing louder as Eddie visibly fought with the compulsion. It lasted for about a minute, then he was finally able to get control of himself.

"There are a lot of ways to use this trick," said Instructor O'Keefe, waving for everyone to quiet down. "You can give a target frequent small undetectable amounts that over time make them more susceptible to your requests. Or you can overwhelm them with an immediate dose, though as you saw, Eddie knew he was being manipulated, so you have to work subtly."

She patted Eddie heavily on the shoulder. "That wasn't so bad, was it? There are a lot worse fates. Yer lucky Priyanka doesn't let me polymorph anymore. Tis a sight to see a man reduced to a simple guinea pig, or a parakeet. But it's hell on resources, and hell on the students. Alright, now for the next demonstration."

Instructor O'Keefe retrieved a small black bead from the table. She held it up.

"Anyone know what this is? Probably not. It's what made that delicious panty-wetting explosion at the beginning of class. Priyanka likes to go on about its formal name, but I like to call it a urine spreader, 'cause everyone within a hundred feet are gonna piss themselves when it goes off."

She looked to Eddie, pointing to the center of the factory. "I want you to run to the center—act like you're goin' out for a throw, like that ridiculous game you call football."

The knotted forehead of concern was back. Eddie made

no move towards the center of the factory.

"Don't worry, Eddie. I'm not gonna hurt ya. And if I do, you won't mind 'cause you'll be dead," said Instructor O'Keefe. "Go on now, run along."

Zayn was surprised when Eddie started jogging away. Maybe it was the leftovers from the suggestive enchantment, which was probably why Instructor O'Keefe performed that trick first.

Eddie made it part of the way towards the center, stopped and held his hands out, as if to ask if it was far enough. But she waved him further towards the center.

While he was running, she turned back towards the class. "This Eddie of yours, ya don't like him? Can be an arsehole, eh? Well, don't ever say that I didn't do anything for ya."

Before anyone could say otherwise, she turned and launched the black bead, the urine spreader as she liked to call it, into the center of the factory where Eddie was just turning around. The bead sped through the air as if it were on a string. As soon as it reached Eddie's location, and right as he was noticing it, she snapped her fingers and Eddie was consumed by a blinding explosion.

When the flash had cleared from his eyes, Zayn looked back to the center of the factory to see a ball of black smoke slowly rising to the ceiling, revealing a stunned Eddie, still standing, completely unharmed.

"You can come back now," said Instructor O'Keefe, waving him in. "Now that you have a good idea of what we can do, I'm going to have you learn how to make a few of these on your own, using mostly mundane supplies."

A group of fifth years walked into the room and took up positions at the various tables.

Zayn led his team to the first table. While the fifth year taught them how to make privacy matches that could hide conversations from interested ears, they discussed how to get out of the bottom group.

"It feels like every time we get close to getting out," said Vin, "we catch a bad break."

"Can't get unlucky forever," said Portia.

"We're being too cautious," said Zayn. "With only four in the group, we can't afford to be average. We've got to be great. That's why I picked you all."

"And we see how that turned out," said Skylar.

"I get it," said Zayn. "I really do. But we can't think of this as high school. We're not here to learn a few things, get some grades, and join some corporate structure like normal folk. When we get out of the Hundred Halls, we're going to be in the thick of things. Our lives could be on the line. And we won't have the instructors to bail us out or tell us it'll all be okay. We've got to think beyond the lessons, beyond the spells, beyond even what the instructors think we should learn."

Vin shook his head softly. "I don't know, Zayn. That sounds like a recipe for doing something really stupid. We're only first years, and barely three months into our experience at the Academy. It's not like it's life or death as soon as we graduate."

Zayn opened his mouth, but he couldn't conjure an argument that would sway them. He could see in their faces that they didn't see things the same way he did. They didn't know how it was in Varna. When he got out of the Hundred Halls, unless he could figure a way out, he'd be forced to work for the Lady, which was like a death sentence.

"Yeah, I guess you're right," he said, grabbing a box of matches. "No one's going to die right away when they leave the Academy."

But some of us might wish we were dead.

Chapter Thirteen
The Hold, December 2013
A morning jog with Instructor Allgood

"Get up, maggots. Time to train."

Zayn cracked one eye open to see Instructor Allgood standing over him in his gray duster, leaning on his clawed staff. He couldn't quite remember what day it was since they all seemed to blend together, but recalled a light dusting of snow in the city a few days ago.

Vin must not have been awake, because from the bed next to him, he asked, "What kind of training?"

The clawed staff moved in a blur. Tangled in his covers, Zayn barely managed to throw himself off the side to land heavily on the floor. The claw end hit right where his stomach would have been.

Instructor Allgood chuckled appreciatively. "How did you know I was swinging for you and not your overly talkative teammate?"

Zayn started disentangling himself from his covers. "Your right foot pivoted to the left, which meant you were bringing the staff in my direction and not at Vin."

"And why would I hit you when Vin asked the dumbass question?" asked Instructor Allgood.

"Because we're a team, and what happens to one, happens to all," said Zayn, standing in the center of the room in his boxers, wiping the sleep from his eyes.

"Good. Maybe you're learning something after all. Get your running gear on, something appropriate for the city, and meet me at the portal. No need to worry about your personas. Today's lesson will not involve them."

After he left, Zayn changed clothes, adding an extra layer for the wintery weather. It was a couple of weeks before Christmas, and a cold front had turned the city hard.

Portia stripped down to nothing before rooting around in her clothes bin, throwing shirts and underwear everywhere. Zayn admired the tight muscles across her back and legs. She was built like a wrestler now, and she wasn't the only one. The months of training had changed them.

When they arrived at the portal, Instructor Allgood took a long look at Skylar's bright pink outfit, but miraculously said nothing. Zayn counted a second miracle when Vin opened his mouth to ask a question, probably wondering where the other first years were, and then wisely closed it.

Rather than the maintenance hallway behind Brightline station, they stepped into a small room barely big enough for the five of them. Instructor Allgood touched some runes on the wall, and the door opened, leading them into a tattoo parlor.

Through the front windows, Zayn could see the Spire, but it was at a different angle. The signage on the window read Empire Ink.

"We're in the thirteenth ward," said Zayn.

Instructor Allgood made no comment, which Zayn took as a compliment.

A man wearing a tailored suit and wire-rimmed glasses

sat at a tattoo station reading the *Arcane of London* newspaper. He looked like he should be sitting in a tearoom rather than a tattoo parlor, and the quality of his clothing didn't match the comic book posters on the walls.

"This is Percival Davies," said Instructor Allgood. "He will be your tattoo artist."

"Cheers," said Percival in upper-crust English accent without taking his eyes off the paper, which Zayn noted was the current day's issue.

"You'll be receiving your first Academy imbuement," said Instructor Allgood.

He put his boot on the nearest chair—receiving an eyebrow raise of disappointment from Percival—and lifted his pant leg, revealing a muscled calf. After a moment of concentration, a tattoo of a bright red rose appeared.

"This rose tattoo allows me to channel my faez into physical strength and speed. When things get dicey, there's no time for spell casting, and in some situations, doing so would break your cover. We use these tattoos to put permanent spells on our bodies, allowing us to channel faez into them at a moment's notice. Think of the tattoo as a predesigned circuit board that only needs your magical energy to activate."

Instructor Allgood reached out with the claw end of his staff and gently pushed Skylar towards the table.

"I've never gotten a tattoo before," she said.

"And I've never had a pedicure, but you can be damned sure I would get one if our patron asked," said Instructor Allgood, pulling his leg from the chair. "You'll need to decide what you want the tattoo to look like. Pick something personal to you. Don't worry too much about what it'll look like on your skin because it will stay invisible unless you want it to appear."

Percival ruffled his papers, then he folded and neatly set them aside. After removing his jacket and gently hanging it on a hook on the wall, he rolled his sleeves up and pulled a new pair of blue rubber gloves from a box, fitting them onto his hands.

Skylar climbed onto the table looking a little pale. She took her shirt off, leaving her athletic bra. Percival cleaned her arm with antibacterial soap rather briskly until her skin turned pink.

"What shall it be?" asked Percival.

Skylar considered his question for a moment before leaning over and whispering in his ear.

"Interesting," he said as the tattoo gun buzzed to life.

Percival worked with supernatural speed. The portrait of a cartoon badger in a tutu came to life on her arm. When he was finished, he pulled out a second tattoo gun and went over the tattoo while whispering arcane phrases. The air had a metallic tint of faez to it.

Vin went next, receiving a towering redwood on his bicep.

"My family's from California, and the redwoods make me feel insignificant and somehow important at the same time," he said.

The interlocking symbol on Portia's arm defied understanding. When everyone was looking at her she explained, "It's the eternity knot." But everyone kept staring, so she added, "My father's a Buddhist."

When Zayn was climbing onto the table, Instructor Allgood said, "He's from Varna."

Percival nodded professionally and started preparing the area around Zayn's elbow. He didn't need to ask what tattoo he would receive, because he knew about the web tattoos from the Watchers in Varna, and now he knew why they were only occasionally seen.

When the thrumming tattoo needle was pressed into the skin above his elbow it made him grit his teeth from the vibration through his bones. The keening of the tattoo gun made him squint as he withstood the low-level pain. His teammates gave him a few questioning glances about the fact that he didn't get to pick his tattoo, but they knew better than to ask him in front of Instructor Allgood.

Zayn admired the finished tattoo in the mirror—the webbing covered his elbow in a pleasing pattern—while Percival threw his gloves in a wastebasket and cleaned up his station.

"Last group," said Instructor Allgood. "I'll see you again next year."

With his eyelids fluttering, Percival nodded his head and said, "Charmed."

He left through the rune-locked door in back.

The urge to ask a question was so apparent on Vin's face that Instructor Allgood gruffly added, "The energies required to keep a permanent portal to London are impossible. *But* he will be back in London before tea time." He tapped the ball of his staff on the tile floor. "Come with me. It's time to put those imbuements to work."

Outside the parlor, the morning was a faint blue nimbus on the horizon. Instructor Allgood shook his clawed staff and it collapsed and folded until he could shove it into his gray duster. The stowing of the staff happened so quickly, it was like a magic trick.

Instructor Allgood took off in a westward direction. He shouldn't have been able to move as fast as he could in heavy boots and a thick weather-resistant duster, but Zayn had a hard time keeping up.

"Channel some faez into your imbuement," said Instructor Allgood over his shoulder to the four of them. "Let's pound some pavement."

He surged ahead, his duster trailing behind him like a cloak. At his size, he looked like a charging bull.

Like a pink comet, sounding off with a whoop of joy, Skylar flew ahead, catching up to the instructor. Vin followed moments later, laughing.

"Come on, *amigo*. Let's fly," said Portia.

It wasn't hard to find the tattoo in his mind, but getting the faez into it took a moment, as if he had to reroute the energy pathways first. When the faez completed the circuit, laughter burst out of his lips unexpectedly.

"*Sí!*" said Portia, her face split with a grin.

They caught up to the others easily. Instructor Allgood let them run as a pack for a few blocks. He shared a crackling newness with the others as if he were alive for the first time.

"Now that you're warmed up, let's start challenging you," said Instructor Allgood.

He veered into a broken-down industrial park, leaping to the top of a chain-link fence and vaulting over.

Zayn poured faez into the imbuement and pushed off hard, flying up and over the fence completely. He went so far that he almost tumbled onto his back, but his faez-strengthened muscles were able to pull him out of the stumble.

"That's the way," said Instructor Allgood.

Zayn thought he was going to head deeper into the rotted-out buildings, but instead Instructor Allgood jumped onto an old diesel tank, his boots ringing it like a drum. Then he leapt through an open window on the second floor of one of the buildings.

The team followed Instructor Allgood through the interior of the building, dodging through old offices, leaping over desks, and climbing rotting stairs until they reached the roof. He went straight for the edge, jumping across a narrow gap to the next building.

The next phase of their rooftop parkour had Zayn oscillating between fear that he might miss and raw adrenaline.

After a few minutes of playing follow the leader with Instructor Allgood, he stopped on top of the tarred roof of a four-story building with a good view of the sunrise.

Laughter hung on their lips like bubbles as they caught their breaths. Vin had tears at the corners of his eyes, and Zayn shared the feeling of being overwhelmed.

"It's good, isn't it?" asked Instructor Allgood.

Zayn hardly knew what to make of the instructor's change. He wasn't their gruff taskmaster, but a cheerful leader.

The pinks of sunrise were deepening to red, and the top of the Spire reflected like a beacon. Early morning gondolas slid through the sky on invisible gossamer threads, catching the sunlight on their windows like morning stars, and for the first time since he'd come to the Hundred Halls, Zayn was truly glad he was there.

"Why did we have to wait so long to do this?" asked Vin, then realizing he had asked a question, slapped a hand over his mouth.

"I will for a short time allow a few questions. The first time faez-running is always the best and it can be a little overwhelming," said Instructor Allgood. "But we wait until midway through the year because your bodies aren't ready when you first arrive. If we gave you imbuements in the first month, you'd tear your bodies apart."

"So that's why you make us kick pads for hours every morning?" asked Zayn.

"Among other things," said Instructor Allgood. "Let me warn you that you are going to be very sore tomorrow, and the next day. From here on out, training in the dojo will involve faez-speed. You need to harden your body to it. There will be more rooftop parkour, and other training. The longer you do it, the more your body will become accustomed to the pulling and stretching, to a point, but that's a lesson for another day."

"I feel like a goddess," said Portia breathlessly. "Or a warrior monk."

Instructor Allgood nodded. "Last trip around the industrial park and then we'll head back to the Hold. You're going to need a hot shower and a good stretching back in the dojo."

Before they resumed their parkour, he said, "I want you to push yourself on this circuit. Don't worry about following me if you're feeling your oats. You should be able to handle anything on the main path—it's marked with green paint splashes. If you're feeling adventurous, you can take the blue path, but stay away from the purple and red, you're not ready for those yet."

Instructor Allgood burst away like the wind, duster flying behind him. He went right over the edge.

"Last one back at the Hold has to serve Eddie tonight," said Portia as she sprinted after the instructor.

Zayn let the others go ahead and took one last look at the sunrise before pouring faez into the imbuement. It was easy to follow the others, noting the green splashes strategically painted on the sides of buildings and marking the roof. Instructor Allgood was a few roofs ahead, bouncing across them as if they were made of trampolines.

As Zayn ran, he channeled more faez, passing Skylar and then Vin in short order. He sensed them straining to catch up, and he hardly felt like he'd reached his limits.

The instructor veered left towards the blue path, and Zayn followed. The jumps were longer, the course more intricate, but Zayn had no problem following.

When Instructor Allgood noticed him behind, he went faster. Much to his surprise, Zayn found he could keep up. This seemed to surprise Instructor Allgood as well as he didn't bother hiding his emotions.

Then Instructor Allgood found another gear, and he

blurred across the rooftops, heading into the purple path, which had seemingly impossible jumps. The instructor flew across a wide gap and landed a good ten feet beyond the edge of the next building.

Zayn followed, and gave it everything he had. The impact to his knees and ankles reverberated through his body, but as soon as he leapt, he knew he would make it across. For a brief and wonderful moment, it felt like he was flying. He wondered if his display might earn them a spot out of the bottom, and he was delighted when Instructor Allgood turned his head to see Zayn following.

His excitement lasted until he reached the apex of his leap, and he saw the landing area. Unlike the other rooftops, this one had partially fallen in. When Instructor Allgood had made the leap, he'd gone an extra ten feet to land on a safe spot.

Zayn wheeled his arms, trying to make the last few feet, but there was nothing he could do. He went through the buckled roof, crashing into rotted beams and the floor beneath it. He felt the world collapsing around him and then nothing.

Chapter Fourteen
The Hold
On a bed, groggy...

Zayn remembered pain, as if every nerve in his body had been turned on, then sweet darkness again. For a long time, he was a speck in the void, a tiny ball of pain in an infinite emptiness.

There were flashes of other, of life: people standing over him murmuring in guarded tones, the knotted brown forehead of a familiar woman, the throat-choking smell of faez.

When he woke enough to piece two consecutive thoughts together, he realized he was back in his room in the Hold. He tried to move, but his body was contained within a cold black carapace of unknown material. Runes covered the hard material. He could feel his bones being forced to knit together.

Zayn had had a cavity once, and when the dentist had put the drill into his tooth, the vibration had been agonizing. This felt like the drill, except it was in dozens of places around his body.

When it grew too much, he passed out again. He woke to find Instructor Allgood standing over him.

"Why are you here?"

His condemnation was somehow comforting. Zayn was able to choke out some words, though they were raspy. "I fell."

"That's not what I asked," said Instructor Allgood.

"I'm here to learn," said Zayn.

"It doesn't look like it," he said and left.

When Zayn woke again, he was looking into his cousin's eyes. The black runed carapace had been removed from his body, but he was in no mood to move anything.

"Hey," said Keelan, barely able to meet his gaze, and in that one word, Zayn knew how close he'd come to death.

"They didn't tell my family, did they?" whispered Zayn.

"No."

"Good," said Zayn, and he tried to sit up, but couldn't muster the energy. "I don't want them to worry. How long have I been out?"

"Nine days and you've still got more time for recovery," said Keelan. "You're way behind. I don't know how you're not going to get sent back home at the end of this. You know that won't go well with the Lady."

There was a long silence in which neither of them made an attempt to say something. His cousin looked over his shoulder. "I have to go."

With no one else in the room, Zayn probed his injuries. His dark skin had been yellowed with old bruises. He saw faint scars where magically induced healing had occurred. The area around his elbow where he'd received his tattoo had a tight bandage wrapped around it. Runes had been drawn onto the bandage.

When Zayn opened his mind to faez, a sharp migraine stabbed through his head. He didn't know if the bandage was blocking him, or his injuries, but he wasn't going to try again. It was like biting an electrical cord.

He was too weak to do much other than sip from the water

tube near his mouth.

Later in the day, his teammates returned. They had bags under their eyes. Down another member, the work he normally carried had to be spread out between them.

"Hey Zayn," said Portia, looking at him with sympathy. "It's good to see you awake. When you went into that building, I didn't think you'd be coming out."

"What happened? After I went in?" asked Zayn.

"Instructor Allgood went in after you," said Vin. "He came out quickly, blood all over him, some of it his. He brought you somewhere, and then we didn't see you for a few days. Then you showed up in the room with all these tubes and wires connected to you."

"I'm sorry, you guys," said Zayn. "I shouldn't have tried to make that jump. I wanted to impress him so we could get out of last place. Now it's going to be impossible."

"Don't worry about us," said Skylar, knocking the hair out of her eyes. "You get better."

They chatted for a while longer, catching up on what had happened while he was out. Another student had dropped out of the Academy due to the stress, and they were sparring with faez-speed in the dojo, which had doubled the number of broken bones a day. It hit him hard how much he wanted to be with them training.

Instructor Pennywhistle knocked softly on the door and asked, "May I speak with Zayn alone?"

They left him with her. She pulled up a chair next to his bed, crossed her legs, and placed her manicured hands on her knees. She wore a fuzzy white sweater and a black pencil skirt. She smelled like lavender. It was soothing.

"I really screwed up, didn't I?" he asked her.

"You have, as your fellow first year Eddie might say, screwed the pooch," she said.

"Is the patron mad?" asked Zayn.

Instructor Pennywhistle considered the question for a moment and replied, "At this moment, she does not know since she is away on business, but let's assume she would be greatly disappointed." She sighed heavily. "Here's the problem. You have a couple of weeks of recovery ahead of you. You damaged your imbuement in the fall, and you cannot use faez until it's healed. There is a chance that your access to faez is damaged permanently. When an imbuement is new, the faez flowing through your body has to reroute itself, but the damage to your arm has blocked that."

"What are my options?" he asked.

Instructor Pennywhistle lifted her chin, stroking her neck in thought. "We at the Academy understand your particular situation is different from the other students. The Lady of Varna can be a difficult mistress to those that fail her."

Feeling there was an opportunity for honesty, Zayn asked, "Why is there a relationship between the Lady and the Academy?"

"That's between Priyanka and the Lady, but I know our patron, and I assume it's for a good reason," said Instructor Pennywhistle.

"But she must know that we're all trapped," said Zayn. "We can't leave, don't get to make our own lives, except that which she gives us."

Instructor Pennywhistle's lips grew thin. "If you want me to tell you the world is a fair place, then you're not as strong as I think you are. The world requires compromise in difficult situations."

"It also requires conviction," said Zayn.

"Says the young man whose uncle paid the price for his, but not his father." She paused while he recoiled. "Of course we know about that. We learn about all of our students so that we might best guide them, and because there are those that would do us harm that we must ward ourselves from."

Zayn looked away, heat rising to his cheeks. Of course, she was right. What convictions had he shown?

"What now?" he asked.

"Like I said, we understand your particular situation is more challenging than the others. Under normal circumstances, we would allow you to heal, and if you did properly, you could rejoin your fellow students. Being as far behind as you are, it would be unlikely that you would pass the year, and you would return to your previous life. But like I said, we understand your particular situation.

"So we're offering a way out. If you fail to continue after your first year, the Lady will not be kind, to you or your family. If you wish, we will not fix the damage to the imbuement, leaving you crippled and without access to faez. We will inform the Lady of the unfortunate accident that caused it—making it clear that it was no fault of yours, a lapse in our rigorous training regimen—and she will take you back into Varna."

"Will she believe it?" asked Zayn.

"We believe so," said Instructor Pennywhistle.

"So if I give up my access to faez and leave the Hundred Halls, I can return to my family?" he asked.

"Essentially," she said.

"Can I think about it?" he asked.

She nodded. "You're a couple of weeks away from being ready to be healed. We'll give you until then to decide. Is that fair?"

"More than fair. Thank you."

Instructor Pennywhistle patted his leg and stood. She looked ready to leave, but turned back to him.

"I'm sure you came into the Academy with certain expectations of what we're about. I know you've seen little more than the Hold and a few wards of the city, but I can tell you that we do important things here, necessary things. If you stayed and put your mind to it, you could become one of our best. I see that in you. Despite your fall, Instructor Allgood was rightly impressed with your making the leap in the first place. Not only the leap itself, but that you were willing to take that chance. You could be great here, if you stay."

She left without giving him a chance to answer.

Zayn slumped back into the bed. He noticed a little Christmas tree in the corner of their room with pink and gold ornaments on it. There were a few presents under the tree, perfectly wrapped. It was then he realized it was Christmas Eve.

He imagined at that moment that Neveah was in the kitchen whistling as she brewed up another delicious meal, while his mom and dad were seated at the counter talking excitedly about their projects, using their hands like conductors. The twins would be causing trouble somewhere in the house, and Imani would be plotting to ruin it as Queen of the Jungle. He could see everything in the Stack, every wall and couch, every painting and pot, from the third-floor slide to the generator in the hand-dug cellar. He could see everything—except himself.

Chapter Fifteen
Varna, July 2012
The best things in life are free

Perched on the light pole above Ms. Gardenia's trailer with a screwdriver stuck between his teeth, Zayn carefully maneuvered his body so he could get access to the cable box. With the small gray door flipped open, Zayn replaced the cheater card with the latest version.

The work was easy, but he had to be careful not to fry the card while installing it. While he worked, the sounds of Castlewood trailer park were all around him: the crush of gravel beneath tires as a rust-tinged truck passed beneath, the shouts of the kids on the swings, the hum of the transformer further up the pole.

When he was finished, he returned to the trailer. Ms. Gardenia was cutting coupons out of the glossy section, the steady snip-snip filling the air. Zayn turned on her TV and flipped through the channels before announcing, "Everything's back to the way it was. You should even get QVC and a few new channels with this filter."

Busy cutting away, Ms. Gardenia glanced up. "What do I owe you?"

"Nothing for me, ma'am."

She paused, the scissors dangling in her wrinkly, liver-spotted hand. "Now, Zayn, you know I can't have that."

"There is something I want you to do, but it's not for me. Mr. Lopez hasn't been feeling great since the medicine ran out. I've heard him mention he had a hankering for your spicy egg casserole, the one you bring to the potlucks. I bet that'd take his mind off the pain if you brought him one."

Ms. Gardenia leaned forward, shaking her scissors at him. "You know I can't refuse that, but what about you, young man? I know you're planning on going to that art school in a few years. Can't you take a few bucks?"

"No, ma'am, but thank you," he said. "I have to get going. Don't forget Mr. Lopez."

As soon as the screen door banged shut behind him, Zayn heard his name from up the street. His Aunt Lydia was outside her house, waving him down with her only arm, a cigarette dangling from her lips.

"Aunt Lydia," he said, leaning down to give her a kiss on the cheek when he reached her.

She had milk chocolate skin with messy light brown hair and smelled like menthol.

"Sweet, sweet Zayn," she said, leaning into her Alabama accent like it was a shovel. "You seen my dumbass son around?"

"He's not dumb, Aunt Lydia, and you shouldn't talk about him that way," he said.

"Well, he may get good grades, but he's always doing dumb things, which means he's probably out causing trouble," she said, taking a drag off her cigarette until the end was cherry red.

"I thought he was stacking wood for Mr. Holland today," lied Zayn.

Aunt Lydia wrinkled her nose. "Maybe so. If he would have had a man raisin' him like you gots, then maybe he wouldn't be so bad."

Zayn swallowed his retort. It was better to let her say her piece and move on; otherwise, she'd keep bringing up his uncle's death until he left.

"Did you need something?" he asked, trying to wring the accent out of his words. "I see you're not wearing your prosthetic."

"Cheap-ass piece of shit broke again," said Aunt Lydia with a frown.

"I can take a look at it if you want," he said, heading towards the front door. "I'll bet it's just a broken wire again."

"It needs a sure-fire enchantment, not some fiddle-dee-do with a screwdriver, no offense," she said, tugging him back. "I know you gots some magic, my Keelan tells me sometimes. Why can't you fix it right?"

"You know why, Aunt Lydia," he said, nodding towards the center of town. "Magic has never been any good in this town. It only gets you the Lady's notice."

Aunt Lydia poked her finger into his arm, nearly burning him with her cigarette in the process. "Well, bless your heart, you like livin' poor. Don't you see them that do what she wants, livin' in those big houses and driving those fancy cars, and want some of that?"

"There's more to life than fancy cars and having people think you're important," said Zayn under his breath.

"Maybe my boy don't have what you have, maybe he needs the Lady's notice. I wish you'd stop filling his head with all that nonsense that magic is bad. Magic like anything else, it depends on how you use it," she said. "You family, you should be lookin' out for him."

Maybe I am, he thought.

"I have to get going, Aunt Lydia. You should come by for dinner," he said. "Mom and Dad miss you. You're always welcome. It'd be nice to have us all together for a nice meal. I can fix your arm while you and Mom catch up."

Aunt Lydia pulled hard on the cigarette until it crackled like a winter fire. She glanced askance, chewing on her smoke.

"No, you tell Sela I ain't feelin' well," she said, holding her palm across her stomach. "I'll catch up with her later."

The dry canal was the fastest way home. Zayn left the gravel paths of the Castlewood trailer park and skidded down the concrete slope.

He found Keelan waiting for him on the path to his house throwing black walnuts at squirrels scampering through the trees. The cicadas hummed their droning chorus, oscillating like ocean waves.

"Is she coming?" asked Keelan, hopefully.

Zayn shook his head. "No."

Keelan went inward. "Thanks for trying. I miss when we all had dinner together."

His eyes were dark with memories. Zayn was afraid his cousin was going to slide into one of his moods, but a playful grin rose on his cousin's lips instead. Keelan launched a black walnut at him, which Zayn easily sidestepped.

In retaliation, Zayn scooped up one from the forest floor and whipped it at Keelan, smacking him right in the side.

"That was a good one," said Keelan, laughing and rubbing his hip. "Remember when we would have those big wars, when every kid in the trailer park came out, and it'd only end when it got so dark you were afraid you'd run into a tree?"

"Seems like only a few years ago," said Zayn.

"I always lost those wars," said Keelan. "Which is why I always made sure I was on your team."

"On my team? Those were your teams," said Zayn,

throwing his arm around his cousin's shoulders.

"Nah, they were yours. You always came up with the best, most outrageous plans, like when we hid in the dumpster waiting with a bucket of walnuts," said Keelan.

"Which, if you remember, failed spectacularly when the garbage truck picked us up, and we only survived by screaming our lungs out," said Zayn.

Keelan shrugged. "I forgot about that. I guess I only remember the ice cream we blackmailed the driver out of to keep us quiet."

Their conversation was interrupted by a bell ringing, which brought smiles to both of their faces. When they were kids, their parents would hang out together. When it was time for dinner, they'd ring a bell that could be heard as far as the east edges of Castlewood.

"Last one does the dishes?" asked Zayn.

Keelan took off running, laughter trailing behind him like a bright banner. Zayn burst after, a grin plastered on his face. The race through the trees was short and sweet, ending when Keelan lunged through the gate with his arms up in victory. Their earlier dark discussion was banished by the flush of adrenaline. They walked with linked arms towards the Stack, the home of Maceo and Sela Carter and their brood of five kids.

To some in Varna, the Stack was an eyesore, a metal monstrosity built on the edge of a junkyard, and only tolerated because it was hidden by a line of vine-choked woods. To Zayn, his brothers and sisters, and when he visited, Keelan, the Stack was like living in a Disneyland imagined by a robot Willy Wonka.

The bones of the Stack were six shipping containers, placed two at a time on top of each other like Jenga blocks and creating a courtyard in the center. Nooks, bridges, and platforms jutted from sections, connecting at others, until it was either an Escher drawing or a Rube Goldberg device. At first glance, some sections appeared perilous, like a bridge made of chain-link fence that crossed the highest level or a whimsical slide that exited the turret at the top of the left stack—which was Zayn's room—and curled its way to the ground.

His father, Maceo, was currently painting a field of sunflowers against a greenish alien sky, beneath which a giant house marched on long metal legs.

"That's ripped, Uncle Maceo," said Keelan. "You should have been a professional painter."

Maceo pulled his paintbrush away, grinning at them. His tight kinky hair had a breath of gray to it that seemed antithetical to the exuberance contained within his gaze.

"I will assume, in the parlance of youth, that 'ripped' is a positive," said Maceo. "And I *am* a professional painter, it's just the pay isn't so great."

"Neither is being a high school teacher," said Keelan.

"I get paid in seeing young minds blossom," said Maceo, pointing his paintbrush at them. He taught ethics and history at the school. "And more importantly, now that you're here, we can get dinner started."

Hugs were shared. They helped him bring the paints inside and washed the brushes out in the outdoor sink, a nice stainless steel one that had been rescued from when the Big Boy restaurant went out of business a couple of years before. Maceo had traded the junk man, Doc Stephenson, a new sign for the sink.

His mom, Sela, was camped at her drawing desk, ponytail bobbing as she worked on sketches of possible new additions to the Stack, alongside reams of mechanical loading calculations. Her cocoa skin glowed beneath the soft lights, and seeing his mom deep in her work always brought a grin to Zayn's lips.

He moved to give her a hug around the time Keelan roared after his youngest sister, Imani, who was wearing her lion costume. She squealed with delight and escaped into the courtyard, where Izzy and Max were setting up dinner beneath the strung-together holiday lights and a canopy of swooping fabrics.

"Time to put the pen down, Mom. It smells like Neveah almost has dinner ready," said Zayn. "And you need more light in here, this isn't good for your eyes."

Sela pursed her lips and raised an exquisite eyebrow. "Oh, really? I seem to recall giving you that advice from time to time." She stopped and sniffed, eyes widening with delight. "Is that masala?"

"You just noticed?"

Sela pushed Zayn in the arm. "I was busy. Oh, I just remembered." She reached down and dug into a battered olive green shoulder bag with patches sewn into it, pulling out a black metal gear about the size of her palm. "Doc found this in the yard. Is this what you're looking for?"

Zayn snatched it away as if it were a hunk of precious gold, spun it around in his hands, and ran his fingers into the greasy grooves. "I think so."

Before he could scurry away, Sela grabbed his arm. "Not until after dinner. Speaking of, did you...?"

He winced. "Sorry, Mom. She said she wasn't feeling good."

His mom's eyes grew watery as she looked away. "That's okay. She needs time."

Zayn didn't bother saying that it'd been years, and more time probably wasn't going to heal things; his growling stomach reminded him of more immediate concerns, like eating.

He found his younger sister, Neveah, in her element, surrounded by steam and spices, shifting pots and pans, coaxing flame from the stove like a magician. A bright red scarf tamed her tight braids, but the beads at the ends clicked together as she moved.

Zayn snuck a salty Kalamata olive from the tray before she could smack his hand away.

"Back, you scamp!"

"Hey, I was the one that got these olives." He shoved the olive into his mouth. "Oh my, that's delicious. What did you do?"

"Chef's secret," she said, bouncing to the oven to pull out a loaf of sourdough bread. Then she paused and looked over her shoulder. "If you even touch this, I will turn you into sushi."

"Real chefs don't threaten their customers," said Zayn, lurking near the olive tray.

"You're not my customer, you're my brother, and until you can get me a shot at a Michelin star, you're not eating until it's ready," she said. "Can you stir the soup? It's the pot on the left."

"They don't give Michelin stars to home kitchens," said Zayn, lifting the lid to the pot and almost forgetting to stir when the delightful aroma hit his nose. "Or to fifteen-year-old girls in Varna, Alabama."

"Well, they should," said Neveah, sternly. "Now go help the twins, you'll eat soon enough."

Izzy and Max were whirling around the outdoor table, a pair of giant wooden spools, setting plates and silverware. Their hair was currently platinum blond and spiked like an anime character as they nosily chatted about their favorite subject.

"What about the zebra—" asked Izzy.

"Oh, that's an easy one," replied Max. "Equus quagga."

"You didn't let me finish," said Izzy, sliding plates across the table. Each one came perilously close to falling off before stopping at the edge. "What about the different types of plains zebra?"

"That wasn't what you were going to ask," said Max.

"Was too."

"Whatever," said Max, with an epic eye roll. "But the answer is equus quagga burchellii, equus quagga boehmi, equus quagga selousi, equus quagga borensis, and equus quagga chapmani."

"Ha! You forgot the equus quagga crawshayi," countered Izzy.

"I was about to say that, but you didn't give me a chance," said Max.

Zayn cut in, not because he didn't enjoy their bantering, but because it could last for days. Just the year before, they'd gone on about the various types of flying squirrels for three whole weeks until the entire house mutinied.

"What do you two need help with? And love the hair."

The twins stopped and glared.

"We did this five days ago," said Izzy, pouting.

"Where have you been?" asked Max.

Zayn paused, reviewing his memory. He'd been working on his art project and doing work around Castlewood for the last week.

"Sorry, you two. I guess my mind is on other things."

They nodded and focused their attention back on folding napkins. Keelan showed up a moment later with a giggling Imani draped over his shoulder.

"The lion tamer has returned!" Keelan set Imani on the ground. "Hey, Izzy. Hey, Max. Or...is it the other way around?"

"Keelan!" said the twins at the same time, rolling their eyes.

Keelan winked at Zayn. Izzy and Max were fraternal twins, not identical, though most people couldn't tell that upon first glance.

"Should we make them wear name tags? Isaac and Maxine. I've got a magic marker around here somewhere," said Keelan, patting his jeans as if he were actually looking.

An ear-busting whistle from the kitchen announced that dinner was ready. Everyone poured into Neveah's space, grabbing plates and bowls that were steaming with food, even Imani in her lion costume, carrying the bread bowl on her head and marching at the front of the procession.

The dinner was a noisy affair, a symphony of conversations and laughter that carried into the night air. They were halfway through the meal when Neveah asked, "Who's in charge of the question tonight?"

"I had last night," said Max with a chicken bone in his fingers, "and Izzy was the night before."

"It's not me," said Neveah, looking up from her carrot soup.

Everyone was quiet for a moment, until Imani shouted, "Keelan's turn!"

His cousin didn't always eat with them, but when he did, he participated as normal.

"Nah, someone else can have it. I wouldn't know what to ask," he said.

As soon as Zayn caught his mother's eyebrow raise, he knew Keelan was in trouble. That arching was like a predator crouching low, getting ready for the pounce.

"Nice try, Keelan," said Sela. "I don't remember whose turn it is, but you haven't gone in a while. Why don't you indulge us with a question."

"Aunt Sela..."

The arched eyebrow went further up, defying gravity and all sorts of rules of physics on the way. "Keelan..."

Keelan set down his fork. "Alright fine. I know I'm not

going to get out of it now. Question time. Damn, I wish I knew it was going to be my turn. The question is...what would you do if you didn't have to stay in Varna for the rest of your life?"

It grew quiet until only the insects in the woods could be heard. Zayn had caught the darkness in his cousin's eyes as he'd asked the question.

The quiet went on far too long, until Neveah spoke up. "Well, duh. I'd go to Paris and be a world-famous chef."

Her response lifted their collective shoulders. Sela reached out to squeeze Maceo's hand. "I'd really love to see the pyramids. Then open up an architectural firm in Tokyo—together, of course."

Imani screamed a little too loud, "I'd be a lion!" bringing laughter.

Max spoke for the twins. "We're only eleven, so we don't have to know yet...but, we'd like to go on a road trip, for like a summer. Grand Canyon and all."

Everyone looked to Zayn. He hesitated, not because he didn't know, but because he avoided thinking about it because it would never happen.

"There's an art school in Toronto, and then after that, wherever the wind took me." He looked to his cousin before he could get misty-eyed. "Your turn."

Zayn thought he knew what Keelan was going to say, something about joining the military, or building race cars, or maybe just "anywhere but here." But it wasn't any of those things.

"I'd want to be with my dad."

Chapter Sixteen
Ninth Ward, January 2014
Don't move or I fireball you

A snowstorm had buried the city of Invictus, turning the bodega into the center of the universe for the locals. Zayn could barely look up, as he rang up the never-ending line of customers with their red noses sticking out of their parkas.

His body had mostly healed from the fall, but a lingering ache stayed with him. The runed bandage remained on his arm, so he couldn't use faez.

"You take care of your wife, Mrs. Kettle," said Zayn, handing cold medicine to an elegant black woman in a designer winter coat. "Rest and a shot of Appleton rum."

Mrs. Kettle winked. "You know my Angela doesn't drink."

"Then you'll have to drink it for her. Uncle Larice got a new shipment of rum in, straight from the heart of Jamaica. Every sip will remind you of sunshine," said Zayn with a smile.

"Nice try, Zayn," said Mrs. Kettle. "You really are a charming young man, but I'm a red wine girl. I like my merlot."

"Respect," said Zayn.

As Mrs. Kettle was on her way out the door, Katie slipped in with the chill wind. Fat flakes of snow dusted her aquamarine hair that went in all directions. Zayn noticed how rosy her cheeks were, how soft her lips looked.

"Careful, Katie," said Mrs. Kettle. "Zayn could sell stripes to a skunk today."

After she left, Katie threw her elbows on the counter, leaving enough room for other customers to make their purchases. She wore a thin Army jacket and no hat or gloves.

"You crazy, Katie. Gonna get frostbite like that," he said as he rang up another customer.

She knocked the snow from her hair with a brush of her hand.

"You know I'm good. This is the city of sorcery, right?"

"It is, Katie. It is," said Zayn, leaning into his Jamaican accent.

"You feeling better? Your Uncle Larice said you had the flu pretty bad," she said, leaning on the counter.

"They had to take me to the hospital and everything," said Zayn. "Wires and tubes and all that. Doctors said it was dangerous."

She reached out and touched his arm. Her lips had bunched up into a little bow of concern, which warmed his heart.

"I'm glad you're better. I was worried about you," she said.

If there'd ever been a moment when he was certain that he could lean over and kiss a girl and not be rebuked, it was this one. But the counter between them and his sore ribs made the maneuver problematic.

"Did you hear about that guy that combusted on Ninth and Arcane?" he asked.

"I did!" she said, eyes wide. "But he didn't spontaneously combust. I heard some fire creature crawled out of the concrete and swallowed him, leaving a burnt crispy behind."

"That's disgusting," said Zayn. "There's been a rash of these weird deaths going on all over the ward. No one knows why."

"There have?" she asked, a glint of worry in her eyes.

Zayn was about to ask her what she meant by that, when she jumped as if something had bit her.

"Oh! I almost forgot, or really, I guess I didn't forget, if I'm telling you, but anyway, we got another gig at the High Dragon. This time, like, an actual Saturday night. The owner loved our music, though he said we were going to have to up the show experience if we wanted to keep coming back. But I've got that covered."

"That's excellent news, Katie. I'm really happy for you," said Zayn, giving her a fist bump. "I wish I could make it."

"Are you sure?" she asked, her fingers kneading into his arm. "I was really hoping you'd be there. I can get you a fake ID."

Zayn realized she was wearing perfume, which she'd never worn before. It smelled good, really good.

"I'm sorry, Katie. I...I'm leaving the city soon. I'm going back home," he said.

The excitement she'd carried into the bodega crumbled. "What? Does this have to do with being sick?"

"There are...some family problems...back in Jamaica," he said. "I need to go back and help."

"Oh, are you sure you can't stay a little longer? The show is in a month. It could be a last night in the country kind of party," she said, biting her lower lip hopefully.

It took effort to get the words out. "I...wish I could."

"But what about your Uncle Larice? He needs your help," she said, then when he didn't reply, she added, "It always seems like when I meet cool and interesting people that they leave."

Katie pulled her hand back as if she hadn't realized it was there.

"Goodbye, I guess. It was nice meeting you," she said suddenly, casting her gaze downward and rushing out the door.

"Great," he said to the empty store. "I can't even leave without screwing it up."

Part of him wanted to wait and see her band, but he knew that was dangerous. It would only make him want to stay, which would only lead to more problems. It was better if he made a clean break without complications.

Zayn was so deep into his thoughts, he barely noticed a short dude with blotchy pale skin and a beard that looked like it'd been through a shredder was standing before the counter. He had wild, nervous eyes and was sweating.

"Can I help you, man?" asked Zayn.

The nervous man thrust his hand out, fingers splayed. "Give me all your money, or I flame you. I can do magic."

When the guy spoke, Zayn recognized him. He was the asshole who'd taken his money in the park on Zayn's first day in the Hall. He was a part of the Glaucos Gang, or something like that.

"Hey man, you don't have to do this," said Zayn, keeping his hands above the counter. He was afraid the guy might recognize him. The only thing keeping him safe was that the last time they'd met, Zayn had been painted gold.

"Don't you tell me what to do. Just get your ass into that cash register and give me what's there. All of it. Right now. I know it's flush with cash. I've been watching you all morning," he said.

Patchy seemed less put together this time. His clothes had holes in them, and he looked more desperate. Zayn hesitated. It'd been a great day for sales, and he knew Uncle Larice had mounting medical bills for a bad back.

"Hurry up," said Patchy, glancing towards the door. "Like right now!"

Patchy strained, and a few sparks came out of his hand.

"You can't do magic," said Zayn, preparing to leap over the counter, but the robber went fishing into his jacket and pulled out a revolver.

Zayn backed away. "Sorry, man."

The end of the barrel looked like a tunnel ten feet wide. He felt like it was an eye following him.

But also, Zayn felt strangely calm. He glanced towards the door as if someone were about to come in. When the robber turned his head to look, Zayn catapulted over the counter, swiping the gun away as his stomach slid across the glass.

The gun went off, exploding the stacked boxes of Belvita biscuits. Zayn grabbed the robber's wrist and slammed it against his upraised knee, forcing him to release the gun.

In a panic, the robber slipped away, but fumbled at the door, trying desperately to get away.

Zayn retrieved the gun and pointed it at the robber, who backed against the glass.

"Stop. Don't move," said Zayn.

Patchy's frightened expression slowly hardened, until he wore a scowl. "You're not going to shoot me."

The robber opened the door and slipped through it, and all the while Zayn kept the gun trained on him. Only when Patchy ran across the street did Zayn allow himself to relax.

With the danger past, a wave of shaking overwhelmed him, until he had to lean against the counter.

"Dammit," he said, smacking his fist against the crumbled biscuits that had exploded when the bullet hit them.

Once he regained function of his limbs, Zayn went around to the back, placed the gun on safety, and shoved it into a drawer. Then he cleaned up the ruined boxes of Belvita biscuits and the shattered flaky crumbs on the counter.

While straightening the products on the shelves that got knocked during their brief tussle, Zayn found a small baggie on the floor with a symbol printed on the outside. The symbol was an upside-down "Y" with a big dot on the top. It was strangely familiar though he couldn't place it. Eventually he decided the symbol just looked similar to something he knew.

But he knew the material inside, or at least had encountered it before. It was the same stuff he'd taken from Patchy in the park. He carefully sniffed the bag before shoving it into a pocket.

Back behind the counter, Zayn couldn't believe how lucky he'd been that no customers had been in the bodega when the robber had attacked. He couldn't imagine what might have happened had Uncle Larice been behind the counter. What if he'd tried to stop the guy? Would he have shot him?

Zayn examined the baggie again. The earlier conversation with Katie about the weird deaths came back to him. There was something familiar in the way the robber had acted, just like the guy who'd turned himself crystalline.

"Why am I even worrying about this? I'm going back to Varna," he said.

But saying the words out loud didn't convince himself that it was what he wanted to do. If he stayed, he might get kicked out at the end of the year anyway, and that would put his family at risk. If he left now, under the pretense of his injury, then he'd be safe, and so would his family.

And he really liked the people from the area. Though working at the bodega was a front for the Academy, he enjoyed his interactions with the people. Was this what Instructor Pennywhistle meant when she talked about "necessary things"?

He felt a duty to the people of the ward, to find out what

was going on with the drug. But he couldn't do that if he left.

The earlier surety that he should return to Varna faded. The injury had given him an out, but now he didn't want to take it. And if he stayed, it'd mean he'd get to see Katie again, assuming their team could climb out of the bottom to have enough free time that he could see her.

If he stayed, it wouldn't be easy. His team was in last place, way behind now because of his injury.

While Zayn was ruminating, Uncle Larice returned from his treatments at the clinic.

"How was business today?" he asked, kicking the snow from his boots as he stood in the open door.

Zayn had been planning to tell him about the robber, but something in the way Uncle Larice unzipped his coat with trembling hands made him change his mind.

"Excellent," said Zayn. "Best day in weeks. I sold nearly half a case of Appleton rum today."

"Good, man. Lord knows I need it," he said, pulling his graying dreadlocks from beneath his hoodie. "So what was it you wanted to tell me before I left?"

"That you should pick up some merlot," said Zayn. "Mrs. Kettle doesn't drink rum."

Uncle Larice gave him the side eye. "*That's* what you were going to tell me? I thought it was going to be something of some import."

"It is important," said Zayn, holding out a fist, his mind made up about whether or not he was going to stay in the Academy. "I've got to look out for my Uncle Larice."

Chapter Seventeen
The Hold, January 2014
At least he maintained trigger discipline

Still hot from his battle at the bodega, Zayn marched into Allgood's room with the pistol in his fist. He'd made his decision and hadn't wanted to wait until his next class. The instructor's hand flinched towards his staff as Zayn slammed the gun on the table.

"Because of this," he said, staring at Instructor Allgood defiantly.

Amusement passed across his face, but not necessarily in a good way. Zayn sensed the instructor was about half a breath away from grabbing the staff and beating the life out of him.

"You asked me why I'm here," said Zayn. "That's my answer. A guy came in the store to rob me. I took the gun from him."

"Why didn't you kill him?" asked Instructor Allgood.

"Because it would have invited questions from the police. I didn't even tell Uncle Larice about it. The robber hit the store during a lull in business," said Zayn.

Instructor Allgood scooped up the pistol and checked the

safety before examining it.

"At least you had the good sense to remove the bullets before slamming it on my table," said Instructor Allgood with a hint of menace in his voice. "But this still doesn't answer my question. If you want to play cop, go join the Protectors."

Zayn's blood was hot, and it was hard to keep the derision he felt from his voice. "For one, I wasn't given an option on which halls I could choose." Instructor Allgood's forehead knotted dangerously, so Zayn quickly added, "And even if I had been given the choice, I wouldn't have picked the Protectors."

Zayn fished through the right pocket in his jeans, pulling out the handful of bullets and the baggie with the Y-pattern.

"The guy was robbing the bodega to pay for this. I think it's the same drug as from before. I don't know what it is, but I think it has to do with the weird deaths going on in the ward. The crystalline man, the one eaten by fire creatures, the lady who melted into green goo," said Zayn.

When he handed the baggie to Instructor Allgood, he detected a twinge of recognition at the symbol, but it quickly disappeared behind his mask of disinterest.

"What does this matter if you're running back to Varna?" asked Instructor Allgood.

"Because I'm not, I'm staying."

"Why?" challenged Instructor Allgood.

"Instructor Pennywhistle told me that the Academy does important work, necessary work. I think I understand that now. I want to be a part of that."

"What you did in the bodega is Protector work," he said. "That's not what we do. We're not undercover cops, we don't deal in petty shit like robbery."

"That drug isn't petty. I think it gives them magic, but it's not working right and it's killing them. If someone has figured out a way to give anyone magic, think how much that would change things, for the Halls, for the world. So it's not just about the bodega, or the ward, but everything," said Zayn.

"You trying to make a mountain out of a molehill?" asked Instructor Allgood.

"Probably," said Zayn. "But I've gotta start somewhere."

"Well, if it is, it's nothing you should be worrying about. This is above your pay grade."

Zayn was confused. "I thought this would be important."

Instructor Allgood crumpled the baggie in his massive fist and threw it in the wastebasket.

"It might be, or it might not. But you should stay out of it. If that drug does what you say it does, then a first-year Hall student in the bottom group would likely only get himself killed. If it's not what you say it is, then it's Protector work, and you shouldn't worry about it either. So in either case I want you to stay away from that drug," said Instructor Allgood. "Anything else?"

Zayn pulled his sleeve back, revealing the runed bandages.

"If I'm staying, I need my magic back," said Zayn.

Instructor Allgood's nostrils flared. "Then remove it."

Zayn realized that Instructor Pennywhistle had tricked him about his imbuement. He tugged the bandage off his arm and threw it in the wastebasket. He gave Instructor Allgood a long look.

"Are you about to ask me to prom? Get the hell out of my office."

Outside in the dojo, Zayn had to shake his hands out.

"You okay, cuz?" asked Keelan, coming from the hallway that led to his room. "You have some heavy thoughts going."

"I do. I'm staying at the Academy."

"You are?" asked Keelan. "I thought they'd given you a free pass back home. No questions asked. I figured you'd jump at the chance to return home."

"They did, but I'm staying, but I need to ask you something," said Zayn, thinking about the reasons that the instructors would lie to him. "And you have to give me the hard truth. No holding back."

"Sure thing," said Keelan. "But you don't need to force a promise from me. I always tell you the truth."

"I need to know what I'm doing wrong," said Zayn. "If I'm staying, I have to get our team out of last place, but it seems like everything I've done has gone ass-end up."

His cousin gave him a funny look. "The cousin I knew from Varna didn't try to save the world all by himself. He always figured out how to get other people to do it for him." Then Keelan looked away towards the instructor's closed door and his face brightened. "Did you hear about Charla?"

The change of subject was obvious, but Zayn let it slide. "No?"

"She got her named coin. First for the class, and one of the earliest ever," said Keelan.

For some reason this didn't bother him as much as he thought it would. Mostly because he'd remembered that he had other reasons to get out of the bottom in the Academy.

"What's that look for?" asked Keelan.

Zayn smiled. "I remembered that in a couple of weeks, there's a band I really want to see."

Chapter Eighteen
Varna, June 2009
A lesson in reverse charm school

The Goon's bluetick coonhounds, Jordan and Barkley, had passed out beneath the row of basketball arcade games as Zayn packed boxes for shipment. Jordan, the bigger one, was snoring, which competed with the occasional beeping from the arcade games and the constant ripping of packing tape.

The Goon had an obsession with arcade basketball games. There were six lined up in the room Zayn was working in, and he'd seen another twenty in the basement. He'd only been working for the Goon for a couple of months, doing odd jobs around the compound, mostly feeding Jordan and Barkley and making the occasional delivery.

Zayn had no idea what was in the boxes he was packing. There were smaller boxes that went into the bigger ones, which he filled with packing peanuts, closed and taped, and then he wrote out a P.O. Box address with no name. No two boxes went to the same state, which Zayn tried hard not to notice.

A gunshot startled Zayn, who nearly cut himself on the tape ripper. He held his breath until he saw the Goon appear in the workroom, a revolver in his hand.

"Bet that scared your hair straight," said Goon, grinning in that way that always made Zayn feel like he was going to take up the banjo.

"No, sir," said Zayn. "I've come to expect it."

The Goon considered Zayn flatly as if he was disappointed that his little joke had gone unappreciated. Zayn hadn't been lying, even if he'd been startled. The Goon liked to pack his own shells in the next room, and had a small firing range for testing.

"You're getting pretty tall now, aren't you?" asked the Goon, still fingering his revolver.

"I suppose," replied Zayn.

He sensed the Goon had something in mind, but kept his head down and dumped more peanuts into the open box.

"What are you now, fifteen?"

Zayn looked up. "Fourteen."

"That would make Imani three now?" asked the Goon in a forced casual way.

"Yes, sir," said Zayn. "Just had her birthday last month."

"And the twins would be eight then. That's a lot of mouths to feed. Your parents have any luck finding new work?" asked the Goon.

"No, sir. Not for long anyway. My mom can find freelance jobs on occasion, but they don't last. Seems like whenever she works with an architectural company for more than a few months, they suddenly stop calling her," said Zayn.

The Goon shoved the revolver into a hip holster. Everyone in the south owned guns, but Zayn had never heard of anyone who owned more than the Goon, and half of them were enchanted with mage-killing bullets due to his paranoia. Last week, Zayn'd found a snub-nosed pistol in Jordan's healthy heart dog food bag. It'd probably fallen out of the Goon's pocket when he was pouring it.

"I heard your father's interviewing at the high school," said the Goon. "I bet that'd be real nice if he got the job. I heard there's an abnormally large number of candidates, what with the recession and all. A good word might go a long way, if he knew the right people."

Zayn wasn't oblivious to what the Goon was insinuating. "A good word would be helpful."

"You have been quite industrious around here," said the Goon. "Jordan and Barkley do seem to enjoy the attention."

Jordan, the larger of the two, raised his head and his ear flopped over. Barkley was still asleep, snoring and twitching his paws.

The Goon smiled big and wide, and Zayn felt like he could drive a train through that grin. "I have a few errands I need to run. Would you like to help out?"

Zayn had been expecting this question for a week, so he didn't hesitate to answer. "Yes, sir."

"Good choice," said the Goon.

The Goon had been wearing Adidas workout clothes, but switched to jeans and a tan jacket, even though Zayn thought that with a name like the Goon he should be wearing overalls. They hopped into the Goon's red Fireball GTX, heading across town going west.

"Do you like Varna?" asked the Goon, in his not-so-obvious way.

"It doesn't really matter whether or not I like it," said Zayn.

"But you wouldn't stay if you didn't have to," said the Goon.

"Yes, sir."

"I was like you once, desperate to get out of town," said the Goon, turning on a blinker, heading onto the old highway that went around the south side. "Prayed to all the gods that I'd have even a spark of magic so I could go to the Halls and escape for a time. You have the faez, don't you, just like your parents."

Zayn hesitated, chewing on his lower lip.

"Don't worry," said the Goon, "I knew your parents in high school. I know what they can do and I know why they keep their heads down." He tapped on the steering wheel. "But my point is that faez or not, everyone comes back to Varna. Everyone. So it's best to start thinking about how you're going to spend that time, make a living, fit into the Lady's little ecosystem."

"You want me to work for you," said Zayn.

The Goon made a sour face. "Now don't say it like it's such a bad thing."

"I'm sorry, sir. I didn't mean it like that. I've been saving up to go to art school. There's a place in Selma, close enough I can come back every month," said Zayn.

"That's fine, you can do that if you want. Art school's only two years. Varna's for life. I can wait if I have to. And you'll need money while you're there."

The Goon looked up and made a hard turn onto a gravel road, giving Zayn the chance to change the subject.

"What do I need to do, wherever we're going?" asked Zayn.

The Goon snorted lightly. "You're a cagey one, aren't you? Can't get a thing past you. Well, I need you to check on an investment of mine, deliver a message. You in?"

Zayn felt his heart boom against his chest. He knew he'd come to this point eventually. And while the Goon hadn't spelled out the deal—work for me and I'll help your family and you personally—it was pretty clear cut. And while he hadn't told his parents that he was doing odd jobs for the Goon, if he started doing outside work for him, eventually they would hear. But neither of his parents were working, and despite Neveah's magic in the kitchen—natural, not faez related—meals were getting thin. Eventually someone was going to have to make a sacrifice.

"I'm in," said Zayn.

"Good," said the Goon. "I'm going to drop you off up the street. You're going to knock on that blue trailer at the bottom of the hill. A William Longer will answer the door, and you will inform him that the bill is due and that you're there to collect it. He'll whine and cry a bit, but tell him that he has to pay or it ain't gonna be good. You got that?"

Though he'd only been working for the Goon a short time, Zayn noticed that when he was delivering a serious, don't-mess-with-me message, he usually fell back into a thick Alabama accent. Otherwise, he could almost sound like he'd gone to a college in Ohio.

"Yes, sir," said Zayn.

The Goon leaned in conspiratorially. "Just between you and me, I'll give him a couple of weeks to get the money. I know they just had a third kid and all. But don't let him know that. It's better that they sweat it. Reminds them of who's in charge." He clapped him on the shoulder. "Now go get my money."

The trailer sat on a scratch of land with an old rusted tricycle wheels up on the gravel driveway. The lawn hadn't been cut in weeks, but that wasn't unusual once you got out in the country. With evening coming on, the cicadas were revving up. Zayn checked down the street as he approached the trailer. If trouble happened, the Goon wouldn't know it.

Zayn felt pretty stupid knocking on the trailer door, a fourteen-year-old kid in Varna, Alabama, wearing nothing but jeans and an art school T-shirt with skin as dark as dusk. It didn't matter that he was collecting for the Goon, the guy would probably take one look at Zayn and fetch his gun. He wiped his sweaty palms on his jeans waiting for William to answer the door after he knocked.

There were sounds of a baby crying. A deep male voice yelled into the back. That was the thing about a trailer, every sound carried to the outside. There might be walls, but there was little privacy. So he heard William's approach before the door opened.

William didn't look much older than Zayn. He had freckles and dusty blond hair, grease stains on his shirt. William's voice shook when he spoke. "You're from the Goon, aren't you?"

A young woman's voice came from the back. "Baby? Who's at the door?"

"Just feed the..." He lowered his voice. "Just feed Jacob, will ya." Back to Zayn. "I'm sorry. The Goon. He wants his money, doesn't he?"

Zayn could see in the guy's eyes that he didn't have it. Looked ready to piss himself and Zayn hadn't said a word. On the way up to the trailer Zayn had imagined all the things that might have led to borrowing money from the Goon like a drinking habit, or gambling, but now that he saw William, he figured he was probably just behind on the bills and trying to cover for his new baby.

"He wants it now," said Zayn, and though he didn't intend to put any menace in it, William reacted as if he'd shouted. Fear was eroding William as he watched.

"I...I don't get a paycheck until next week," said William. "I'm doing everything I can. My hair's practically falling out from worry. Look, please, mister, can you say something to him, make him understand?"

Zayn swallowed. He knew what he was supposed to do. But seeing the guy up close, watching the screws unravel until his limbs were practically falling off, was hard. The crying baby seemed to grow louder than the cicadas.

He looked down the street, to check that the Fireball GTX

hadn't snuck up the hill. "Look. The Goon needs his money, and I'll tell him about the paycheck, so don't miss it, but he's not going to do anything to you right now. So you and the missus can rest easy. I imagine that baby is quite a handful."

For a moment, he thought William was going to hug him. "Thank you, sir. Thank you. I sorely do appreciate it. May the Lady bless you."

"Don't forget you got to pay," said Zayn. "He won't be so forgiving next time. Promise me you'll pay."

"I promise. I promise," said William, nodding enthusiastically.

"Goodbye," said Zayn, walking back across the lawn while the screen door banged shut behind him.

He slid into the Fireball next to the Goon. "Did he crap himself like I thought he would?"

"Yes, sir," said Zayn.

"And you put it to him good? No quarter?" asked the Goon with a hard stare as he held onto something he was wearing beneath his shirt, an amulet perhaps.

"Yes, sir," said Zayn. "I thought he was going to puke on my shoes."

The Goon chuckled, slapping the steering wheel a few times. Zayn had half a breath out, a tortured sigh, when the Goon spun on him hard. The revolver was pointed into his gut.

"When I ask you to do something and you say you're going to do it, you'd better do it. If you're not going to, then tell me, but I cannot abide a liar in my house."

"I..."

The Goon's eyes narrowed. "What?"

Zayn closed his eyes for a moment, composing himself. His knees were shaking.

"I screwed up."

"You're damn right you did," said the Goon, searching his

face as if he were deciding whether or not to pull the trigger. Then he sat back, removed the barrel from Zayn's side, and placed it back in the holster.

The Goon revved the engine and did a quick U-turn, spinning gravel into the trees. When he spoke again, the earlier anger was missing, replaced by cold intention.

"You ever do that again, I'll make you and your family pay for your mistakes," said the Goon. "Do you understand me?"

"Yes, sir."

The Goon said nothing more the rest of the trip. He dropped Zayn off up the road from the Stack, handing him a roll of bills.

"See you tomorrow," he said before driving away.

Bewildered, Zayn didn't move for the next minute. Then he counted the money, finding four hundred dollars in twenty-dollar bills. There was no way his parents would believe he earned that kind of money doing odd jobs around town, so he decided he'd run by Aunt Lydia's trailer first and give her half. She hadn't spoken to his mother since Jesse's death, so he didn't think she'd start now. The news that he was working for the Goon was safe for now, though eventually he'd have to figure out how to tell them.

Chapter Nineteen
Uncle Larice's Bodega, February 2014
Merlot diplomacy

The doorbell rattled while Zayn was sitting behind the counter in the bodega, Peter Tosh playing lightly on the speakers behind him. The sounds of tires cutting through the icy slush on the streets grew loud before being muted.

"Mrs. Kettle, how was your trip to Tokyo?" he asked.

She slipped her leather gloves off, one at a time, tugging from the tips of the fingers. "Mildly successful," she said, looking a little weary. "I'll be going back in a few weeks to finish the deal. We're selling a new line of enchanted beauty products, but we're stuck on the finer points of who pays for the logistics and port fees."

She looked up, her pinched consternation turning to surprised relief. "But you don't care a bit about boring business deals. How is your uncle doing?"

"Better, he's responding to the treatments," said Zayn. "And for the record, I do care about boring business deals. I don't intend to work in my uncle's bodega for the rest of my life. I could learn a thing or one hundred from you."

Mrs. Kettle gave him an appraising look. "Well, I'm

exhausted today, but maybe later this week I can stop by and regale you about patent law and the logistical nightmare of shipping products with an expiration date. It's not as interesting as what the researchers do, but it's just as important."

"That would be solid of you, respect," said Zayn.

He reached under the counter and pulled out a velveteen drawstring bag in the general shape of a wine bottle.

"This is for you, ma'am."

"For me?" she said, holding a manicured hand to her chest. "I don't understand."

"You said you liked merlot, so I found a nice bottle for you. If you like it, we can stock some," he said, watching her reaction carefully.

When her gaze fell upon the label, a little hiss of surprise slipped out.

"Chateau de Chevalier 2008," she said with a perfect French accent. "A Bordeaux? How did you...? Oh, it's divine." She hugged the bottle to her chest, a feralness to her grin. "How much do I owe you?"

"Nothing, ma'am." He winked. "First one's free. Want to make sure you like it."

After purchasing a few other items, Mrs. Kettle left, looking absolutely possessive about her new bottle of wine. What she didn't know was that it had a mild suggestive in it.

During the next two hours, he gave out three more gifts—a package of Lindt dark chocolate bars to Ms. Gonzalez to feed her sweet tooth, a special razor for Mr. Vonla's wiry beard, and tickets to the Raspberry Girls tour for Jenny from the expensive flats. Each gift contained a nearly undetectable enchantment that would make its recipient more suggestible to him. He didn't expect to need it, but it didn't hurt to be prepared either.

During the afternoon lull, Zayn chugged an energy drink—

he hadn't slept but a few hours a night for the last week—and put the "Closed" sign on the door.

Using a piece of long string that he'd pre-enchanted, a tablespoon of salt, and a hunk of dark chocolate, Zayn set up a trap in front of the counter. Then he grabbed the final two packages and left the door unlocked.

He jogged three blocks south to the rent-controlled apartment area. By the time he got to the Korean grocery store, his legs were splattered with muddy slush. He knew a spell that would have protected him from the elements, but Zayn the Jamaican wouldn't have known it.

He found Skylar stocking the juice section in back, wearing a New York Islanders hockey jersey with her hair pulled back in a ponytail. She wore the frown of a bored retail worker, which probably wasn't an act, especially wearing the least fashionable clothes that he could imagine.

Zayn held his finger to his mouth to signify silence, then pulled a matchbox out of his inside pocket. He struck the match, letting it flare briefly, then blew it out.

As the smoke trailed from the burnt stick, he said, keeping his voice barely above a whisper, "Okay, man. It is safe to talk."

Skylar could barely contain herself. "What's going on?"

"Ji-yeon," he said, using her persona name.

He pulled a baggie from his pocket. He'd found this one in the alley near the bodega. "Have you seen this pattern before?"

Her forehead rumpled with thought.

"Maybe? It looks familiar, like I've seen it before." She shook her head. "No. That's not it. It just looked like something else. Why?"

"Keep an eye out for it."

Skylar sniffed the baggie. "What is it?"

"A drug of some kind. It might give people magical ability,

but eventually it turns on them. You know all those weird deaths in the area?" She nodded. "I think this is the cause of it."

"What does this have to do with anything? We need to be focused on getting out of the bottom," she said.

"This *is* our ticket out of the bottom," he said. "If there's a drug on the streets that creates magic, then this is major. It could change everything. Figuring that out would put us at the top."

Skylar nodded slowly. "But why did you come here, instead of telling me back at the Hold?"

"I think some of the other teams have been spying on us," Zayn lied.

"I'll keep my eyes and ears out," she said.

What he'd said was partially true. He didn't know if the other teams were spying, but if the instructors were then they would be in trouble. He was certain that the instructors knew more about the strange drug that gave people magic abilities than they were letting on, which was why Allgood had told him to stop worrying about it. But he had no plans of doing that. Not only for Academy reasons, but because he didn't want to see anyone else in the ninth ward get hurt.

When Zayn returned to the bodega, the salt was scattered, the piece of chocolate was missing, and the length of enchanted string was shorter than when he'd left it.

Privately amused by what the unsuccessful trap had told him, Zayn cleaned up the mess, flipped the sign to "Open," and moved behind the counter as the late afternoon rush began. Despite the exhaustion that went down to his toes, Zayn felt better than he had in months.

Chapter Twenty
Second Ward, March 2014
Charm school dropout

"Today you're going to practice the art of magic in espionage," said Instructor Pennywhistle, crossing her arms across her electric blue bodysuit.

The rest of the class looked equally dressed up. Before they'd left to travel across town to the second ward, Instructor Pennywhistle had unlocked a new room in the Hold filled with rows and rows of clothes. Skylar had practically fainted in excitement.

Now they stood inside a side room next to a repurposed high school auditorium. Thin panes of glass in the door revealed hundreds of tables with a chair on either side, typically filled with a man on one side and a woman on the other, though some had a male-male pair, or two females. They were congenially chatting, but there was a nervous air to the room.

"That looks like speed dating," said Keelan.

"Right you are," said Instructor Pennywhistle. "Raise your hand if you think magic can be helpful for espionage."

Twenty-nine students considered the question before slowly raising their hands.

"What might you do to steal information from a diplomat, should you be given the opportunity?" asked Instructor Pennywhistle.

"I would enchant them into giving me the information," said Charla, giving the rest of the class a salacious wink.

"Yes, you could, and then they would know you took it from them, they would file charges with the embassy, which would cause an international incident, and the information would be worthless because they would know you had it," said Instructor Pennywhistle, and Charla's shoulders sank.

"Why would you teach us all these charm and influence spells if we're not supposed to use them?" asked Skylar.

Instructor Pennywhistle smiled at Skylar, then lifted her chin and asked, "Would anyone else care to try?"

There were no takers, until Andrew spoke up. "I would get a hotel room next to theirs and use a dream thief spell to sneak inside their mind while they sleep and get it that way."

"Except most diplomats are trained in the arts of dream fighting. They would likely identify your presence, trap you in the dream, and break your will until you were a gibbering idiot," she said. "Though I suppose that would be an improvement upon the answers I'm being given. Anyone else?"

"For starters, I wouldn't use any magic," said Zayn.

Most of the class looked back at him as if he had defiled the room with his voice.

Instructor Pennywhistle raised an eyebrow. "Explain."

"I would assume that important people understand the power of magic and would prepare accordingly. And even if you could figure out a way around their defenses, there are these rocks I read about that the maetrie use, quazaefs I think they're called, and if you have one in your pocket, you can tell if someone has cast magic on you," he said.

"Those are good points, but they don't explain how you

would get the information," she asked.

He hesitated because he hadn't thought through the answer to its conclusion, but the way Instructor Pennywhistle was standing at attention, watching him closely, gave him the encouragement that he was on the right track.

"I...I might..."

Their stares felt hot on his cheeks. *What would he do?*

Someone muttered, "Country boy," drawing laughter from the rest of the class.

Zayn swallowed hard, trying to loosen his tongue from the roof of his mouth.

"I might find leverage over them. Possibly blackmail them into giving me the information. Maybe something about their family, or something awful they did in their past. Then they would want to hide the fact that I knew it, even from their bosses, so they didn't get in trouble too," said Zayn.

He knew he'd said the right thing when a tiny curl of a smile caught the corner of Instructor Pennywhistle's lips. He was the only one to see it because she returned to her studious mask once everyone looked back to her.

"For once, Zayn is right," said Instructor Pennywhistle, "though I wouldn't go so far as use blackmail. Too crude, and usually backfires. Better to find reasons for the target to give you the information freely, because they want you to have it. Now watch as I convince one of you to do what I want."

With everyone's eyes on her, she strolled across the front, curling around where Eddie was standing. As she moved closer, he stood up straighter. She put her hand on the back of his neck, and his face went through contortions of concern and pleasure.

"Instructor...?"

She smiled sweetly at him, showing her teeth, licking her lips. Instructor Pennywhistle whispered to him, lips nearly grazing his ear, sending waves of jealousy through the room. Eddie blushed like the breaking day, pink and red, before glancing at the rest of the class as if he'd forgotten they were watching. He looked back to her with a question on his face, and she nodded slowly.

Eddie shook his head as if he couldn't believe he was about to say what he was going to say. "The eagle has landed, the fat man walks alone."

The class burst into laughter, and Eddie laughed along with them. He looked back to Instructor Pennywhistle for confirmation, but she was standing in front, picking through his wallet. When she pulled a condom packet from the back, the laughter doubled.

"This looks like it's been here a long time," she said with a wink.

"Hey!" said Eddie as he ran up to retrieve his wallet.

"Did anyone see me take his wallet?" she asked, to which no one replied. "I didn't think so. I got you to focus on me, on what I was doing with my lips and face, and while I leaned over to whisper in Eddie's ear, I took his wallet, which he didn't feel because"—she looked to him—"what did I say?"

"Say the eagle has landed, the fat man walks alone, or I put this knife into your back," he said.

"I had no knife, but I kept my fingernail shoved into his lower back and slipped the wallet out while he was focused on the potential for evisceration, all without a breath of magic." She clapped her hands, then held them in front of her. "Now for today's challenge. In that room of a couple of hundred horny twentysomethings are twelve students from the Academy, upperclassmen of course, and none that you've met before, properly disguised and with back stories. As much as you don't know them, they don't know you either. Your task is to figure out who is a fake and who is really here to find a date.

If you think you've found one, give the Academy student one of these business cards."

She handed the business cards out. Before they got to Zayn, Vin raised his hand. "But they're blank."

"Exactly," said Instructor Pennywhistle. "You're not here for a date. If the person across from you is an Academy student, then they'll get up and leave with you. If you're wrong, and they look at you like you're an idiot, then you're out, and you have to leave and return here. If they figure out you're an Academy student, then you're out. If anyone detects you using magic, you are also out. There are twelve fakes out there, and twenty-eight of you. Next week's rankings will depend on how well your team does today. Good luck."

The room descended into chattering as each team plotted strategy. Zayn joined his team. The glances from Vin and Skylar that said "you're not going to screw this up too, are you?" were obvious.

"We're going to get this," Zayn said confidently.

"I don't know how you can be cocky," said Vin. "We're still in last place. You know if you hadn't decided to come back, Instructor Allgood was going to give us another member for the team."

"That doesn't matter. Today we're getting out of the bottom," said Zayn. "So going out there looking like our dog just died is not going to get us any dates."

"We're not here for dates," said Vin.

"Of course not, but you can't let them think that," said Zayn.

Exasperated, Vin said, "Let's just go. I want to get this over with."

The others filed out, though Portia gave him a nod before she left. After they were gone, Zayn filled out a profile on the speed dating app, creating an alter ego that he thought would be believable. He was memorizing his information when he realized most the groups had left.

"Shit," he said, hurrying into the auditorium.

There was a quiet hum of conversation, and the room was awash with hormones. Zayn was studying everyone's faces until he remembered he was supposed to be looking for a date. He opened up the app on his phone and started looking through the faces and profiles for clues on who might be an Academy student.

There had to be at least two hundred people in the room, not including Academy first years, which made taking a random guess out of the question. Realizing that he was standing back for far too long, Zayn pressed a couple of faces that seemed interesting and was surprised by a confirmation and a table number.

He found table forty-two on the far side of the auditorium, resisting the urge to study people along the way. A petite girl wearing a tight green dress and too much eyeliner was seated across from him.

He offered his hand, pausing to shape his words correctly and without his Alabama accent. "I'm David Williams. It's lovely to meet you."

"Sarah Overton," she replied, giving a nervous sigh. Her forehead was strained, and she glanced around the room. "This has been more than I expected. Not a place for introverts."

"You're my first date, or meet, or whatever we're supposed to call it," he said, giving what he hoped was an appropriate nervous laugh.

"Are you an introvert or an extrovert?" she asked, studying him intently.

Am I? Or is David Williams? Shit. This is a question I should know right away, which means she's an Academy student, and she knows I am too.

The words careened through his head. "I like to think of myself as an extrovert, but wow, this is a lot. So maybe I'm really an introvert. Today at least."

Feeling as if he'd bungled his answer, he adjusted the collar on his shirt.

"Really?" she asked with her head tilted.

Sensing that he was busted, Zayn reached into his pocket for a blank business card. If he gave it to her before she called him out, then he'd be okay.

"Yeah," he said, holding the card under the table. Should he give it to her? Was he making a mistake?

He shoved the card back into his pocket. "I'm sorry. I'm fibbing a little. You said you were an introvert, and I felt bad that I'm not. I'm definitely an extrovert, but a bad liar."

When her glossy lips broke with a grin, he knew he'd saved it, and that his initial read had been incorrect.

"Thank you for being honest," she said, leaning forward. "I could tell that you're not an introvert. Like right away."

He had a pleasant conversation with Sarah, and then the timer on the table dinged, and he moved on, giving her profile an interested tag. While he was studying the app for his next "date" Keelan walked out of the room with a stunning redhead behind him. She carried a blank card in her slender fingertips and a barely concealed scowl.

And almost as soon as Keelan had left with the Academy student, Eddie got up from his table cursing, bringing the eye of everyone in the room. His date looked bewildered as he marched out. She gave an exaggerated shrug.

The two hours went by quickly. Zayn would find a new table date, chat for a few minutes using made-up details about "David Williams" on the spot—which he found he was exceedingly good at—and then move to the next. He thought he'd hate this part, lying about himself, obfuscating his true nature, but he found he rather liked it. It was like wearing fresh new clothes.

At Varna High, he'd never been interested in the drama club, mostly because he didn't want to stick out, but now he regretted not joining. There was a certain freedom to pretending to be someone else.

During those two hours eight more fakes were uncovered, none by his team, and both Vin and Skylar were knocked out. They were trending towards last again, and as much fun as Zayn was having, he had no idea how to spot the fakes.

When the ninth fake was uncovered by Andrew, almost at the same time that Portia was knocked out, Zayn knew they'd be in last place again, unless he could miraculously pick out the final three without getting caught.

Frustrated, Zayn went into the bathroom to think, washing his hands and staring at himself in the mirror. *How do I make them give themselves away?*

There wasn't enough time for speed dates. People were starting to leave, which meant that it would get easier and easier to spot the fakes. And he couldn't stand in back and study the remaining people, that would give him away, which was what had happened to Vin.

"I need a misdirection," Zayn muttered to himself, thinking about how Instructor Pennywhistle had stolen Eddie's wallet. He'd been trying to head straight at the problem, but that's not what he needed to solve it.

When a skinny guy wearing a too-large suit stumbled into the bathroom, going straight for the sink, and using a damp paper towel to wash the sweat off his forehead, Zayn had an idea. After checking to make sure no one else was in the bathroom, Zayn waggled his fingers, letting faez fill his mind. When the spell landed on Skinny Guy, he twitched.

"You okay, there?" asked Zayn, putting his hand on

Skinny Guy's shoulder.

"This has been a disaster. My hands are sweaty. I can see it in their eyes when I shake their hands that they're not interested," he said.

"You look like you're too warm in that suit," said Zayn.

"I am...yes, too hot," said Skinny Guy.

"There must be a fire somewhere, maybe in the basement. It's not your fault. But you can be the hero, save everyone, if you pull the fire alarm," said Zayn.

Skinny Guy nodded, almost a little too enthusiastically. "Yes, fire."

"Pull the alarm, before it's too late," said Zayn.

Skinny Guy moved like an automation back into the auditorium. Zayn realized he'd put the charm on a little too heavily, but that would be alright as long as he did as he was told.

Zayn positioned himself near the exit with a good sightline on the auditorium. When the fire alarm sounded, he watched for those that didn't move right away, looking like they were going to stay regardless. It helped that his fellow first years reacted similarly, proving his hypothesis.

The lady in charge of the speed dating session yelled, "Everyone out! Everyone out! Orderly line!"

Zayn moved to the door, holding it open for the others to pass through. As the final three fakes—which included Sarah Overton, his first speed date—passed his location, he shoved a blank business card in their hands, to be rewarded with wide-eyed understanding.

He left the auditorium last with a triumphant smile on his lips. The next day was Friday, which was the last day of the week, and when Instructor Allgood announced the group rankings, they would no longer be in last and just in time to make Katie's concert.

Chapter Twenty-One
The Hold, March 2014
An electrifying evening of music

Zayn leaned into the door, softly knocking to get their attention. He was met with smiles of greeting.

Vin spoke first. "I'm sorry I doubted you. And you were right, I needed more confidence. I got outed by an Academy student who wasn't even at my table."

"No worries," said Zayn. "Just own it next time."

"Thanks for winning that competition," said Skylar. "That almost makes up for being unconscious for a couple of weeks while we picked up the slack."

Skylar held her fingers an inch apart. She had a wry smile.

"Next time I know, no purple path," he said, then he looked to Portia. "Are we good?"

"Always have been. You stuck up for me when Eddie was an asshole that first day," said Portia.

"So what now?" asked Skylar. "Are we going to use our extra time on that thing you talked to us about outside of here?"

"No. I think we should take a moment and celebrate.

Enjoy our newly earned freedom. Go out on the town. I haven't seen anything but the Hold or the inside of the bodega," said Zayn. "It's the city of sorcery, we should get to enjoy it, right?"

Their bright grins told him they agreed with his idea. His insides warmed and his face hurt from smiling.

"You clearly have something in mind," said Skylar, "and if it involved dressing up, I'm in, but only if you guys let me pick your outfits."

"There's a band I want to see," said Zayn. "Shall we raid the hall closet for proper attire?"

The four of them went to the disguise room and spent the next two hours finding clothes for the evening. Skylar was in her element, digging through the racks until she found a set of clothes that matched their ward nine personas and still took into account their individuality.

Vin wore tight black pants and an aqua-patterned button down with ample chest hair showing. Portia wore a skimpy red number that she looked like she might burst out of at any moment, while the outfit Skylar picked was little more than two handkerchiefs with oodles of brown skin revealed.

Skylar had tried to pick out a tight-fitting suit and bow tie, but Zayn waved them off—even though he rather liked them—because it wouldn't match the Jamaican Zayn's personality. In the end, he ended up with jeans and a V-neck shirt.

When they arrived at the High Dragon, there was a line out the door. The sign on the place was a dragon lounging on a throne of gold coins with smoke rings slipping from his lips.

They stood in line for a few minutes before Zayn said, "This is silly. Come with me."

He received funny looks from people as he walked around the velvet rope and straight up to the bouncer with the other three in tow.

"Hey man," said Zayn, laying on his Jamaican accent. He

reached out to clasp hands, adding a spell of suggestion to it. Not enough to be noticed by anyone in line, in case there were hall mages waiting to get in, but enough to sway the bouncer's attitude. "We're friends of the drummer. She said to come straight up front."

His wide face crinkled with understanding. "Zayn? Yeah, she said that you might show up."

Zayn had to choke back his surprise, hiding it behind a cough. He hadn't told her that he was coming since the last time they'd talked. She'd barely been by the bodega since the day he told her he was leaving. He'd only planned to say hello and check out her band, but the fact that she'd left his name with the bouncer. The implications left him a little dizzy as he strolled into the High Dragon.

The bar was built in a semicircle with the stage at the center. The warm-up band, Fresh Fish, was playing loud and fast with two guitars and three horns. The area around the stage was packed with people. A huge animatronic dragon head blew smoke into the room, and the lights sparkled against the fog.

Vin got them drinks. Zayn didn't bother asking what it was, and they lifted their glasses in toast.

"To not being in last place!" said Zayn, having to shout over the band.

"To not having to wash dishes!" added Skylar.

"To Zayn's daring!" said Portia.

They looked at Vin, whose face went through contortions of thought. "To...forgetting about school for a night!"

They clashed their plastic cups together, spilling stickiness over their hands. Zayn took a healthy drink. His throat burned as the liquid went down, and when he belched a puff of flame came out.

"What was that?" coughed Zayn, waving away the smoke

from his mouth.

"Dragon's breath," said Vin.

He put his meaty hand on Zayn's shoulder and squeezed. "It'll put hair on your chest."

"And on your back and palms," said Zayn, banging on his chest to get the warmth to subside, "and before I know it, I'll be a wolfman."

Before Zayn could go looking for Katie, they made three more toasts. By the last one, Zayn felt like he was floating. When he'd first come in, the music had been loud and annoying, but then he felt it pulsing through his feet. He'd never danced, except around the living room with Neveah and the twins, but he felt the urge to rush the stage and feel the press of people around him.

Zayn gave a small cheer that was swallowed by the cacophony, but it felt good to let go.

"You look like you're having a good time," said Portia, sipping on a neon green drink.

After a moment of thought he said, "Yeah, I am. I've never been out, really never drank before."

"Then you should be careful," she said.

"But I don't *want* to be careful," he said, laughing. "I've had to be careful all my life! It feels good not to worry, at least for one night."

"Sí, it does," said Portia, finishing half her drink and wiping her mouth with the back of her hand. "In Mexico City, I had to work at my father's business, doing the accounting for him."

"What's his business?" asked Zayn.

"He used to own a restaurant, good enough to make the El Universal," she said.

"Used to?"

Portia stared into the distance. "Some criminals told him

he had to pay them or they'd burn the place down. He didn't pay. They torched it."

"I'm sorry," said Zayn.

"It's okay. He got insurance money, and because I no longer accountant, I can come to Hundred Halls," she said, shrugging. "Maybe someday I will find those criminals and teach them a lesson, but probably they are dead already."

Portia finished her drink and went for another one. Fresh Fish finished their set. The crowd in front of the stage dispersed, and thumping dance music came on. Zayn was checking out the animatronic dragon when Skylar grabbed his hand and dragged him onto the dance floor, where Vin and Portia already were.

They were the only ones dancing, as everyone else had gone for drinks. For a big guy, Vin was an excellent dancer. When Zayn raised an eyebrow in his direction, he leaned over and said, "I took six years of ballet until I grew eight inches and put on fifty pounds."

Zayn had almost forgotten why he was at the bar until he saw a flash of aquamarine hair on the empty stage. She was wearing tattered jeans and a white tank top.

"You made it!" she said, sitting on the edge of the stage and kicking her feet.

Zayn found himself strangely fascinated by the definition in her arm muscles.

"You've got guns," he said, reaching out and poking her arm.

"You're drunk," she said with a laugh. "Are these your friends?"

He was having such a good time, he almost forgot that he was supposed to be working in the bodega. "Yeah, man. Uncle Larice introduce me to them a few months ago."

Skylar wandered over and stuck out her hand, which

Katie accepted. "You're cuter than he mentioned."

"You work in the Korean grocery store, don't you?" asked Katie.

Skylar hid a demure giggle behind a cupped hand, reverting to her fake persona. "I'm going for another drink. Nice to meet you, Katie!"

The other three went towards the bar, leaving him alone with Katie. The closeness between them was like a magnetic field. The hairs on his arm were buzzing.

"I'm glad you came," said Katie. "I wanted to see you one last time before you go back to Jamaica."

"I'm not going back," he said. "I can stay."

"What changed?" she asked, face lit with animation.

"I was letting the world push me around," he said. "But I'm over that now. I'm not going to let it."

A guy with a guitar near the back of the stage yelled her name.

"I have to go," she said. "We're almost ready to start."

"Have a great show," he said, remembering to add, "respect."

He was about to turn away, but she grabbed him by the shirt and yanked him towards her. They banged teeth as their lips mashed together, but quickly moved past the awkwardness. She tasted sweet, but there was also a familiar metallic taste that lingered on his tongue.

Katie hooked her leg around his knee, drawing him closer until there was no air between them. She had her hand on the back of his neck, jamming his mouth against hers. His skin was on fire.

Then she pulled away, hopping up and jogging towards the back. "See me after the show."

It sounded more like a command than a question, one he was happy to oblige.

As he turned around, he nearly fell over from deliriousness. He stumbled back to the bar where the others were. Someone tried to hand him a drink, but he waved it off.

"You okay, Zayn?" asked Skylar, tongue resting on her teeth playfully.

"No." He paused. "Yes? I don't know."

Before anyone else could ask him a question, Katie's band went on, and fans rushed the stage. Katie started off a song with a skillful drum opening, and before Zayn knew it, he was bobbing along with the music.

The singer for the Sticky Wickets had a smooth voice, and his lyrics swirled around Zayn's head. It didn't help that he was still high on Katie's kiss and more alcohol than he'd had in his life.

Katie played with a kinetic energy that made it seem like she was on fast-forward, even though the beat held multiple layers. Occasionally, she shot sparks from the end of her drumsticks and then made them levitate, spinning them like a top. Zayn hadn't known she knew magic, but it *was* the city of sorcery, so he knew he shouldn't have been surprised.

The crowd was into their music. People in front were hopping up and down like pogo sticks. There was an electricity in the air, like everyone knew this band was going to be special and they were getting to be a part of it.

Feeling overly warm, Zayn headed for the bathroom to throw water in his face, thinking better of it when he saw the swampland that was the sink counter. It looked like someone had been swimming on it.

Zayn was about to leave in search of a less flooded bathroom, when a dude with long hair burst out of a stall. He had crazed eyes, and Zayn wondered if he'd have to defend himself.

"Rock on!" said the guy, and then he made devil horns

with his fists, and lightning crackled from them before he left.

He looked like a kid after his first rollercoaster ride, or someone who'd watched *Bill and Ted's Excellent Adventure* too many times.

Zayn was about to follow when he saw the baggie on the ground. He knew what it was before he picked it up. The symbol on the front was the same as the one on the baggie he'd found at the bodega. The thought sobered him up quickly. He shoved the baggie in his pocket and went looking for Sparky.

When he returned to the main area, he tried to find him, but the stage lights were flaring through the smoke and he couldn't see further than ten feet. He was getting a throbbing headache from the noise.

He found the others trying to get the bartender's attention for another round, but people were jammed against the bar. Zayn gathered them in and showed them the baggie.

"Where'd you find that?" asked Vin.

"Some guy in the bathroom. He came out of the stall and shot lightning out his hands like it was the first time he'd ever done magic," said Zayn.

"This is that stuff you told us about?" asked Portia.

Zayn nodded.

"Are you sure we're not going to get in trouble for investigating this?" asked Skylar.

"We might," he said. "But if we can get this stuff off the streets, wouldn't it be worth it? I know I'd hate to see anyone else in the ward get hurt."

Instead of answering, Skylar handed the full drink she'd just ordered to a girl with pink pigtails walking past.

"I'm in," she said.

"What's he look like?" asked Vin.

Zayn gave a brief description.

"What do we do if we find him?" asked Portia.

"Convince him to go outside. We need to talk to him, find out where he's getting it," said Zayn.

They split up, heading through the crowd. Zayn went towards the stage. Every bit of him wanted to forget about Sparky and revel in Katie playing the drums, but he kept his head down, searching the faces in the crowd.

When Zayn saw a crackle of lightning spark over the crowd like a Tesla coil, he knew he was close. He found Sparky thrusting his fists in the air like a pair of pistons. His skin was turning translucent, and he had plenty of space around him, because more lightning coiled in his chest like a snake.

He had a sweaty, delirious face, and Zayn knew it wasn't just from the dancing. The reports of people spontaneously combusting or turning into goo suddenly made sense to him. It was the drug. It gave the users the ability to channel faez and do magic, but it turned on them because their bodies couldn't handle the power.

But this wasn't some drug-addled bum on an empty street. This guy was standing in the middle of a crowded bar, and while no one would get near him, they weren't running away either, probably thinking he was part of the light show. If he turned into a human ball lightning, a whole lot of people would get hurt.

"Hey man," said Zayn, trying to get his attention. When his fingers brushed his shirt, he got a nasty shock. "Hey man, can I talk to you?"

Sparky took no notice of Zayn's attempts. He kept pumping his fists in the air and shouting randomly.

"Hey, I need to talk with you outside, please," said Zayn, shouting over the music.

Realizing that he was too far gone, Zayn tried the spell he'd used on the guy at the Speed Dating event, when he got him to pull the fire alarm.

"Come with me, now," said Zayn.

This time, he got a reaction, but it wasn't the one he wanted. Sparky spun on him, eyes glowing white.

"Don't you mess with me," he said, then threw lightning towards Zayn.

He barely got out of the way, and it was a miracle no one got hurt as the arc ricocheted off a metal scaffolding, flew through the air, and bounced off the dragon's nostrils.

As Zayn pulled himself from the sticky floor, Sparky ran through the crowd, screams following as people received shocks from incidental contact.

Zayn followed him to a back exit. When he hit the alleyway, he saw Sparky turning onto the street at a full sprint. Zayn checked behind him, but none of the others had seen him leave. He thought about going back for them, but was afraid he'd lose the guy if he did.

"Shit."

He let the door close behind him and ran after Sparky, hoping he could get back to the High Dragon before Katie's set ended.

Chapter Twenty-Two
Tenth Ward, March 2014
Following a shocking individual

It wasn't hard to track Sparky. He kept shooting off random bolts of lightning that would jet into the low cloud bank in the sky, or crackle against the upper floors of apartment buildings. The problem was that he was fast. Zayn was already a block behind, the distance growing greater by the second.

After a few blocks of running full out, Zayn heaved to a stop and bent over at the waist, hot breath coming out of his lips like mist. The air was chilly but he was warm from running. An ambulance siren sounded from somewhere behind him.

"I'm an idiot," he muttered, remembering his imbuement and pouring faez into it.

He caught up to Sparky on Ninth Street, near the Korean grocery store where Skylar worked. The occasional car motored past, but this area of town was shut down at this time of night. Sparky had stopped. He was standing like a pole at the corner, arms down by his sides.

Zayn stayed on his side of the street. "Hey man, are you okay?"

When Sparky spoke, his mouth was a hive of electricity.

"Stop following me."

"I only want to help," said Zayn. "That stuff you're taking is dangerous. It'll kill you."

"But I need it," said Sparky, staring at his hands.

Only the distance between them saved Zayn when Sparky shot a thick bolt of white-hot energy across the street. When it passed Zayn as he dove, it burnt the bottoms of his shoes before blowing the windows out of an electronics store.

With broken glass scattered around him, Zayn scrambled to his feet, prepared to dodge again, but the glowing energy inside of Sparky had diminished.

Zayn saw his chance and started moving across the street, slowly, with his hands up, as if he were trying to corral an escaped pet.

"I don't want to hurt you, but you're going to get someone killed if you keep doing that," he said, checking behind him in hopes that his friends might have found him.

With the energy discharged, Sparky looked sweaty and worn out, like he'd had the flu all night. His eyes were cavernous.

"Stay...back."

Zayn stopped halfway across the street. He thought about trying the charm again, but it hadn't worked the last time. He'd have to do this the old-fashioned way.

"Do you have a name?" asked Zayn.

"Jeffrey."

"Hello, Jeffrey. I'm Zayn."

Jeffrey's forehead bunched up. "Are you from Jamaica?"

"Ya man. I am. And I've seen some others like you and it didn't end well for them," he said.

"But it gives me magic," said Jeffrey in a breathless delirium. "I had no idea that it would feel so good. It's better than sex."

"It's killing you. Even for trained mages faez is dangerous, and it's especially dangerous for mages without a patron. If this drug is giving you magic, then you should be worried."

"I don't feel worried."

Zayn cast about for another tactic. "Do you have a family?"

"No, why?"

"Brothers, sisters?" asked Zayn.

"A sister. Jessica. She lives in Philadelphia with her husband," he said.

"Think about her. Think about how sad she would be if you died," said Zayn.

"She would be. She's pregnant. Told me they might name the baby after me."

"Great," said Zayn, taking tentative steps towards Jeffrey. "Then you should stop taking it. Does that drug have a name?"

"Alpha."

"You should stop taking Alpha right away. Do you have any more?" asked Zayn.

Jeffrey's hand went reflexively towards his front pocket. "No."

"Jeffrey, you know you do. Think about Jessica. Think about her baby, little Jeffrey. You want to see him, right?" asked Zayn.

After a moment, Jeffrey gave a slow steady nod.

"Then pull it out, and throw it away. No more Alpha. No more dangerous magic," said Zayn.

Jeffrey reluctantly reached into his front pocket and dug out two baggies filled with a sparkly powder. He stared at them longingly.

"Where did you get those?" asked Zayn. "So I can make sure no one else gets hurt."

Jeffrey weaved like a snake in a trance, and then he came out of it. "The moon lady gave it to me..."

His voice trailed off, and Zayn had started to close the final distance between them when he heard shouts from up the street.

"It's him! He's this way!"

Vin was running up the sidewalk towards them. In the dim streetlamps, he looked like a menacing hulk.

"This is a trick, isn't it?" said Jeffrey, ripping open both packets and emptying them into his mouth before Zayn could stop him.

When Jeffrey's skin turned translucent with light, Zayn fled the other way. A bolt of lightning charred a blue Volvo near him, melting its tires to slag.

Zayn didn't bother looking back. The hairs on the back of his neck told him that Jeffrey was chasing him, and catching up. A second bolt hit the traffic light, showering him with sparks.

Further up the street, a car was headed his way, but wisely made a tire-screeching U-turn. Zayn wished he had such a quick getaway.

When he took a left, he found the way blocked by construction fences and detour signs. Zayn looked for a way past the chain-link fences, but the gates were chained and locked. Trapped, Zayn turned and faced Jeffrey, who had slowed as well.

He looked like a human candle with flecks of lightning jumping from his brow and sparks spitting from his hands. When Jeffrey shot another bolt, only Zayn's enhanced reflexes saved him from annihilation.

"Stop, Jeffrey. Think about Jessica. Think about the baby," said Zayn, but Jeffrey kept coming.

Zayn went for the fence and made it halfway up before another blast of electricity turned the whole thing into hot fire. His muscles contracted, squeezing his fingers around the metal wires, cutting them. His back arched and he smelled his hair crisping.

When it was over, he collapsed onto the pavement. His limbs shook. It was a miracle he hadn't wet himself. Zayn struggled to his hands and knees, but the effort took his last reserves of energy.

Zayn looked up in time to see Jeffrey lift his hands again. Lightning scintillated across his body.

Zayn was tensed, hoping he could throw himself out of the way, when a shadow rose up from the street and struck Jeffrey in the head. He collapsed, knees buckling and body jackknifing into the concrete.

Portia stood in the space that Jeffrey had only just occupied. Her dress was ripped and tattered, split up the sides from the chase. The other two came running up, looking similarly disheveled, but there was no time for small talk. Jeffrey's unconscious body looked like a bottle of lightning, and the glow was growing stronger.

"Run!"

No one took any further prodding. They fled, and though Zayn's muscles ached as if he'd finished two consecutive marathons, the fear of being turned into charred ash pushed him.

When Jeffrey exploded, it knocked them off their feet. Windows in the nearby buildings shattered. Zayn ripped the skin from both palms when he hit the concrete. The concussive blow rang in his ears.

It took a minute for them to recover. No one got up. They sat on the street, admiring the destruction that they'd only barely avoided.

"I think I'm sober now," said Zayn, to murmurs of agreement from the others.

"What do we do now?" asked Portia.

Zayn picked tiny rocks from his palm. "We don't tell Instructor Allgood, that's for sure."

"Why not?" asked Skylar. "I thought you said this was our ticket out of the bottom?"

"We didn't learn anything new. Nothing we can use," said Zayn, then remembering Jeffrey's comment, he added, "Well, he did say something about the moon lady but I have no idea what that means."

"That seems vaguely familiar," said Skylar.

"Never heard of it myself," said Vin.

Portia merely shook her head.

When they finally got up, they limped their way back to the nearest train station and ignored the stares from the other passengers at their state of clothing. The whole way back to the hall, it wasn't his near-death experience with Sparky that weighed on his mind, but that he missed meeting up with Katie after the concert.

Chapter Twenty-Three
Varna, June 2005
A sticky hot day in Alabama (but aren't they all?)

Nothing good had ever come of young men without something constructive to do. It was an aphorism his father had relayed to him time and time again, but it was too damn hot to do anything else.

His mom, Sela, had tried to get them to stay at home, but the Stack, despite being a creation out of the mind of MC Escher, was made of shipping containers, which in the summer, turned to giant ovens. Everyone had been lounging in the courtyard, beneath the colorful drapes—yellows and oranges—hung between the shipping containers, providing shade. The terrible twins had adorned themselves in armor made of pegboard and shoelaces, and had been launching skirmishes all day, so he and Keelan took off into the woods, headed east on the railroad tracks that went around town.

The vine-choked trees turned the tracks into a strange verdant corridor. Zayn, in jeans and with his shirt off and tucked into the back of his pants, was walking across the left track, balancing on the hot steel, while Keelan was on the right. Neither had fallen in more than a hundred yards.

"Is Uncle Jesse really going to work for the Lady?" asked Zayn.

"He's not working for her, but the Speaker," said Keelan, reflexively touching the side of his face where a bruise stained his jaw.   Neither one of them had talked about it, and Zayn knew better than to ask.   The answer would usually be: "I tripped in the kitchen" or "I was jumping on the bed and fell off."

"I thought he hated the Lady," said Zayn, pausing for a moment to catch his balance.

"What does it matter?   He says we still gotta eat, and nothing happens in Varna without her permission," said Keelan.

"Do you hate her?" asked Zayn, though it wasn't really what he was asking.

Keelan half-shrugged, nearly falling off the track in the process, before wheeling his arms around his head and righting himself.

"I hate that we can't leave town, but I love that I get to do this"—an illusionary topless dancing girl in a hula skirt appeared on his palm—"and not go mad.   The Lady might have poisoned us, but at least there's a good side."

"You're not supposed to do magic," said Zayn.

"Are you going to tell on me or something?"

Zayn shook his head.   "No way.   But it makes sense why we're not supposed to.   If she thinks you're good at it, you get sent to the Halls to become one of her Watchers.   Then it's like you're not even a person anymore."

"Better a Watcher than going nowhere in this town," said Keelan, then he added with a grin,   "Or getting eaten by her."

"She doesn't eat people," said Zayn.   "Name one person that's gone missing."

"I don't know.   That's just what I heard.   Maybe she

gets them from out of town." Keelan paused, hunching his forehead. "Do you feel that?"

At that moment, a vibration hit Zayn in the heels. "Train coming, we should get off the tracks."

"If you do, then you lost," said Keelan, grinning.

"We didn't agree on any contest," said Zayn, glancing at the curve in the tracks that they couldn't see beyond. The train whistled in the distance, though with the heavy foliage surrounding them, it was hard to tell how far away it was.

"Fine by me if you want to get off. Then I'll be the winner," said Keelan, placing an imaginary crown on his head.

"I'm not getting off," said Zayn, using the distraction to surge ahead of his cousin.

"I knew it!" said Keelan, laughing as he tottered forward, arms pinwheeling.

They made it another thirty feet before the train appeared around the bend. The vibration made Zayn's teeth hurt, but hadn't affected his progress. He nearly fell off when it sounded its horn.

The moment of distraction gave Keelan a chance to take the lead. Zayn lengthened his stride to catch up as the train was bearing down on them.

"We should get off," yelled Zayn as the train sounded its horn again.

"You can if you want," said Keelan, laughing and nimbly hopping forward like a mountain goat as if his earlier struggles keeping balance had been an act.

When the train was a hundred feet away, Zayn felt the rumbling in his gut. He'd heard stories of kids getting too close when a train went by, and getting sucked underneath, crushed beneath the wheels.

"We have to get off!" yelled Zayn as he tried to keep up with Keelan.

They were shoulder to shoulder. The train blasted its horn again. The train was so close it looked like a tsunami of steel approaching.

The heat and the noise surrounded him. Zayn could hear the clacking of the wheels like hammer strikes in his ears. The glare of the front grill burned his eyes. He heard shouting from behind him, though he still sensed Keelan at his right shoulder.

With no room left, Zayn threw himself off the track, the wall of wind throwing him into a spin. He landed hard on the rocks, parallel to the tracks. The train whipped past him like a massive metal snake.

Then as fast as it'd come, it was gone, the caboose sliding away. Zayn looked across the tracks for Keelan. He didn't remember seeing him leap. Searching those last frightening moments, he swore the train had hit him.

Ignoring his bloody arms and the aching of his lungs, Zayn moved across the tracks, steeling himself for the moment he found Keelan's body. There was no way that he had avoided the train.

But there was nothing on the other side. No body. No blood. Nothing.

"Keelan?" called Zayn, then louder, "Keelan?"

When he heard the laughing from behind him, Zayn started to understand what had happened. Climbing from behind a couple of bushes, Keelan appeared. He was back about fifty feet from where Zayn was standing.

"You sonofabitch," said Zayn when he reached his cousin. "You could have got me killed."

Keelan was laughing, tears in his eyes, hand quivering in front of his mouth. He was laughing so hard his knees were shaking.

"You didn't have to stay on that track. Your dumb ass

didn't want to lose," said Keelan through the tears. "It wasn't even that good of an illusion, but you fell for it."

Zayn pushed him in the shoulder. "That wasn't cool."

When Keelan stopped laughing and Zayn caught his breath, they left the tracks, cutting through the woods to head back towards town. Zayn wanted to jump in the pond near the Stack.

In the woods, the thick air was claustrophobic and the insects came out. Zayn didn't feel like talking to his cousin, so the only noise was them pushing their way through the brush and the occasional slap at a buzzing mosquito.

"Zayn, stop," Keelan said suddenly.

"Screw you," replied Zayn, marching forward.

"No stop, really."

Zayn prepared to wheel on his cousin and give him a piece of his mind, when he saw the giant web inches from his face. He skidded on his heels, and his nose gently kissed the web. At the top corner of his vision, he sensed the spider's approach, and he threw himself backwards.

"Thanks," mumbled Zayn as he watched the purple-veined spider creep down the web on spindly black legs.

They watched the arachnid investigate its web, checking the area Zayn had touched and repairing the small rip. As he watched, the hairs on his arms rose.

"That's a big one," he opined.

"Purpura domina aranea," said Keelan, "and no, not big, maybe an inch, inch and a half. Supposedly they can get as big as four or five inches under the right circumstances."

"I don't want to know what circumstances those are," said Zayn, shivering. "When did you learn so much about spiders?"

"Duh," said Keelan, throwing out his hands.

"Oh, yeah. Your dad," said Zayn, remembering Uncle Jesse's predilection for learning facts about all manner of animals.

"Anyway, seems stupid not to, given where we live," said Keelan, staring intently at the spider that was perched in the middle of the web preening. "They eat insects, make webs when they live outdoors, obviously, but will switch to hunting if they're indoors. Those are the bigger ones. They'll eat small frogs, crickets, larger prey. They're cousins to the achaeranea magicaencia, but most of their branch of the spider family tree is empty, no one knows why."

"They probably ate their part of the family tree," said Zayn.

Keelan moved near the web, a look of rapture on his face. "I have that old aquarium. I wonder if I took it home if it would grow bigger. Wouldn't that be cool?"

"Uhm, no? And aren't you worried about it spying on you?" asked Zayn.

"Even if I believed that the Lady could see through them, what do I have to hide?" said Keelan, who looked like he'd thought about this before.

He yanked his shirt from the back of his pants and held it out with two hands. The spider, sensing the danger, scurried upward, but Keelan was too fast, and snatched it off, pinching the shirt at the top to make a little bag.

They made their way back through the woods. Zayn kept quiet and his distance, eyeing the shirt clutched in Keelan's fist as if he expected the spider to slash its way out and crawl up his cousin's arm. Keelan, on the other hand, looked content and completely at ease holding a spider in his shirt.

Exiting the woods near the culvert that went behind the trailer park, they ran down the concrete slope. Zayn turned left around the time he heard Keelan chuckle.

"Check this out, cuz," said Keelan.

Further up the other way, a tall gangly kid was sitting near a puddle of water with a couple of toy cars, running them across the concrete and making car noises.

"Is that one of the Clovises?" asked Zayn.

"Roy," said Keelan.

The Clovis family lived in the trailer park. Their father worked for the sheriff's office and their mother had died a few years ago to breast cancer.

"What's the dumbass doing playing with toy cars?" said Keelan. "Ain't he in the grade above you?"

Zayn nodded. He saw the look in his cousin's eye and he didn't like it.

"Let's go, Keelan," said Zayn. "I'm hungry and I really want to wash this blood off my arm."

"Give me a sec," said Keelan, jogging towards Roy Clovis, who was facing away from them.

"Keelan," Zayn said under his breath, but he ran to catch up.

"Hey Roy, what ya doing?" asked Keelan, holding the shirt in both hands in front of him.

"Oh, hey, Keelan right?" asked Roy with a soft smile. "Just killing time. Wanna join me?"

"I do," said Keelan with a hard edge.

Zayn saw what was going to happen before it did. He tried to reach his cousin first, but Keelan opened the shirt, slinging the spider at the Clovis boy.

Roy didn't understand what had happened until he looked down and saw the purple-veined spider crawling up his chest, and then he started screaming.

"It's one of the Lady's spiders," said Keelan, "so don't kill it or she'll come after you."

His face etched with horror, Roy cried, "Get it off, get it off, get it off," as his hands hovered above the spider, which was leisurely making its way up his chest.

Zayn pushed his cousin. "What are you doing? Get it off

him."

There was a perverse, almost strangled look in Keelan's eyes. As if he knew he shouldn't be doing this, but couldn't stop himself. Zayn had seen the look in his uncle's face after he'd hit Keelan, which since they'd gotten older, only happened when no one was around.

"If you want it off, you do it," said Keelan, pushing him back, then running away in the opposite direction, neither towards his trailer or the Stack, as if he were too ashamed to be seen by anyone after what he'd done.

Roy's screams had grown louder, and Zayn was afraid some adults might come investigate. Using the shirt he pulled from the back of his pants, Zayn knocked the spider off his chest. The critter had two broken legs when it hit the concrete. Zayn stomped it, putting it out of its misery.

He looked up in time to see Roy throwing a punch, hitting him in the shoulder.

"What the hell? I got it off you," said Zayn.

"He's your cousin and you gotta remember there is more of us than of you and him," said Roy, wiping his tears with the back of his arm.

"But I didn't do it," said Zayn, holding his arms out.

"You didn't stop him either," said Roy, and he marched back towards the trailer park, leaving Zayn alone with a smashed spider beneath his shoe.

Chapter Twenty-Four
Uncle Larice's bodega, March 2014
Three parts trouble, vision not included

Zayn was snoring at the counter in the bodega. He'd been this way for the past half hour, and it didn't help the full body ache he had from the encounter with Sparky. Zayn let his fake snore rise in crescendo, before falling away to a breathy hiss.

Sparky had given them a few leads on where the drug was coming from, and they'd all agreed that they would keep an eye out.

He was so focused on his deception, he almost didn't hear the door slip open, or the pad of silent, soft feet. Zayn waited a full minute before popping up and scurrying over to the door. The callolo, sensing the trap, leapt, but Zayn was already there.

The orange tabby hissed at him, and if Zayn hadn't been paying attention, he might have missed the creature's hands turning into cat's paws.

When Zayn reached into his pocket, the callolo arched its back, its eyes darting for a route to escape. Zayn started to worry when the domestic cat paws transformed into nasty feral bobcat claws.

He yanked the chocolate bar from his pocket and

brandished it like a weapon.

The callolo's olive green eyes narrowed. Zayn waved the chocolate bar.

"This is for you," he said. "I want to be friends."

Then he slowly set the chocolate bar on the ground and moved behind the counter.

As soon as he wasn't blocking the callolo's escape, it leapt forward, grabbed the chocolate bar, and slipped out the door. Zayn didn't know what the people on the street would make of an orange tabby with a chocolate bar in its tiny hands.

Zayn locked up the store and went after the callolo. It wasn't hard to follow, at least for the first two blocks. Since the weather had warmed, the city was laden with tourists. He only had to follow the direction they were staring, incredulous looks on their faces.

After jogging another couple of blocks, the easy trail ended. Zayn pulled a divining rod from his back pocket and waited for it to tug him in a direction. He'd placed a enchantment on the chocolate bar and linked it to the rod.

The tugging pulled him across the street to the park where he'd set up as the Statue of Liberty on his first challenge. A skating rink had been built onto the pond; it wasn't cold enough, but magic could do wonderful things.

The chase led him around the skating rink and the mermaid statue. He passed the old woman with her cat on a leash. She was talking with a young man in a hoodie. When the trail came out the other side of the park, he wondered if the callolo had tricked him.

A few people gave him funny looks, but he ignored them and kept following. The callolo was leading him on a big circular route. Zayn was worried the creature was headed back to the bodega when the trail stopped cold. He craned his head in all directions, looking for the orange tabby, only to find a torn chocolate wrapper by the curb.

Zayn confirmed it was the bar that he'd given to the creature. He wasn't disappointed, since he wasn't even sure befriending the creature would work. The information he'd found about them was thin. They'd been originally bred to hunt therianthropes like werewolves, but like most well-intentioned breeding programs, life found a way, and enough of them escaped to form colonies. They tended to live in packs of five or ten, laying claim to a small town, and moving around in the form of cats or raccoons. People often thought that raccoons were smart because they could get into cabinets and garages, but those were usually the shape-shifting callolo. The solo callolo was rare, which was why Zayn thought he might be able to befriend it. They were highly intelligent, though typically kept to scavenging and thieving.

On the way back to the bodega, he was busy thinking about how he might track the callolo again, when he saw a woman who looked a lot like Instructor Pennywhistle get out of a ghost taxi outside a bookstore called Howling Madwoman Fortunes and Spells. At first he wasn't sure if he was mistaken, but then he saw her walk and knew it had to be her. She'd modified her appearance enough to appear different at first glance. She carried a package, tucked against her side.

He stood back while she went into the store. She stayed inside for a few minutes before leaving, heading the opposite direction. She still had the package when she left.

Curious, Zayn approached the bookstore and peered through the glass. He couldn't see anyone. He thought for a long moment about whether or not he should go inside. If she found out he'd been spying on her, it wouldn't go well for him. But on the other hand, he'd never really understood why she'd deceived him about the imbuement bandage.

He went inside. The shelves were filled with books:

magical histories, biographies, picture books of spell effects, and so on. There was a rotating kiosk with necklace charms, the same crap sold in every other store in Invictus. Further in the back was a big glass case with ancient-looking tomes in them. They were probably worthless, distressed to look old for know-nothing tourists.

He didn't see another customer anywhere. He was about to head deeper into the store when a woman addressed him.

"Can I help you?"

Zayn could have sworn that no one was at the counter a moment before.

"Hey, I was just checking your store out."

The woman was middle-aged, with straight black hair, and wore a Rolling Stones T-shirt. She had multiple piercings on her eyebrow, a nose ring, and a tattoo of a Mexican sugar skull on her neck. She had other tattoos on her arms, but the way she looked directly through him made it hard to look away.

Zayn pointed to his neck. "Day of the Dead? Are you...?"

In an East Coast accent, she replied, "Choctaw. I like skulls."

"Oh," he said, feeling embarrassed by what he'd implied.

"Can I help you?" she asked again with no change of expression on her face. A little nameplate clipped to her shirt read, "Snow Owl."

"I...don't know, Snow Owl."

She looked down at her chest as if she'd forgotten she was wearing the nameplate. "The name is Amber DeCroix." Her forehead creased. "Are you looking for someone?"

"No. Just browsing."

"Do you need a reading or need to talk to the dead?" she asked.

"A reading?"

She frowned. "Yeah, like a fortune."

When he hesitated, her lips came together as if she were growing suspicious.

"Yeah, a reading. Sorry," he said. "I'm a little spacey today."

"Give me your hand," she said.

Her grip was strong. She held his wrist with one hand and spread his palm with the other.

He heard talking in back, and was turning to see if anyone was there when he felt a sharp prick on his palm.

"Ow, that hurt," he said, and tried to pull away, but she had him held tight.

A fat bead of blood was building up on his palm. Zayn grew worried that he'd made a mistake in allowing the reading, and that she wasn't human as he'd first thought. While most supernatural creatures didn't dare attack humans, especially in the city of sorcery, where there would be swift reprisal, it did occasionally happen.

Amber pulled his hand to her mouth. He fought it the whole way, but she was considerably stronger than he was. When her tongue darted out to lap up his blood, he expected something inhuman coming out of her mouth, but it appeared to be a human tongue.

When she was finished, she let go of his wrist. He rubbed the life back into it. He'd thought she was going to read the lines in his palm or something like that. His only experience with a seer was the Goon, and he only had visions that affected himself.

Amber said, "Pottery," by way of explanation for her strong grip. Then she closed her eyes and turned her head a little, as if she were sifting through information from his blood.

After a good half a minute, she said, "Oh, shit."

When she opened her eyes, she looked upon him with

pity. If it were an act, it was a pretty good one.

"I saw three visions, which is unusual," she said in a manner as if she were explaining how much it was going to cost to get a car fixed. "In the first, I saw your hands covered in blood after killing a man."

"Who was he?" asked Zayn, thinking about Priyanka's question.

"I couldn't see his face, but his life was tangled in webs."

The Lady, he thought. When he was finished with his learning he would be hers to command. Whatever doubts he had about Amber the Choctaw's ability to read his future was washed away with the involvement of the Lady.

"The second?" he asked softly, as if his voice might break glass.

"Heartache," she said, her face wracked with emotion as if she had experienced whatever he was destined to. "I'm sorry. Any attempts at a relationship will only end in tragedy, maybe not at first, but eventually. There will be moments of happiness, but in the end, you are destined to be alone."

"That can't be true, you can't have seen all that," he said.

She ignored him and spoke about the third vision, growing visibly distressed as she said, "I tasted death in your blood. So much death. I don't understand." She shook her head, looking him directly in the eyes. "Who are you?"

"No one important," he said, and heard more voices gathering in back, or maybe inside his head, he wasn't sure. "I should go. How much do I owe you?"

"Nothing. But never come back here. Ever."

Zayn left the Howling Madwoman Fortunes and Spells, feeling Amber's gaze upon him until he was around the corner. While he'd been in the store, the power of her reading had left him somber. But as he made his way back to the bodega, that feeling of oppression left him, and the certainty that he'd felt at the reading was truly gone.

By the time he returned to the bodega, finding Uncle Larice behind the counter, he'd forgotten the reading.

Uncle Larice's wrinkled dark skin held shadows around his eyes. "You know you're not supposed to be wandering the city."

"It's okay, Uncle Larice. I'm trying to solve your orange tabby problem," said Zayn.

Uncle Larice didn't look like he believed him. He gave the closed door a long look, sighed and said, "I know what you're learning in that hall. I've had enough of you working in my store to understand, and to know when you've been lying to me. And you are. I won't tell Carron about it, I like you too much, and not just because you've doubled my business this last month. But know that he is a hard man, and that hall is hard business. If he says something, you do it. Don't mess around. I don't want to see you get hurt."

Chapter Twenty-Five
Near the Glitterdome, March 2014
Datus interuptus

After a spate of storms had blown through Invictus, Zayn was in the second ward on a date with Katie. It was the first weekend Zayn had felt safe enough with his team's position in the hall that he could take some time to explore the city. It was also the first time he'd seen her since their kiss.

Tourists were out in full force, snapping pictures at every building as if they were about to sprout arms. The clear day made the Spire visible from the outer wards. It was a tall tower of glass and steel rising above every other structure in the city. When Zayn looked at it, he imagined the city as a giant wheel.

"What do you want to do now? There's a Garbage Kings concert tonight at the Glitterdome. I hear they have a killer show with illusionary mock battles over the crowd and mass audio charms to make you think you're hearing voices in your head. I'm sure we could score some tickets from a street vendor," said Katie.

Her hair was in a bright blue Mohawk and her lips glowed faintly. Zayn resisted the urge to reach out and tussle her hair.

"I've really never understood the appeal," he said.

"What about ice skating? There's a park nearby. I love the way the blades cut across the ice like worms," she said.

"Honestly, I'm happy just wandering around without something to do," he said.

"Okay," she said, shoving her hands into her jacket pockets. "But you seem distracted. I thought you were taking me out on a date, but you've barely talked."

He glanced sheepishly at his shoes. He'd been thinking about how he was going to get his named coin from Instructor Allgood. It seemed like everyone had theirs except him.

"Sorry. I haven't really seen the city, and it's a bit overwhelming," he said, which was mostly true. A good lie, Instructor Pennywhistle taught, contained enough truth that you could sell it honestly.

He bit his lower lip. "How's da band?"

"Great," she said, brightening at his question. "We're booked into the summer. That show at the High Dragon really kicked things into gear for us. We've played every weekend since. The only problem is our manager says we need to up the stage show to make it to the next level. Tours are expensive and we don't have the money for travel yet, but we don't want to get stuck in the small venues for the rest of our lives."

"That reminds me," said Zayn. "I did not know you could do magic. Isn't that dangerous without a patron?"

"That's just Hall propaganda so they can keep their monopoly on magic," said Katie with considerable distaste. "It's not like I don't think that faez madness is a thing, but you have to use a *ton* of magic for that to happen. A few concert enhancements won't hurt me."

"Just to make sure, this is your ability, right? Not something else?" he asked.

"No, what are you talking about?" she asked.

He studied her face. It appeared she was being truthful. "Nothing," he said.

He felt relieved even though he knew he shouldn't have been. Using magic without a patron was dangerous in itself, though the negative effects didn't come on as rapidly. But he didn't actually know how much magic was too much when it came to faez madness. He'd been protected from that since he'd been given the Lady's poison, so it was never something he gave much thought.

"Can you do magic?" she asked with a hopeful glint to her eyes.

"No. Dry as a bone," he said as they passed the Orpheum Theater with its glittering lines and theatrical posters. "But it would be nice, right?"

"Totally," said Katie. "What hall would you join if you could?"

"I have not really thought about it," said Zayn.

"Oh, come on. Everyone thinks about it, even if they don't have a speck of magic. *Especially* if they don't have a speck of magic. I would join the Daring Maids for sure," she said.

"What? Not Stone Singers or the Dramatics?" he asked, nodding towards the Orpheum Theater for extra emphasis.

"No way. The Stone Singers are just civil engineers with perfect pitch, and the Dramatics are...well...too drama for me. They're not real enough. And I think it's awesome what the Maids do in poor countries, protecting young women from those creepy-ass terrorists."

The way her eyes lit up, Zayn believed that she would join the Maids if she could. He'd seen pictures of the Maids before, striding streets filled with rubble, ghostly armor protecting them from a hailstorm of bullets. Zayn imagined Katie busting through a concrete wall to save a bunch of kids from kidnappers.

"What about you?" asked Katie, studying him intently.

He'd been truthful when he'd said that he hadn't really thought about it, but he said the first thing that came to mind. "The Animalians, I think. It would be cool to talk to animals, live amongst them. Somehow I think they would be not as messed up as we are."

The way the smile spread across her face told him that his answer was to her approval. She hooked her arm around his and squeezed.

"I was so praying that you wouldn't say Assassins," said Katie, almost offhandedly. "I hate those murderous pricks."

"Why?" asked Zayn, almost too quickly. She gave him a curious stare. "I don't know much about them. Did they do something to you?"

"No," she said dismissively. "But they're like the opposite of the Maids. The Maids stand up and fight for people, while the Assassins sneak around and murder good people in the dark."

"What if those are bad people that need to be killed?" he asked, thinking about whoever was making the Alpha drug, ruining people's lives all over the city.

"Do you agree with them?" she asked, releasing his arm and stepping away.

"Just playing devil's advocate," he said. "I mean, what would you do if you had a chance to take someone out who was doing horrible things? Someone who would never get caught otherwise."

"Oddly specific," she said, crossing her arms.

Feeling suddenly exposed, Zayn said, "Not at all. In Kingston, we had a class on ethics, and one of the questions was about that very subject."

The question hadn't been in Kingston, but presented in his home by his father the high school ethics teacher, but he felt it was close enough he could easily get away with the lie.

"So would you do it?" he asked.

"No way. I wouldn't do it. Because it wouldn't be me," she said. "And you can't be responsible for everyone else's decisions. Doing it would...I don't know, break me or something. You?"

"I don't know," he said, thinking about Priyanka Sai's question at the beginning of the year. "I think it's one of those things you wouldn't know until you were presented with it. I'd like to say that I wouldn't, but part of me thinks that I should. Either way I'd feel awful."

"That much is true," said Katie, who seemed to have forgiven him for his initial answer because she leaned over and pressed her lips against his cheek in a warm kiss. The soft touch sent a pang of want through his midsection. When she pulled away, his cheek tingled where her lips had touched him.

"Oops," she said, grinning and licking her finger to wipe off the lipstick adhered to his skin. "I got some on you."

"It feels like my cheek is dipped in mint," he said. "Is that how your lips feel?"

"Oh, watch this," she said, eyes twinkling with mirth. She formed her mouth as if she were blowing. A gossamer bubble sprung from her glowing lips, scintillating in the sun. The fledgling bubble wobbled on her mouth until the breeze caught it and pulled it away. It floated upward until he couldn't see it anymore.

"Magic?"

She squinted with one eye. "Sort of? It's the new lipstick brand from D'Agastine. Lets you make bubbles just by blowing. The higher-end stuff turns the bubbles into little horses or pegasus, but they didn't give us any samples of that. The middle school and high school crowd is going crazy for it. They can barely make it fast enough."

"You work at D'Agastine?" he asked incredulously.

"Yeah," she said, tilting her head. "I thought you knew that."

"I guess I didn't make the connection with the lab tech thing," he said. "What do you do?"

"I work for quality control on the fifth floor. They give me the latest recipes, and I test them to make sure they're mixed as they expected. I run the gas chromatograph, or spectrometer. None of the magical equipment. It's boring work, but I'd rather spend the time thinking up new songs than trying to impress my bosses to get moved into the real research areas on the eighth floor."

Zayn's whole face felt tingly, and not from the lipstick. He'd been walking by the D'Agastine building for months and had never realized that they actually mixed product in it. He'd always thought it was a marketing department, and that they made the products in other countries.

The lipstick imbued the wearer with minor magical ability, which wasn't so uncommon, as the alchemy business had been around for centuries—even his sister Neveah had coveted the eye shadow that helped you see heat signatures to help her cook better. It was how the patron of the Alchemists Hall, Celesse D'Agastine, had made alchemy into a global empire.

Wouldn't the Alpha drug be the next logical step? A powder that could give people the ability to use magic? Such a drug would be ludicrously valuable. And if they were making it in the building, how would they test it? It didn't seem such a stretch they might be giving it to people on the streets to see how it worked.

"What's wrong?" asked Katie, searching his face. Her hand was on his arm. "You look like you've seen a ghost."

"I...I remembered something I was supposed to do for my

Uncle Larice. I totally forgot," he said.

"You have to leave?" she asked.

Zayn sensed not only disappointment, but betrayal. If she didn't consciously know he was lying, she sensed it deep down, by the look in her eyes. But the D'Agastine office building was closed on Sunday only, which meant that he needed to go now if he was going to snoop around.

"I'm sorry," he said. "I wouldn't if it weren't important. I'm an idiot for not remembering earlier."

She took his hand and tried to smile, but a frown had settled in. "I was hoping we could go to dinner. Maybe you could spend the night. My roommates are out of town."

Zayn swallowed. Her hands were so warm in his. It was tempting. He liked her a lot. The girls in Varna had been like Gretchen—beautiful but all the same. But Katie was her own little microcosm, the science-y rock goddess in a lab coat. Maybe he could check out the office building later.

When Katie bit her lower lip he felt like he was falling. The soft tips of her fingers caressed the inside of his wrists until he couldn't hear his thoughts anymore.

"I...I have to go," said Zayn, and even as he said the words, he couldn't quite believe they were coming out of his mouth.

"Are you sure?" she asked, wounded.

"No, I don't want to go," he said, "but I have to go just the same. Duty calls. Respect."

He left her in front of the Orpheum Theater. Against the backdrop of the eager theatergoers hurrying inside to purchase tickets for their favorite show, she looked lost, like a girl out of place, drawn into the picture even though she didn't belong. He looked back, catching a glimpse of her before the swell of the three o'clock crowd exiting the theater surrounded him. It was the last time he saw her alive.

Chapter Twenty-Six
Ninth Ward, March 2014
After ruining a perfectly good date

As soon as he saw the forty-foot mural of Celesse D'Agastine on the side of the office building, he remembered the words of Sparky on the night he exploded.

"The moon lady gave it to me..."

The patron of the Alchemist Hall stood before a giant alien moon, her blonde hair blowing in a soft breeze. The guy had been out of his mind that night. Zayn didn't really think Celesse D'Agastine had given the drugs to Sparky. It'd probably been one of her underlings.

Zayn meandered past the front door of the office building, covertly examining the security measures. There were badge swipes, arcane detectors, and a security guard desk—currently occupied.

Shit. There was no way he was going to waltz into the building and root around without serious countermeasures. He could have lifted Katie's badge, but it wouldn't have given him the access he needed.

He was thinking about other ways to get inside the building when he remembered someone he knew that probably also worked for D'Agastine.

Not only did he know her, but he knew where she lived. Zayn formulated a plan on the way over.

Zayn was relieved when he found that the expensive flats north of the bodega did not have doormen. That might have complicated his ruse.

Before he pressed the button to ring the appropriate flat, Zayn balled up his fist and slammed it into his jaw with faez-speed. The impact knocked him to his knees and brought tears to his eyes. Then he used the Five Elements to sear his jacket, crisping the edges black.

After he rang the bell twice, Mrs. Kettle's voice came over the speaker.

"Hello?"

Zayn conjured his Jamaican persona, adding liberal amounts of grief and terror.

"Mrs. Kettle. It's me, Zayn. I'm so sorry to come to ya, but I need help and I didn't know who to turn to," he said in a quivering voice.

"Zayn? Just a moment, I'll ring you up."

The door buzzed and Zayn went in. She was waiting for him at the entrance to her apartment in jeans and a gold-and-black top.

"Oh dear, are you okay?" she asked, leading him into the apartment.

"Yes. No. Uncle Larice is gonna be so mad," said Zayn. "I was taking the week's haul to the bank. He always did it hisself, but I asked. He wasn't looking so good, and I wanted to show him that I could do more. But then this man came up, he was sweaty and twitchy, told me he knew what I had. Blasted me with fire magic and took the money. I don't know what to do."

Mrs. Kettle marched over to the phone. "I'll call the police, right away."

A stab of fear went right through him. The cops would make a mess of his story.

"No!" cried Zayn, improvising. "You can't. I screwed that up too."

With the phone in her hand, Mrs. Kettle tilted her head at him.

"The locals, they require a fee, they call it a Priority Fee, ain't no different than in Kingston," said Zayn. "But Uncle Larice's treatments, they cost a lot of money, so when the cops came around, I didn't pay them."

Mrs. Kettle put a hand to her mouth. "Those monsters. What can I do to help?"

"I need to borrow five hundred dollars," he said, noting that she didn't even flinch at the number. "It's only until next week. I'll contact my da and he'll send money back. I send remittance every week, so he's got the money, and I'll take a second or third job and make it back as soon as I can."

She waved her hand at him. "Don't you worry about a thing. You're a good kid and I adore your Uncle Larice. I'm pleased you came to see me. Let me grab the money out of my room."

Mrs. Kettle disappeared into a back room. Zayn quickly surveyed the room, looking for her purse. He didn't see it, but he found her ID badge on a lanyard, hanging by a portrait of her wife. As he had hoped, the badge had a D'Agastine Cosmetics symbol.

But Mrs. Kettle returned before he could reach the ID badge. She laid five one-hundred-dollar bills into his hand.

Before she could move away, he let out a little groan and fluttered his eyes.

"Zayn! You didn't tell me you were injured."

She grabbed his arm, steadying him.

"I'm fine. I tried to keep him from taking it, but he hit me," said Zayn. "I swear if I ever see him again, I'm gonna make him pay."

Mrs. Kettle tisked him. "You'd best forget about the money, and move on. Violence never solved anything. Sometimes these things are the price of business." She gave him a stern look. "But next time, pay the damn cops."

"Yes, ma'am," he said, hanging his head in faux shame.

"Now let me get you an aspirin and a cold towel," she said.

Mrs. Kettle disappeared again, and Zayn went right for the lanyard, pocketing it before she could return. He wouldn't be able to do anything if she noticed it was gone. He was hoping to get in and out of the D'Agastine office building and return both the money and the lanyard before the night was over.

Zayn took the aspirin from her, but declined the cold towel.

"I really need to get to the bank drop," said Zayn. "If I get it in before 5 pm, it'll be in the account the next day."

She patted him on the shoulder. "Come see me if you have any more problems. I'm happy to help."

"Thank you, Mrs. Kettle," he said, leaving her flat.

He wasn't sure what his story would be when he returned the money, but that wasn't the most pressing problem. He had to break into a heavily protected office building without getting caught.

Chapter Twenty-Seven
D'Agastine Office Building, March 2014
Preparing to do something stupid

After picking up a brown jacket and hat from the thrift store and wrapping his fire-singed jacket into a shipping box, Zayn strolled into the D'Agastine Cosmetics office building. The main hallway had a combination metal and arcane detector at the front, making passing deeper into the building impossible without going through it.

The security guard barely looked up from his desk. He was watching a video on his cell phone with an ear bud in one ear. Zayn noted the arcane detector on the guy's uniform, which would sound an alarm if it detected faez. Zayn had been planning on charming his way into the building, but he'd have to find another way.

The security guard tapped on the desk. "Leave the package here. Have a good day."

"Thanks, man," said Zayn, copying Eddie's New Jersey accent. "You got a bathroom around here? I'm majorly clenching right now."

Without taking his eyes off the video playing on the cell phone, the guard extended his arm towards a hallway. Zayn waddled into the bathroom. He went right to work, pulling huge strands of toilet paper, wadding them up, and tossing them in the toilet. He had to flush a couple of times before he got it to back up—the D'Agastine office building had good water pressure—and then he opened up the lid on top and jammed the float into place so it would keep running. He'd fixed many a clogged toilet in the Castlewood trailer park, so he knew his way around one.

Zayn washed his hands thoroughly before jogging back to the security desk.

"Hey man, do you got a janitor around here? I swear I didn't use much paper, but it overflowed and it's still running," he said.

As if on cue, a trickle of water sneaked out the bottom of the bathroom door into the hallway.

"You gotta clean that up," said the security guard, half-standing with the ear buds dangling from his ear.

Zayn started backing towards the door. "I ain't no janitor, man."

"That ain't cool," said the security guard, hesitating between staying at his desk and going to find someone. "Can you stay here while I get him? He's on the fourth floor."

"Are you crazy? What if someone comes in like your boss or something? They'd put me in jail for impersonating you," said Zayn.

The water was filling the hallway. The guard looked constipated from the indecision, which was exactly Zayn's intention. He'd learned from the Goon that you could get people to make the decision you wanted by giving them no time to think about it.

The guard looked at him. "Can I send you up to get him?"

Zayn glanced longingly at the front door. "I don't know. I've got a bunch more deliveries to do."

"Come on, you're the one that did this," said the guard, thrusting his finger at him. "You have some responsibility."

Zayn let his reluctance show in a longing glance towards the exit. "I'll go."

The guard badged him through the glass doors and switched off the detectors for a moment so Zayn could pass through.

"Fourth floor?" asked Zayn, receiving a thumbs-up before the guard went tiptoeing into the bathroom hallway, his black shoes making little splashes.

Zayn hoped the clogged toilet would keep the guard busy enough that he didn't check the monitors to see that he wasn't on the fourth floor.

The elevator went up to the tenth floor, but he hit the eight button. Blood was pumping through his veins at Mach five. He could barely contain his excitement at getting this far. He just hoped that Mrs. Kettle's badge got him into the right rooms.

He knew he couldn't spend a long time searching, so Zayn burst from the elevator, panicking for a moment when the motion detection lights came on, before pressing his nose against the first windowed door to find a conference room. Zayn kept going until he found the laboratory.

He pulled Mrs. Kettle's badge out, gave it a kiss for luck, and swiped the door, breathing a sigh of relief when the little green light came on.

He had never been inside a real laboratory before. Zayn's only experience had been high school chemistry, so he only had a cursory idea of what he was looking at. But he did know what the drug looked like, and how it was packaged.

After a quick search, he knew the drug wasn't being made in the room he was in. There weren't any powders. It looked like they were developing a lotion that would keep hands soft during the winter months based on the notes written on the wipe board. They listed the fifteen different versions they'd created, giving them a score from C- to F.

Zayn left that lab and went into the next. Again, his search proved fruitless. In this one, they were making a blush that could notify the wearer when the person they were talking to was interested in them. The scientists in this lab seemed to be getting closer to a working formula based on the board notes.

Realizing that he only had to check the wipe board, as each lab followed the same structure, Zayn went running from room to room, glancing at the board before checking the next.

The D'Agastine Cosmetics laboratories were dreaming up products like fingernail polish that changed colors based on the wearer's mood, a shampoo to give hair ghost-light, and sunscreen for those with *albino hemophagism.*

Zayn banged his hand on the wall in frustration when he realized that either the drug wasn't being made here, or it was on another floor. He'd been away too long, and eventually the security guard was going to get suspicious, but on the other hand, he'd never get another chance.

He slipped into the elevator and punched floor nine. The badge swipe beeped at him, so Zayn used Mrs. Kettle's ID. Once again, the light turned green and the elevator started moving upward.

The ninth floor was filled with smaller laboratories. It looked like they were doing the higher-end research up here. Zayn didn't see product notes on wipe boards. Instead, it was chemistry notations along with alchemy descriptors.

As he looked through the first door's window, he had the gut feeling he should leave. He'd been in the upper floors too long, he was using a stolen badge, and eventually the guard would figure out the janitor wasn't coming.

Zayn badged into the room, making a quick sweep, looking

for any signs of the Y symbol. He didn't find any baggies, or anything that looked like the Alpha drug.

Knowing he was out of time, Zayn ran by the rest of the rooms, looking through the windows on the doors before coming back to the elevator. Without more time, he had no way to tell if they were manufacturing the Alpha drug in this building. For all he knew, they could be making it somewhere else, or they weren't making it in the first place.

He hovered his finger over the ten button in the elevator. *What if it was up there?* He'd almost worked himself up to press the button when the elevator lurched into motion. He almost convinced himself that he'd accidently pressed it until he realized he was moving downward.

Zayn had a strong suspicion this was not going to be good. The ride to the bottom seemed to take forever. Feeling like a dog in a cage, he prepared to bolt out the door on faez-speed.

When the door opened, he was faced with a group of people blocking his way. There were at least five security personnel, and not the wimpy door clerk kind. He was also staring at a thoroughly disappointed Mrs. Kettle, who had her arms crossed and a frown on her face that made Zayn feel like he'd murdered her first child.

But none of these were what kept him from leaping out of the elevator in an attempt to escape. Because he was staring at a tall blonde woman with high cheekbones with an air one only saw in royalty, or in those rich and powerful enough to think they were. It was the woman from the mural on the side of the building.

Celesse D'Agastine.

Chapter Twenty-Eight
Varna, April 2010
The Lady's plantation in the daytime

Doing stupid things without planning had been a habit from Zayn's earliest years, and had nearly gotten him killed more times than naught. One such time was when the Goon had brought him to the Lady's plantation on an errand.

The towering oaks and verdant lawn looked almost welcoming in the daytime, a far cry different than the shifting pools of shadow at night when Zayn came with his family for the Ceremony. Zayn leaned against the porch column as the Goon rang the buzzer. The door opened far too fast for someone not to have known they were coming.

A Watcher stood in the opening, wearing her dark sunglasses like a mask. Zayn pulled himself away from the column and straightened his shirt, feeling like he was about to be inspected.

"I need to see her," said the Goon in an aggressive tone that made Zayn flinch.

"She's busy," said the Watcher in a passive voice that still managed to sound threatening. "Come back tomorrow."

"Tell her I'm here and she'll see me. I have something for

her," said the Goon.

The Watcher looked over the Goon's shoulder to Zayn. He had the sudden urge to run until the Goon let out a sharp laugh. "Not him. He's with me. I have information."

"Tell me and I'll pass it along," said the Watcher without a trace of inflection.

"No way," said the Goon. "That ain't how I work. I only talk to her."

The Watcher looked annoyed, which was like saying that a brick wall was annoyed, but that's what Zayn sensed.

"I apologize, but you cannot see her today." The Watcher paused as if she were unsure how to proceed. "But you may be of help with another matter."

"Go on," said the Goon, laughing. "Spit it out, or do you only spit from your backside?"

The easy and condescending way that the Goon spoke to the Watcher appalled Zayn, not because he didn't despise them also, but because they were the Lady's enforcers. That the Goon didn't fear the Watcher gave Zayn a deeper understanding of his position in Varna.

"I will explain if you step inside," said the Watcher with another glance towards Zayn.

The Goon shrugged and followed her inside. Zayn wasted no time as soon as the door shut, and cupped his ear against the door.

"...the Lady is unhappy with"—the name was garbled—"and needs him to be reminded of her expectations."

"What did he do this time?" asked the Goon.

"It wasn't what he did, but what he didn't do. He's as fragile as an insect's wings."

"How reminded should he be?" asked the Goon.

"There should be no doubt about the message," said the Watcher.

A foot scuff warned him that they were returning outside. Zayn threw himself against the column, hastily taking up a casual position, then once again straightening himself as the Watcher's gaze fell upon him.

But the length of time she stared at him twisted his guts a full three turns until his forehead broke out in sweat.

The Goon sensed the attention, and with an amused chuckle added, "There's something about him, ain't there?"

The Watcher slanted her lips crossly at the Goon. "There will come a time when your cleverness catches up with you."

When they hopped into the Fireball, Zayn asked, "What are they?"

The Goon glanced out the window as if they might hear. He waited until the Fireball was headed on the highway away from the plantation to explain.

"They're the kids Varna sends to the Hundred Halls," said the Goon.

"I...I know that," said Zayn, though he'd never heard anyone actually say it. It was one of those things everyone knew but no one discussed.

"Another reason you'd be better off working for me," said the Goon. "The Lady does something to them."

A whole host of thoughts flew through Zayn's mind, like a flock of ravens taking flight. They rode for another mile before Zayn spoke up. "I want to do the next job for you."

"What did you say?"

The Goon's hand went towards his hip holster.

"I listened at the door," said Zayn. "I know it was stupid, but I didn't like the way she was acting, like she was going to do something to you."

"And you were going to somehow stop her?" asked the Goon, raising an eyebrow.

"Maybe help you, or something," said Zayn.

"There ain't no fighting the Lady, or her Watchers for that matter. You might have heard my rough talk, but that's just a way that I gauge where I'm at in the Lady's graces. That I'm still allowed to speak that way lets me know where I stand. People in town think I'm untouchable, and I am, to everyone but her. But I only stay that way as long as I'm valuable to her. That works the same for you. And while I appreciate the sentiment about coming to my rescue, putting your ear to the door was dumber than painting a fence with a chicken sandwich."

Despite the Goon's gentle reprimanding, he seemed to hold the news of Zayn's new allegiance with appreciation, ending with a short nod.

The Fireball arrived at a small neighborhood behind the Castlewood trailer park. Aunt Lydia always said they built the neighborhood in spitting distance of the trailer park so the poor sons of bitches had someone to look down on in their shitty ranch homes.

"Alright," said the Goon, motioning towards a house on the other side of the street. It was one of the nicer homes, a sign of someone on the move. "That's the house."

"What do I need to do?" asked Zayn.

"You need to put the fear into 'em," said the Goon, and his face turned mean and old, as if he were something else entirely. The veins on his forehead seemed to writhe, and his mouth, normally full of teeth, seemed suddenly toothless.

Zayn recoiled into his side of the car, and then the Goon broke out laughing, and the horrible visage was gone.

"Was that magic? I thought you didn't have any?" asked Zayn.

"I don't," he said. "But it helps if you look like the kid from *Deliverance* banged Elmer Fudd. But you need to let them know about the Lady's displeasure in a permanent way, while not impacting their ability to still do the Lady's business."

The Goon unstrapped his revolver and handed it over. Zayn put his hand on the grip and gently pushed it away, receiving a glare from the Goon.

"I'll do it my way," said Zayn, holding his hand out and letting electricity crackle over his fingers. He'd been practicing the Five Elements in the woods behind the Stack when no one was watching.

The Goon watched the display of magic with hunger. "God, that is the sexiest thing ever. It is a cosmic injustice that the Lady's poison protects us from faez, and yet I have not a drop in me. You're like Emperor Palpatine."

Zayn let the electricity fade. It was more show than sting, but the Goon didn't have to know that.

"Go get 'em, boy," said the Goon, as if Zayn was a bloodhound on the hunt. Before Zayn could slide completely out of the Fireball, the Goon grabbed his arm. "And don't forget what I said last time. I'll know if you screw me on this."

As Zayn marched away from the vehicle, he glimpsed the Goon holding the amulet on his chest beneath his shirt. After some research on the internet at the school library, Zayn had come to the conclusion that it was a Betrayer's Lock. It sensed betrayal by reading the intentions of those around the wearer and it was supposedly foolproof.

As Zayn approached the home, he took a good look around to figure out who lived there. For personal safety, Zayn had always stayed out of the neighborhood, so he didn't know from his own experiences. Pounding his fist against the door, Zayn hoped that it wasn't someone his family had good relations with.

Angry steps approached and the door swung wide, revealing a surprised Mean Clovis.

"What the ever-loving—"

The words died on Mean's lips as he glanced to the cherry-red Fireball GTX up the street. Everyone knew the Goon's car, and it was evident that Mean knew who Zayn now worked for.

In the years since the Clovis brothers had beaten him and Keelan out back behind the Varnation Garage, Mean had doubled in size and somehow looked like he'd packed in four times the weight. In town, there were rumors that Mean was good enough to play football professionally, though he'd never be allowed because he was from Varna. Under different circumstance, Mean Clovis could break Zayn with one good punch, but these weren't those circumstances.

With electricity crackling over his outstretched hand, Zayn backed Mean into his house.

"I didn't do anything," said Mean, his forehead creasing with confusion.

"It's not you that failed the Lady," said Zayn, making the connection. "But your dad."

"He's not here," said Mean, hopeful. "Nobody's here. It's just me."

"I'm sorry," said Zayn, slowly advancing, sparks jumping from his fingertips. "Then you'll have to relay the message."

As big as Mean was, the threat of the Lady's vengeance turned him into a blubbering idiot. His voice cracked as he said, "But I didn't do anything."

Zayn knew how it must look to Mean. The biggest Clovis brother had roughed up Zayn and his cousin on more than one occasion, and now the tables were turned with the Goon waiting in the wings in his Fireball GTX, and the Lady's word backing the both of them.

It was a lot to handle for Mean Clovis, as he genuflected to one knee, holding his hands up. Zayn grabbed him by the wrist. His hand looked like a child's on Mean's arm.

"Your father is in big trouble with the Lady." He screamed

into Mean's face, making it loud enough he could be heard outside. "And after I'm done with you, you're not going to be at school for the next week."

There was nothing but white in Mean's eyes. Zayn could have knocked him over with a breath. Zayn turned towards a knickknack shelf with a row of porcelain figurines lined up along the edge. They were collector figurines of the Hundred Hall patrons. Zayn recognized the towering figure of Invictus on the end.

He kicked the shelf over. Half the figurines shattered as they hit the linoleum floor.

Mean stepped forward with fists at his side. "Those were my momma's."

That truth hit Zayn squarely in the gut, but he didn't have time for second thoughts. "Remember that you're not going to be at school for the next week."

The twin emotions of confusion and rage had taken over Mean's face from the display, a little spittle hanging at the corner of his lip.

"I don't understand," he quivered.

Zayn shocked Mean. His arm recoiled against his chest.

"You're not going to be at school for the next week, and your father is going to fix whatever he did, beg the Lady's forgiveness, whatever he needs to do," said Zayn.

"I...I will," said Mean.

"Do you! Do you!"

Zayn pushed Mean over. The big kid landed on his side with his hands still up, forehead writhing with confusion.

"You're not going to be at school the next week," said Zayn.

"I'm not?"

Zayn kicked him in the gut, not hard, but enough to get his attention. "You're NOT going to be at school next week!"

The moment Mean's eyes went wide with understanding,

Zayn shocked him again, to hide his own complicity in the subterfuge. He didn't know how specifically the Betrayer's Lock worked, but he assumed it had to do with intention. Magic could make miracles out of mist, but it never worked exactly as people expected. Zayn hoped to exploit that.

"Scream if you understand," said Zayn.

When a weak cry came from Mean's trembling lips, Zayn said it again.

"Scream!"

Zayn shocked him again as the cry came out, twisting it into a tortured wail.

"Do you understand!"

With tears in his eyes, Mean nodded his head. Zayn marched out the door before his mind might recognize the big guy's expression.

When he got back into the car, he was shaking. The Goon had his hand on the locket beneath his shirt. He was studying Zayn as if he didn't believe what he saw. When the Goon's hand went to his revolver, Zayn's heart stopped cold.

But when he reached out, the gun wasn't in his hand, but a bottle of water. A straggled cry caught itself in Zayn's throat.

"I bet that felt real good after what that sonofabitch did to you on the day of your uncle's funeral," said the Goon, breaking into a grin as he handed over the water.

Zayn found himself fighting back tears. "It did."

"It's tough the first time, making a person know you mean it like that, but it gets easier, I swear to you," said the Goon.

"I bet it does," said Zayn, chugging the water to hide his anger.

"I heard his screams from here. You must have put a real licking on him. I wanted to see it myself, watch you shock the piss out of him, make him cry like a bitch, but I didn't want to get in the way of it. His daddy is gonna remember that," said the Goon.

And at that, Zayn understood that the Goon had sent him up to the house, knowing that Deputy Clovis wasn't at the house, and that it would be the oldest son, Mean. What better way to teach someone how to do your dirty work, than to add a bit of revenge.

When the Goon dropped him off that night, he had a wad of cash in his pocket. Zayn didn't bother counting it—he was going to give it all away. Instead, as he walked the path back to the Stack, he made a promise to himself that one day the Goon would pay.

Chapter Twenty-Nine
Second Ward, March 2014
Learning the art of being alone in jail

It took two days of waiting in the city jail with faez blockers snapped to his wrists before anyone came to see him. He'd expected questions about why he'd broken into the D'Agastine Cosmetics building, or if he was working with anyone. No one even asked his name, which at first he thought was odd, until he remembered that this was the city of sorcery, and there were mages who could find out anything about him without ever having to speak to him.

When he'd asked about his one phone call, the jail clerk had laughed at him and told him Hall students didn't have the same rights. As the only magical university in the world, the Hundred Halls had a special deal with the United States government, so the city of Invictus was in some ways a separate entity, much like Vatican City in Rome.

Zayn spent the time hunched on his bed with his arms around his knees. At least they'd given him his own cell. But this was a curse as well, because if there'd been someone else in the room, he could have at least distracted himself with idle conversation.

He didn't regret what he'd done, only that he'd gotten caught. It wasn't like he'd made a mistake. Mrs. Kettle had decided to come into work that day to get ready for her trip back to Tokyo. When the security guard went to issue her a new badge, he noticed the recent swipes. Once they saw Zayn on the upper floors, they called the real security, who notified Celesse D'Agastine.

The jail clerk banged on the bars. "Time to go."

Zayn thought he was getting moved to another facility, but the clerk unlocked the suppression cuffs and led him to the front.

Instructor Allgood was waiting for him, gripping his clawed staff so hard that his scarred knuckles were white. The clerk tried to get the instructor to sign the clipboard. Instructor Allgood growled and the clerk wisely scurried back to safety.

After two days of silence, Zayn couldn't help but ask a question as he followed Instructor Allgood down the sidewalk.

"What's going to happen to me?" asked Zayn.

A rumble like distant thunder came from Instructor Allgood's chest. Zayn buttoned his lips together, but kept an eye out for signs of what was going to happen to him.

They took the red line to the outer city. Instructor Allgood sat silent and impenetrable, leaving Zayn to feel like a dead man walking.

Instructor Allgood brought him to a crappy hotel in the eleventh ward and paid the clerk with a wad of bills.

Instructor Allgood shoved the room key into Zayn's chest. "Don't try to tell me why you were in the D'Agastine Cosmetics building, because I don't care. You're too dumb to follow directions and that's all that matters to me. But the patron is out of the country on business, so we're stuck with you until then. When she returns, she will decide your fate and you will most likely return to Varna, and I don't give a crap what the

Lady does to your dumb ass.

"I don't know how long she'll be gone, so you stay here. There's a deli up the street, I'll pay them in advance for your meals. You can be here or there. If I see or hear about you going anywhere else, using magic or your imbuement, I will come back and deal with you my way, and then you won't have to worry about what the patron or the Lady will do."

When Instructor Allgood stormed out of the front door, the metal handle bent in his grip. Zayn turned around to find the hotel clerk had fled.

By the time Zayn made it to his room, he was completely numb. It felt like he'd fallen out of himself, that he was in some weird alternate world where nothing made sense. He curled up on his bed, clutching his fists against his chest, waiting for someone to come back and tell him it was a joke. But no one came, eventually the numbness wore off, and he was left with complete desolation.

Chapter Thirty
Eleventh Ward, March 2014
Hello from the other side

There weren't a lot of things to do in a crappy hotel in the eleventh ward except kill the occasional cockroach that made tentative forays into the room, and read the pile of dog-eared romances someone had left in the waiting room downstairs.

Zayn wanted to call his family and hear their voices for comfort, but he was too embarrassed. Every time he worked up the nerve, he imagined their looks of disappointment.

It wasn't like he didn't have the money. The bills that Mrs. Kettle had loaned him were still in his wallet. He'd also considered leaving the city, but he hadn't had the Lady's substance in over a month, which meant he wouldn't get far before the effects would start to kick in.

After he'd read through the romance novels twice, gone to the deli about a hundred times just to get out of his room, and had a thousand conversations with himself about whether or not he should call his family, Zayn started wondering how his teammates were taking what had happened.

Did Instructor Allgood leave them as a team of three? Or did he give them someone from another team to even things out. He imagined that either way, they probably hated him. Assuming they even knew about what had happened.

Zayn dared the internet cafe next to the deli long enough to do a search on the D'Agastine Cosmetics building and if any break-ins had been reported. The whole time he was there he felt like he was being watched, but he chalked that up to anxiety, as he learned that his ill-fated attempt had been suppressed, probably by Celesse D'Agastine herself, who would have thought it bad publicity to acknowledge a lapse in security.

As spring arrived in the form of heavy winds and the occasional rain shower, Zayn began to worry that they'd forgotten him. It'd been two weeks since Instructor Allgood had dropped him off at the hotel.

Zayn spent a lot of time sitting outside the deli people watching. The feeling of being watched never really went away, but his anxiety had faded. He usually spent it in a daze, which was the safest way to pass the time, until the day he saw a girl with bright aqua hair.

Katie's name leapt to his lips, but then he realized it wasn't her. But it got him thinking about her, and how he'd disappeared without saying goodbye.

At first he tried to convince himself that she didn't care about him that much anyway, and was going on tour that summer with her band, but the more he thought about it, the more he convinced himself to call.

Finding her number wasn't too difficult at the internet cafe. He bought a burner phone and brought it back to his room.

It rang eight times. Just as Zayn hovered his thumb over the end call button, he heard Katie's voice.

"If this is a telemarketer, I'm going to report you—"

"Katie!"

Zayn yelled her name into the phone in his excitement.

"Zayn?"

"Yeah, it's me," he said.

"You sound different?" she asked, reminding him that he hadn't been using his Jamaican accent.

Not wanting to get into further trouble, Zayn let the accent flow back into his words. "Must be the connection."

There was a long pause of shared silence. He didn't know what to say without giving anything away, but the joy of hearing Katie brought him to say, "I missed you" at the same time she said, "What happened?"

"I got in trouble," said Zayn. "Bad trouble. I'm sorry, Katie."

"Are you still in the city?" she asked, and the hope in her question made his heart break. If there'd been any doubt that she liked him, it was washed away in that one question.

Suddenly his mind whirled with ideas. Maybe he could make a deal with the Goon when he returned to Varna. He knew the Goon had a ready supply of substance. That would allow him to go on tour with Katie and her band. He could be their stage show. He'd have to come clean about certain things, but he didn't think that would be a problem.

"Yeah, Katie," he said. "I am. I would love to see you."

"I would love to see you too," she said, but there was hesitation in her voice.

"But?" he countered.

"There are complications," she said.

Zayn realized there was real fear in her voice. He'd been so excited about talking to her, he hadn't been listening, but he was now.

"Are you okay?"

She hesitated. "Yes, sort of. We ran into trouble raising funds for the tour. Most places don't want to pay us until we've played. So we were caught in the middle. I didn't realize how expensive it was going to be, buying a van, bringing our own gear, getting the right stuff to keep up the stage show."

The last part, *getting the right stuff to keep up the stage show*, made him realize there was something he'd been missing during all their interactions.

"You can't do magic, can you?" he asked.

"No," she said, quiet and soft.

"You've been using Alpha, haven't you?"

After a long pause, she replied, "I have. How do you know about it?"

"I hear things at the bodega," he said. "You have to stop. It's dangerous. People die from it."

There were tears in her voice when she responded. "But we need it for the show. Only the damn stuff is ten times the price it was a few weeks ago. To have enough for the summer tour, it's impossible. We barely pay for our shitty flat on our salaries. We needed a way to keep going, keep the dream alive."

"Katie, what did you do?" he asked.

"I...I'm sorry," she said.

Then he heard a banging in the background like someone knocking on the door.

"Shit," she said softly.

"Don't answer it and don't use any more Alpha," he shouted into the phone, but it was dead. She'd hung up on him.

Zayn took a long look at the phone and then the hotel bed. He ran out the door at a full sprint.

Chapter Thirty-One
Varna, August 2013
Earlier on Ceremony night

Only the naive or desperate used magic they didn't understand, but living under the Lady's eye, people were sometimes both.

Zayn stood at the far end of the line of towering oak trees, watching the town of Varna assemble before the Lady's plantation, dressed in their Sunday best. He wiped his sweaty hands on his pants and took a steadying breath, catching the scent of flowering magnolias that had been coaxed to life with her sorcery. He moved around the wide trunk to get a better view, throwing himself behind it again when an old wood-paneled station wagon came rumbling onto the lawn.

It was a miracle Aunt Lydia's car still worked after all these years. Keelan got out first, marching up the lawn before she could even get out. She wasn't wearing her prosthetic, leaving the sleeve of her dress defiantly empty.

While it might have been her own personal thumb of the nose at the Lady, it was also a reminder to Zayn of the risks he was taking, both for himself and his family.

Once she was halfway up the lawn, Zayn moved to the station wagon and climbed into the passenger seat. He found the dog-eared spell book in the glove compartment. It was thin, filled with dodgy spells that were more likely to get you killed than to work, but Keelan had probably tested them out, to figure out which ones worked.

But that wasn't why he'd been lurking at the back of the lawn. He'd already suspected that Keelan was planning on stepping forward during the Ceremony.

Zayn hurried to his rendezvous location, finding three figures huddled behind the oak. He knew them at once by their voices.

"Hey, fellas," said Zayn, when they turned.

It was Wheezer, Rock, and Mean Clovis. They'd been huddled together whispering when he walked up.

"What a sweet Southern surprise," said Wheezer. "If it ain't Zayn Carter, who thinks he's too damn good for the rest of us."

"It's nice of you to notice, Wheezer. I've been working real hard on impressing you. But now that my work's done, I can go back to being a slacker," said Zayn.

Wheezer's mouth hung open for a good ten seconds. "See, that's what I'm talking about—you thinking you're too good for us, making comments like that."

"He's a real shit, that one," said Rock, moving to cut him off.

Zayn held his hands up. "My apologies for disturbing you. I'll kindly move on."

Mean, who stood in back, had said nothing so far.

"You know," said Wheezer, "there's no one else out here to stop us if we decide to stomp you into the ground."

"The Lady will know," said Zayn.

"The Lady can kiss my ass," said Wheezer.

"Try saying that inside," said Zayn.

Before he could queue another quip, Wheezer struck

him across the jaw. He didn't hit him cleanly, since the blow careened off his shoulder first, but it hurt.

"You're an asshole, you know that," said Wheezer, looking ready to throw a second punch.

Not wanting to get into a fight with three Clovis boys, especially on the night of the Ceremony, Zayn said, "You got me good, Wheezer."

"And I'm going to get you good again."

Before Wheezer could step forward, Mean grabbed his shoulder, and since he outweighed his younger brother two to one, he didn't go anywhere.

"Why don't you two go inside," said Mean. "I'll finish this off."

When his brothers lingered, Mean added, "Go now, or I'll whip you both later."

Shaking their heads, Rock and Wheezer disappeared into the darkness.

Mean stepped forward, fist resting in his other hand. He checked over his shoulder.

"Sorry about that," said Mean. "I couldn't get them to go inside."

Zayn rubbed his jaw. "It's okay. Didn't hurt too bad."

Mean's forehead was hunched with concern. "You sure you want to go through with this?"

"I am," said Zayn, handing over a small vial. "This will make it seem like you're sick. You good with the spell?"

"Been practicing with it for weeks. It's serious business," said Mean. "Kinda almost makes me want to go to the Halls."

"That can be arranged," said Zayn.

"Nah," said Mean. "I don't want what happens after. Which is why I don't understand why we have to go through all this trickery."

"I have my reasons," said Zayn.

"I think I know why, but I'll keep them to myself," said Mean.

"Thanks again for agreeing to this," said Zayn.

"I owe you for what you did back then," said Mean. "I owe you ten times over. Tricking them like this is worth it, even if I don't totally understand."

"You will someday, I hope," said Zayn. "We should get inside. You go first, and then I'll follow."

Without warning, Mean leaned forward, gave him a half-hug. "Thank you, Zayn."

"Thanks, Roy. You take care of yourself."

Zayn waited a full minute before he moved out of the shadows. His heart was jumping around in his chest the whole time. As he approached the white plantation steps, his cousin was sitting there, staring at the stars through the trees.

Chapter Thirty-Two
Ninth Ward, March 2014
Do not return to sender

Magic was important. It damn well made the world go round, but it wasn't as important as the people you cared about.

A vague remembrance that he wasn't supposed to be leaving the eleventh ward came back to him as he climbed onto the red line train. It was the evening rush hour, so he had to jam himself into the crowd near the door, receiving frowns and mumbled disagreements for his efforts.

It was entirely possible that Instructor Allgood had placed an enchantment on him that would notify him if he left the area, but Zayn didn't care. He could only think about Katie, the fear in her voice, and the insistent banging on the door.

The flat she lived in bordered on the poorer section of the ward. A couple of guys kicking a soccer ball around on the sidewalk barely looked at him as he dashed through the front entrance of the building. He bounded up the stairs to the fourth floor, where Katie and her flatmates lived.

The door was open. The lock had been broken. Zayn imagined a faez-amped kick could do the job.

Wary that whoever had done that might still be in the flat, he didn't just charge in. He stepped in quietly. The flat was an open plan in a big L-shape. A ceiling fan in the central part of the room rattled as its blades spun.

Thoughts of stealth fled his mind when he saw Katie's fallen form near the couches on the far side. He ran over and had just placed his hand against her bruised neck to check her pulse when a short dude with pale skin and a patchy beard came around the corner with a handful of Y-baggies and cash.

Zayn recognized him right away. It was the same guy who'd tried to rob him at the bodega and taken his money in the park. This was too much to be a coincidence.

Before Patchy could get any ideas, Zayn shot a force bolt at him. It narrowly missed him, shattering the framed poster of the Wiznards musical on the wall. The robber ran out the door, dropping baggies and cash along the way.

Zayn went after, chasing him up the stairs and onto the roof. There were at least forty feet between Katie's building and the next, so Zayn had the robber trapped.

"Why did you hurt her?"

In the dying light, the robber lifted his fist and extended a single middle finger before fleeing off the building. He leapt, plummeting out of sight.

Zayn made it to the edge in time to see the robber on a distant, but slightly lower rooftop, perfectly unharmed. The robber waved to him, before disappearing through an emergency exit.

Zayn ran back, to give himself room to jump. He tapped into his imbuement, picking up speed as he neared the edge. Then at the last second, he remembered his fall when training with Instructor Allgood, and pulled up short, cursing as Patchy reached the sidewalk and fled out of sight.

"Katie!"

He returned to her fallen body with hopes that she was merely unconscious. He placed his fingers against her neck, but he'd been running and it was hard to feel a pulse with his heart beating so hard.

Zayn leaned over her mouth, placed his cheek against it. He felt nothing. He shook her softly, as if he were trying to wake her.

"Katie, wake up," he said. "Please."

He sat with her long enough for his heart to calm enough that he could check her pulse. Nothing.

The words of the fortune-teller, Amber, came back to him. *Any attempts at a relationship will only end in tragedy.* He'd hoped her telling was a gimmick, but now he knew the truth.

His whole body was numb. He put his hand to his mouth, squeezing his hands into fists to keep himself from sobbing. Except for the bruises around her neck, she looked like she was sleeping. He brushed her aquamarine hair with his trembling fingers.

"I'm so sorry. I came as fast as I could," he said, feeling empty and cold.

As he knelt by her side, hands shaking, he realized that if her flatmates came home, it would look bad, criminally bad. But he also didn't want her killer to get away. He'd known that she had a cache of Alpha. Had she stolen it? Or used the magic that it provided to take it?

Zayn collected the fallen money and Alpha baggies, shoving them in his pockets. He checked the drawer where she'd kept them, but there was no clue as to where she'd gotten it.

When he was prepared to leave, he took one more look at her fallen form.

"I wish you could tell me what happened."

Then he remembered that she could, but it would require help, and that would complicate things further with her dead body involved.

He oscillated between leaving her, knowing that would mean her killer would likely get away with it, or taking her body, and putting himself deeper into trouble.

"Shit," he said, moving towards her bedroom. "I hope this is what you want."

He found an Army rucksack in one of her flatmates' closets, along with a gray hoodie he threw on. He neatly folded her knees to her chest and her arms around her knees, then gently placed her body into the rucksack, zipping it closed when he was finished.

"I'm so sorry," he said.

Before he lifted her, Zayn put a Look-Away enchantment on himself. Despite the weeks in the hotel, he was still in peak shape, and carried the sack over his shoulder with ease.

Walking down the stairs, he saw familiar faces coming in through the front door. Her band was returning home. Zayn kept his head down and hoped the Look-Away enchantment would be enough to protect him.

They were busy talking about a new song when they went up the stairs past him. Zayn kept going, pausing long enough at the door to hear them exclaim when they noticed the break-in. He whispered another apology before he headed towards the nearest subway station.

Riding the crowded subway with his girlfriend's dead body in a duffle bag at his feet made Zayn feel like at any moment, someone was going to point at him and call him a murderer. He hadn't done the deed, but moving the body made him feel like he'd become an accomplice.

When he reached Madwoman Fortunes and Tomes, he took a deep breath before going in. It was more likely than not that this visit would result in him going to jail, but for Katie's sake, he had to try.

The little bell rang softly as it closed behind him. No one was behind the counter, and the store was empty. A prickly sense of danger settled into his shoulder blades. He had the urge to flee, as if a vast presence was looming over him, ready to strangle him where he stood. He knew it could be a big mistake to ask for her help again, but he had no other choice. Zayn took a deep breath, readying himself for whatever would happen.

Chapter Thirty-Three
Madwoman Fortunes and Spells, March 2014
Was definitely not invited back

Zayn gently set the rucksack on the floor and went in search of Amber DeCroix. He found her in the back, sitting at a table made of a carved tree trunk, drinking a cup of coffee and reading from paperback called *The Lies of Locke Lamora*.

"I thought I told you not to come back," she said, hard and serious. The sugar skull tattoo on her neck shifted.

The urge to flee hit him again in his gut. "I had to, it's important. You said you can talk to the dead?"

Amber studied his face, and he studied hers. There were a lot of things she hid behind—the tattoos, the piercings, the general air of ambivalence—but Zayn sensed those were in place to give people a sense of calm. As she drank him in, he felt the danger she posed as if he were perched precariously on the edge of the Grand Canyon with a strong wind at his back, or dining on steak in a cage full of hungry great white sharks.

He wasn't sure what prodded him to say it, maybe it was the years working for the Goon, which taught him the value of trade, or maybe it was an innate sense of self-preservation.

"I will pay whatever price it requires," he said.

The smile that grew on her lips, showing hungry white teeth, made him shudder in response.

"Bring me your burden and then we'll talk about the price," she said.

Zayn hauled the rucksack into the back and unzipped it. He hated the feeling that he was desecrating Katie's dead body, but he hated the idea that her killer had gotten away worse. Amber did not seem surprised by the body.

"I couldn't stop her killer," he said. "He jumped off a forty-foot building without getting hurt. I need to know why she died."

"For revenge?" asked Amber.

Zayn pulled a baggie of Alpha from his pocket. Her eyes betrayed recognition.

"You've seen this before, haven't you?" he asked.

"You're not my only customer," said Amber.

"Katie got mixed up in this stuff somehow. Maybe she robbed her dealer or something, I don't know. But it's not good. It gives people magic, for a short time, and then it eventually kills them. I want to stop whoever is making this, and she's my only link to whoever that is," he said.

Amber moved to the front door and locked it, flipped the sign to closed, and pulled down the blinds.

She stood across the body from him and said, "I will give you an opportunity to speak to your girlfriend. For now, the window will be small and she will be in great distress, but you can ask your questions."

"Is this truly her? Her soul or spirit?" he asked.

"Maybe," said Amber, "but truly no one knows. Do you want to do this or not?"

"What's the price? I said I'd pay it, but I want to know what I'm getting into," said Zayn.

Her eyes were dark and hungry. "Today, nothing. But at

a later date, I will come to you for a favor, and you will grant it, no questions asked."

"Anything?"

"Do you want to find your girlfriend's killer or not?" she asked.

"Why at a later date?" he asked.

A curl of a smile caught the edge of her lips. "I think you know the answer, based on what I tasted from your blood."

She waited for him to figure it out, which he did. The implications for the dangerousness of his situation grew deeper. "I've got nothing to offer right now, or maybe I do, but it's not worth much. You're placing a bet on me. If I don't die over the next few days, the bet pays off. But you tasted my blood, glimpsed my future, so you think you have inside information."

"But a bet nonetheless. Prophecies and readings are not guaranteed. They are but statistics ran through a sieve of magic. Truthfully, in the majority of them, you are dead, but the others," she cooed with excitement as she ran her fingertips down his arm, "those are *delicious*."

"And in the end, if I don't do the favor for you?" He held his hand up. "I'm only asking to understand, not because I plan on betraying you."

She ran her thumb across her lower lip and for the first time, Zayn noticed how bloodred it was.

"You die," she said.

"Count me in."

Her pierced eyebrow rose with amusement. "That easily?"

"In the majority of my futures, I will die. So why not do the best that I can while I'm alive and make it worth something," he said.

"But what if I told you that to manipulate you, to get you to agree? That if you don't make a deal with me today, your chances of living go way up. What would you do then?" she asked.

He tried to hide his own amusement. She clearly wanted him to twist on the conundrum of free will versus prophecy, but what she didn't know was that was one of his father's favorite dinnertime questions. Zayn had thought through this dozens of times, so he didn't have to dwell on it too long. For him, the conclusion he'd come to was that trying to pick the most profitable outcome always ended in disappointment. The best course was to be true to yourself and let the wheel spin where it may.

"I still make the deal," he said.

"Fair enough," she said. "Come here and give me your hand again."

She didn't prick his palm this time, but plucked a strand of her glossy black hair and wrapped it around their clasped hands. Then she spoke in a deep voice, something he could barely hear, let alone understand. It was as if the earth itself were speaking through the grinding of stone.

The longer she spoke, the hotter his face grew. By the end of her binding, he wanted to rush outside into the cool evening air, but then it was over, and relief flooded back in after she released his hand.

She had a softer expression when she looked upon him again. Gone was the hard edge and the feral threat.

"Come now," she said, motioning for him to be seated across from Katie's body. "Let us speak to the dead."

Zayn matched her reverence. Amber took a few moments to straighten Katie's limbs and fix her hair. She treated her like a mother to her child, before sending her into the world.

"When I bring her spirit back, she'll be in distress. First you'll need to calm her, soothe her, and tell her everything's going to be okay. Only then can you ask her questions, but tread carefully, or you'll get no answers."

Zayn expected Amber to start chanting, or draw runes on Katie's skin. Instead, she went inward. Amber's throat moved up and down as if she were swallowing, until her shoulders bent forward at an angle that would have broken another person's shoulders. Then she spit something into the palm of her hand. It looked like a round, black pebble.

Amber squeezed Katie's mouth open and dropped the pebble inside. Then she massaged her throat for a few seconds before placing her palm on Katie's chest.

"Katie, can you hear me?" asked Amber.

When Katie's lips moved, Zayn jumped, but he quickly settled himself.

"Yes," said Katie's dead body, but the word came out strangled and weak. "Why does it hurt? Everything hurts."

Amber nodded towards Zayn.

"It's me, Katie. Zayn. I'm here with you. It's going to be alright," he said.

"Then why can't I see you? It's so cold. Where am I? I didn't think it was winter anymore," said Katie.

"It's because you—" He almost said that she'd died, but Amber shook him off. "You got hurt. But you're going to be okay. You're in the hospital. The cold is part of the healing."

As he spoke, Amber's face went through contortions. She didn't look happy about what he'd said. Zayn shrugged at her. If she hadn't wanted him to say certain things, she should have told him.

"I...I am?" asked Katie.

"I need to ask you some questions, Katie," said Zayn. "It's important if we want to stop the people that hurt you."

"It's so cold..."

The pain in her voice almost made him give up right then, but he knew Amber would still require him to honor his side of the bargain if he did.

"Katie. How did you get the Alpha? The magic drug. How did you come by so much?" he asked.

"I'm sorry, I know I shouldn't have taken it. But it was so expensive," she said.

"I know it was expensive. But how did you get it? Did you rob him?" he asked.

"No. I took it from his apartment and then he came back, and he choked me. He choked me!" Her voice cracked. "He's still choking me. Zayn. It hurts so much. It's all pain. All pain. Please, let me go. I know what happened. He choked me. Please let me go."

He went numb with indecision. He hadn't known it was going to be so hard.

"Katie," he whispered, and Amber made a face at him that he translated meant he was running out of time.

"Katie," he said, stronger. "Focus on the robber. Where did you go? Where is his apartment?"

"Zayn, please," said Katie, who sounded like she was in unimaginable pain. "It hurts. Let me go."

"The robber," said Zayn, "where is his apartment?"

"I can't. I can't," she whispered.

Zayn sensed he was losing her. He had to find out where he lived or it was all for naught.

"Katie. This robber, he killed you, and he's going to get away with it unless you tell me where he lived. Please," he said, imploring her with all his being.

He was met with silence. Amber's expression left him less than hopeful. She was about to remove her hand from Katie's chest, when those cold lips moved one last time.

"Where the ice worms play..."

At first he thought she'd gone mad, but then the answer popped into his head.

"Near the skating rink!"

He didn't get an acknowledgement, but he didn't need one. He knew that was what she meant because she'd wanted to go ice skating on their last date. The blades of the skates made lines across the ice that looked like worms were crawling beneath it.

But his victory felt short lived as he realized what he'd done. Across from him, Amber looked exhausted.

She squeezed Katie's throat until the black pebble popped out of her mouth and then swallowed the stone. Amber set her hand against Katie's forehead.

"She rests...for now," said Amber. "I should have warned you not to tell her that she was dead."

"Why?"

"It's dangerous to let them know," she said. "But it appears that your gambit was successful."

Zayn put his hand on Katie's shoulder. The skin was cold.

"I'm sorry I had to do that."

Amber eyed him warily. "What will you do with the body?"

Zayn opened his mouth but no answer came out because he had none. "I don't know. I hadn't thought about it. If her body shows up now, they'll wonder how she died."

"I can take care of the body for you," said Amber, strangely calm.

"You're not going to..."

Amber frowned. "I do not eat bodies. I will treat her remains respectfully. But no one will ever know that she died."

It was too much for him to think about. He was barely coming to grips with the fact that she'd died, let alone what he was supposed to do with her body. It was hard enough focusing on what he was going to do about the robber, and more importantly, the Alpha supply.

"Yes, please take care of the body," said Zayn. "But I'd like a moment to say goodbye first."

Amber stood, touched him on the shoulder, and disappeared into the back.

Zayn put his hand on her stomach at first, but the stiffness and cold reminded him that she was dead, so he pulled it back against himself.

"Katie," he said. "I really liked you. You were new and different, and since everything so far hadn't been going to plan, you were the first thing that happened to me that made me feel like things might be okay. And while I'm sorry that I didn't get to spend more time with you, I'm more sorry that you didn't get to do what you loved with your band. You *were* that rock goddess on the drum kit. I wish you were alive so you could keep playing. So you could go on tour with your friends in an old cramped van and make music in strange cities."

He reached out and fussed with the front of her hair, making it arch over her forehead. He liked when it did that.

"I'm sorry that you died. But I'm not sorry that I met you. I plan on finding out who's making this stupid drug, and...and, well I don't know yet, but I'm going to stop them. Somehow."

He found the courage to hold her cold hand, and sat with her for a while. Tears came, slow at first, then streaming down his cheeks. He wiped them away with the back of his hand.

"Goodbye, Katie."

Chapter Thirty-Four
Ninth Ward, March 2014
One short of being a team

Everything that had happened to Zayn since he'd come to the Hundred Halls had felt removed, like he was playing a game or watching a movie about someone else. They'd never felt real because the consequences had been temporary. He'd bounced back from whatever failure he'd endured.

But Katie wouldn't return from her mistakes, and even though he'd had no part in her decision to get involved with the Alpha, he was impacted by her death in more ways than he'd considered.

So when he was surveilling the park in which he'd spent his first day as a member of the Academy, and found the guy who had strangled Katie with his bare hands, he didn't immediately march over and unload every ounce of faez he had at the guy. And not because he didn't want to. Seeing Patchy blithely wandering the park, occasionally chatting with fellow walkers, acting like he hadn't just ended the life of a promising young woman, made Zayn shake with rage.

But rushing into things had spelled trouble for him, like when he'd leapt off the building trying to impress Instructor Allgood, or when he'd broken into the D'Agastine Cosmetics building without much more than an inkling of a plan, or the time he'd tried to fool the Goon. Maybe he felt guilty for leaving the date with Katie. Had he stayed with her, he was sure she would have invited him back to her flat. Things might have been different after that. He might have seen evidence of the Alpha, might have kept her from making a terrible mistake. Might have.

But he didn't just want to kill him, he wanted to stop Patchy and the Alpha. So he watched him for a few days, identifying his fellow dealers—the other guys that had harassed Zayn—and more importantly, where he was getting it.

Then he left messages with his former teammates to meet him at Lilac's Coffee and Casters.

To his relief—and surprise—they came in at the same time, warily glancing out the windows as if they expected Instructor Allgood to come crashing down on them.

"I wasn't sure if you would come," said Zayn.

Portia slid into the opposite side of the booth first, followed by Skylar and Vin.

"We weren't sure we would either," said Portia. "You haven't made it easy on us this year."

"If you don't like what I have to say, I'll understand," said Zayn, pulling out a privacy match and striking it.

Vin would barely look him in the eyes. He looked ready to dart out the door at any moment.

"If an instructor comes here, I'll tell them you were just saying your goodbyes," said Zayn.

"We're not supposed to talk to you," Vin said under his breath. He bared his teeth in rage. "We finally get out of the bottom, and you have to go and break into the D'Agastine Cosmetics building? What were you thinking?"

Three sets of eyes regarded him with suspicion. "I thought I'd found who was making the Alpha drug, the one killing people on the streets."

"You mean the one you were told not to investigate?" asked Skylar, incredulously.

"The one that killed Katie," said Zayn, remembering too late that no one probably knew that she was dead.

"The girl from the band?"

He nodded. The news changed Vin's expression from anger to embarrassment.

"I'm so sorry," said Skylar.

"She was mixed up with whoever's selling the drug," he said.

Vin scrunched his forehead. "So the D'Agastine people killed her?"

"No," he said. "I was wrong about that. Stupid, too."

Skylar's face brightened. "Did you really break into that place with like, no planning?"

"Yeah, but I got caught," he said.

She blinked a few times. "You realize that's where they make their super-secret stuff. Major multinationals would love to know what they're doing and you just waltzed in and were wandering the upper floors where they do that research? That's like breaking into Willy Wonka's factory for a makeup hound like me."

"So you don't think it was stupid?" he asked.

"Of course it was stupid, but I'm still impressed," she said flippantly.

"What do you want from us?" asked Portia.

"I want to stop the Alpha," he said.

"Why?" asked Portia. "Why do you care? Is this revenge for Katie?"

"I'm not going to lie, that's part of it. He strangled her with his bare hands. She had bruises all over her neck. He doesn't deserve to live." Zayn gathered himself. "But it's more than that. The drug. This Alpha. It's dangerous. Dangerous to the people that use it, and even more dangerous if they figure out how to make it without it killing anyone. Imagine if magic were for sale, for anyone. The price would be astronomical. Whoever could make it would suddenly be a major player on the world stage."

His teammates leaned back into the bench. Portia whistled softly between her teeth.

"Is that why the instructors didn't want us to investigate it?" asked Skylar.

"Yeah. They gave some bullshit answer about it being Protector work, but let's be real, if they could control it, they would. Anyone would," he said, lighting another privacy match.

Portia leaned close and whispered under her breath. "If you think we're going to support you against—"

He held his hands up. "No, no. You misunderstand. I'm still a member of the Academy, for now. And I want to stay a member." *I have to.* "But they're not going to take me back unless I prove that I'm worth it."

"They'd more likely kill you. Us too," said Vin, shaking his head. "This is crazy. We should go back, tell Instructor Allgood, before we get kicked out too."

"Why didn't you ask your cousin for help? Isn't he family?" asked Skylar.

The real answer was that he didn't want to get Keelan involved with something that might tempt his worst impulses, but he couldn't tell them that, so he said, "I asked, but..."

"He was smart enough to decline," said Skylar.

The other two nodded their heads in agreement and slid from the booth.

"Wait," said Zayn, reaching out to keep them from leaving. "I know you want to do this. You didn't come to the Academy of the Subtle Arts to be an average mage, let alone on a last-place team."

"What are you talking about?" asked Vin, though Zayn noted he stopped leaving.

He took a deep breath. "On the first day, you took a risk and sandbagged, so you could get on a top team. You don't do that unless you're willing to fail."

Their faces kept a mask of indifference.

"I don't know what you're talking about," said Portia. "I didn't even plan on being in the Academy. I wanted to join Alchemists."

"You're wrong, Zayn," said Vin.

Skylar sighed. "You're grasping for straws. We should go."

"Before you go," he said, "think about this one thing. You came to the Hundred Halls and *specifically* the Academy of the Subtle Arts to be the best. While it hasn't worked out this year, there's still time to recover. Help me take down these Alpha dealers, figure out where it's coming from. I promise you it'll make up for everything that's happened. Put us right back at the top."

Vin stood up. "And you back in the Hall. This isn't about us. This is about you and a last desperate attempt to stay in the Academy."

Skylar and Portia followed him out of the booth.

"Bye, Zayn," said Portia. "It was nice to meet you. I'm sorry it didn't work out. And I'm sorry about Katie, she seemed very nice."

Vin and Skylar noised their condolences, but in the end, the three of them walked out of the coffee shop.

Chapter Thirty-Five
Tenth Ward, April 2014
Not rushing into danger for once

Zayn had given the others a few days to change their mind, but when no one contacted him, he knew they'd made their decision, which meant he had to follow through with his crazy plan by himself.

He wished he had more time, but Instructor Allgood could show back up at the hotel room any day, and his chance at stopping the drug would be over.

What he'd learned since scouting the park from a nearby café was that Patchy and his fellow gang members made their deals in the quiet places between the trees, passing drugs and money in a not-so-cleverly disguised handshake. But what confused Zayn was that he never saw them dropping off their money or picking up new drugs. In fact, one of the lesser members got pinched by the cops on patrol. Zayn watched as they patted him down, emptying out his pockets, finding nothing but a ratty wallet and a hard comb. This was a surprise to Zayn, as the guy had just completed three deals right in a row, which was probably how the cops had spotted him.

It wasn't until the third day that he finally learned how

they were moving the drugs and money around without getting caught. Zayn had given up watching the gang members, since it was clear he wouldn't learn anything more from them. And he knew they weren't clever enough for sleight of hand since their deals were so obvious.

Zayn was watching the older lady with the cat on a leash when he noticed that she crouched down to pet the long-haired cat frequently. This by itself was not that abnormal until he spied the cat handing over a wad of bills to the older lady, who slyly slipped the money into a pocket as she stood. Had he not encountered the callolo at the bodega he might have dismissed what his eyes had seen—a cat with small monkey hands. She owned a callolo just like the one he'd befriended.

Once he understood how the drugs and money were being passed around, everything else became clear. The gang members dropped the money on the ground while the lady came up behind them to collect, using the clever callolo to obfuscate the transfer. He never did detect how they were hiding the drugs, but once he knew she was the lynchpin, he decided to make his move.

The simplest plans were the best plans. Zayn followed the old lady with the callolo cat when she left the park that evening. He had ear buds in—not connected to anything—and nodded his head as if he were listening to music.

He stayed a block back, watching her transform her movements. In the park, she'd hobbled like a pensioner killing time. On the street, she took long powerful strides like a queen making her way towards a regiment of saluting soldiers.

A few times, his shoulder blades itched as if he were being followed as well, but each time he checked, he didn't see anyone.

He expected the old lady to turn into the three-story shotgun-style housing near the park. She seemed like the kind of elderly rich widow who would live in one, but against his expectations, she kept going, into the seedier part of the ward, on the edge of the ninth, where Katie had lived with her flatmates.

When she pulled out a jingling ring of keys and opened a metal door on a large warehouse, Zayn hung back at the corner until she went in. Then he went down the alleyway to the back of the warehouse, since it was likely that the front was being watched.

The warehouse wasn't like the others in the area. It didn't take much investigation to see that it was built like a bunker. The windows had bars *and* sheets of metal behind them. The building had strong bones and had been reinforced.

He saw signs of warding—runes etched into the door frame—on the back entrance. Thankfully, one of the first things the Academy taught was how to bypass door protections, since you couldn't be much of a spy or assassin if you couldn't get in the room.

Once inside, he crept down a long hallway with numerous doors on either side. Looking through the windows he saw offices on the left and laboratory equipment on the right, though he could tell that most of it hadn't been used yet. It looked like they were about to take their operation to a bigger scale.

He paused at the inner door leading into the warehouse. He wasn't sure he'd learned enough to convince Priyanka Sai that he should stay in the Academy. It was possible he *might* have learned enough, but he had to be sure.

Zayn slipped through the door into darkness. He sensed a vast open space and squeezed his eyes shut so he might reduce their blindness. He wished he had an imbuement that would help him see in the dark.

After a minute, he could make out the edges of large

shelves with boxes packed tightly. It was too dark to make out the labels. He crept forward until he reached a wider space. The hairs on the back of his neck were at attention. Zayn turned his head to listen, when the lights flashed on, blinding him temporarily.

When he could see again, he found himself surrounded by Patchy and his friends. The old lady was standing across from him with her arms crossed. The cat, without the leash, was crouched at her heels, holding a small, but deadly looking knife.

"I'm afraid, young man," she said, shaking her head, "that you are in a world of trouble."

Chapter Thirty-Six
Tenth Ward, April 2014
Neck deep in trouble

There were a lot of things Zayn felt at that point: fear, anxiety, the lizard-brain need to flee, a spike of adrenaline for that final and inevitable battle to the death. But none of those were *useful*. The brain, evolved over millions of years, had not yet learned to cope with the subtleties of human behavior, which was why it took every bit of Zayn's self-control to project not the raging cocktail of useless emotions coursing through his veins, but the confidence of a prized rooster strolling into a chicken coop.

"That would be one way to look at this," said Zayn, spreading his hands as if he were the ringleader at the circus, "but it would be a narrow, short-termed viewpoint at this moment of time, rather than the enormous opportunity that it is. It might almost be *life-saving* as well."

The guy with the patchy beard bared his teeth ferally. He and his friends seemed different in the warehouse, changed. His patchy beard—no, fur—was thicker, and it appeared he was wearing a bushy cloak.

"For you, you stupid piece of shit. You're the asshole I

robbed at the bodega."

"Tried to rob," said Zayn, a secret smile on his lips. "How did that work out?"

"Hush now, Levi," said the old lady. "While it's likely that he's just stalling, we *are* running a business, so it would behoove us to listen, perchance that he has something of value to offer."

"Screw the offer, Sandy. Let me throw him off the building and see if he can fly," said Levi.

Sandy turned an icy glare on him. "Need I remind you that you work for me and I don't give a damn if he pricked your sniveling pride. You can go back to living under bridges and picking through garbage cans like you were before I found you if you'd like."

The rebuke crumpled his shoulders as if they were mere paper. Cowed, Levi hissed at Zayn again.

"You may proceed," she said. "Though I warn you my tolerance for chicanery is quite low."

"I understand your caution," said Zayn. "You've got a world-shaking product and you want your grand launch to be glorious." At the mention of the grand launch, Sandy grimaced, so Zayn continued, "Ahh...I see your product is still having issues. Having your customers explode really cuts in to your repeat business."

"The whole thing is worthless unless those issues can be resolved." Her brief congenial air turned hard. "But you've been talking a lot and not saying much. You spoke of short-term views and opportunities, but you haven't said anything about either. Get to the point or I'll let Levi teach you to fly."

At the second mention of flying, Zayn pieced together what had been bothering him about Levi and his friends. He should have known from the moment he saw the callolo at the old lady's side.

"Glaucos Sixers," said Zayn, feeling a little stupid for not seeing it before. "Glaucomys. Flying squirrels. You're were-squirrels. She must have found you with the callolo. That's how you survived jumping off that building."

When Levi's head twitched to the right, Zayn knew he'd made a mistake.

"Jumping off that building? You're the guy who chased me after I killed that thief," growled Levi.

"You killed my friend," Zayn barked back.

Levi turned towards Sandy. "He's not here for business, he's here for revenge."

Zayn was already moving before Levi finished his sentence, but Sandy was faster. When he saw her fingers move in complex shapes and heard the words from her lips, he knew that he'd underestimated her by an order of magnitude. He didn't make it two steps before the air in his lungs vanished.

His chest heaved, trying to pull in more oxygen, but it was as if she'd vented his chest into space. No matter how he sucked in, there was nothing.

Zayn tried to launch a force bolt at her, but the effort of making magic while having your chest caved in was impossible. Levi and his gang circled him as spots in his vision formed, slowly connecting.

When he was on his knees, the only clue that something had changed was that Sandy, Levi, and the others were no longer looking at him. They were staring at something behind him.

A pair of knives flew over Zayn's head. One hit Sandy in the shoulder, breaking the spell she had on him.

Air flooded back into his lungs, a glorious rush of oxygen. He barely recovered before Levi tackled him. Using the techniques he'd learned with Instructor Allgood, Zayn shifted his weight, throwing Levi into a pile of boxes.

When Zayn saw his rescuers, he was overwhelmed with joy. Standing near the entrance where Zayn had come in were his teammates. Portia had a pair of wicked blades, Vin held his fists before him like hammers, and Skylar crouched against the wall, holding shadows around her like a cloak. And last, and most unexpectedly, was an orange tabby cat with tiny hands. It was the callolo that had been stealing from the bodega. He knew in an instant that it'd been following him for weeks. It must have led the others to the warehouse.

Zayn winked at his teammates. "Did you guys get lost on the way here?"

His quip landed without response as doors opened from other parts of the warehouse, and the rest of the Glaucos Sixers flooded in, leaving them horribly outnumbered.

Chapter Thirty-Seven
Tenth Ward, April 2014
All you ever need is your team at your back

The only fight Zayn had ever gotten into was with the Clovis brothers. It'd been three against two and they'd come out with the worse end of the deal. The odds in his current situation were dramatically worse.

Zayn didn't know who threw the first spell, but in moments the warehouse exploded with force bolts, wind darts, rock smashers, flame jets, and water bombs. He threw himself into a shelf of boxes to avoid the crossfire, hoping they weren't filled with bricks.

The boxes flew out the other side, the crash of glass clear above the cacophony of battle. Zayn climbed over the crumpled cardboard, the fragile glass containers inside crackling to pieces, leaking a bitter smelling yellowish liquid that seemed vaguely familiar.

Two gang members caught him as he climbed to his feet. Zayn tapped into his imbuement, filling himself with strength and speed. He kneed the first attacker while ducking under a fist, flipping the second attacker over his shoulder on the follow-through. Two quick strikes to the neck left them both unable to continue the fight.

Zayn moved on, firing force bolts when the gang members were at a distance, striking with his fists and feet when they were up close.

To his left, Vin brought devastating blows against his opponents, taking them down with his fists. Even naturally, he was built like a forge, but the imbuement made his strikes one-hit knockouts.

Skylar floated through the warehouse, appearing like a moray eel, snatching gang members into the darkness, spitting them out like bones. Before long, they were looking over their shoulders in fear, expecting her to come for them next.

Portia was the opposite of the silent Skylar. Blades flew from her hands as she screamed obscenities in at least a dozen languages, following with more knives until the gang members were running away, only to find knives in their backs.

Finally, the little orange tabby callolo was locked in hand-to-hand combat with its opposite number. They leapt across the shelves and boxes, bouncing and slashing with claws and steel.

And while the gang members had been taking Alpha and using elemental magic, they were untrained, mostly hitting friends rather than the Academy students.

Zayn thought the battle would be short and sweet until a concussive boom shook the warehouse. Standing at the center, surrounded by runes in a circle, Sandy threw her hands high, chatting in a tongue-splitting language. As she spoke, a mist appeared from the edge of the circle, billowing outward.

The gang members disengaged from their individual battles and climbed the shelves, leaping upward in short soaring bursts, like crickets dumped from a glass jar.

Vin was the closest. He backed away, but not fast enough. As the mist touched him, his knees buckled and he fell to the concrete in an awkward jack-knife maneuver.

"We have to get out," said Zayn, but when he looked to the door, it was gone. Either Sandy had hid it with illusion or completely removed it through other means. The runes and the missing door suggested she'd expected him.

"We have to get Vin," said Skylar, edging towards the mist. "What if it's killing him?"

"She'd be killing the others if that was true," said Zayn, "but if we're all asleep, we're as good as dead, so start climbing."

As Zayn reached up to grab the next level of shelves, a force bolt came flying down from above, slamming him in the shoulder and knocking him to the ground. The mist was near his face.

Zayn skittered backwards on his hands and feet like a crab as more elemental blasts rained down. He jumped onto the steel structure, using the shelves to protect himself as he climbed.

Skylar and Portia had found other locations to climb, but they were drawing more fire and the gang members had the upper ground, which was giving them an advantage. Portia paused to throw a pair of knives, but an exploding ball of earth knocked her from the third shelf to be swallowed by the mist.

"Just climb!" yelled Zayn, scurrying up the outer steel structure as force bolts blasted the cardboard boxes into shreds.

Zayn saw the orange callolo bounding up a shelf, leaping and climbing as if its tail were on fire. He didn't see its opposite number, which suggested he'd won his battle. Zayn was glad to know the creature wasn't injured.

He reached the top before Skylar, ending up in a place not far from the under-structure of the roof. He took position and returned fire at the gang members who were trying to knock Skylar off, giving her a chance to make it to the top.

While the battle turned to a stalemate, the mist rose higher. Before long, the lower half of the warehouse was filled. A gang member who tried to jump across from one row to another caught an updraft of mist and went immediately limp, bouncing off the cardboard boxes and falling into whiteness.

"We have to get to the old lady before the mist reaches us," said Skylar, ducking an errant blast.

"Can you see her?" asked Zayn, craning his neck, only to yank it back when shattered glass sprayed across him when a cardboard box was annihilated.

Skylar fired force bolts into the mist. "I don't know where she's at."

They had fewer elemental blasts to avoid as the gang members slipped out a hatch in the ceiling. An ocean of mist swirled two levels beneath him. Zayn leapt across the gap to the next shelves over to get a better shot at the old sorceress.

When he saw Patchy at the hatch, rage grew in him. He ran across the top of the shelf towards the exit.

"Don't leave, Zayn!" cried Skylar. "If we leave they're going to die!"

"I have to stop him," said Zayn, jumping the gaps between the shelves until he reached the hatch, which closed the moment he arrived.

Zayn pushed on the trapdoor in the ceiling, but they'd latched it, or pushed something heavy over top. Summoning reserves of faez he didn't know he had, Zayn thrust upward, knocking the hunks of concrete from the door.

"Don't leave me!" cried Skylar from across the warehouse.

"He killed Katie," replied Zayn as he leapt through the hole and broke into a full sprint. Patchy must have thought he couldn't get out, because he was strolling towards the edge of the building, but once he saw Zayn, he took off, leaping from a fifty-foot edge and spreading his arms, soaring across the gap to another building at least forty feet away.

As he approached the gap, Zayn realized the distance was similar to when he'd fallen during his training with Inspector Allgood. But he was determined not to fall this time. He pushed himself towards the edge, harder than he'd ever pushed himself. He would get his revenge on Katie's killer.

Chapter Thirty-Eight
Tenth Ward, April 2014
There's no "I" in Team, but there is a "Me"

As the gap approached with frightening speed, Zayn heard Skylar's faint cries from inside the warehouse. He told himself that she would be fine and the mist would only knock her out until he could return afterwards.

He needed revenge on Katie's killer. He wanted it because even though she had made mistakes, she'd deserved to live out her dreams with her band. She'd deserved to travel around the country, sleeping in seedy motels and playing dive bars. Who knew if she would have made it or not? It didn't matter because that wasn't the point.

He wanted it for her because he'd wanted it for himself. Being born in Varna had left him few choices. The only choice you really got was how much of your life you were willing to give up to the Lady for whatever she called rewards. His parents had made their peace with living on scraps, and he'd made his peace with what opposing the Lady might cost. But Katie, even though he hadn't known her until this year and she wasn't even from Varna, he'd wanted to know that she'd gotten out, was living her dream.

But when he heard Skylar's cries a second time, he pulled up short, skidding right to the edge. Zayn watched Levi and the other gang members fleeing from the warehouse. He knew in his gut if he didn't go after him now, he'd never see him again.

Zayn made it back through the hatch before the mist had completely filled the warehouse. Skylar was throwing bolts randomly, hoping to hit the sorceress and stop the mist.

"I thought you left me," said Skylar accusingly.

Zayn took a look at the warehouse. There was no way they were going to knock her out before the mist claimed them, and she was probably shielded in the circle of runes.

"Go for the windows," he said.

The outer walls were covered with windows, but those had been covered with sheet metal and bars. Zayn sent force bolts into them, sending arcs of broken glass across the warehouse. It took a couple of rounds, but then pieces of the sheet metal fell away and the mist started draining outside.

"It's working," said Skylar, who switched from hunting for the sorceress to knocking out windows.

The mist, which had almost reached them before they'd knocked out the windows, was rapidly draining. Zayn silently hoped the mist wasn't dangerous as he'd thought or he'd just killed anyone who was walking past this street.

When the mist had emptied enough that they could see the sorceress, they both switched to firing blasts at her, but as he'd suspected, the elemental magics bounced off an invisible shield.

"We can't get through," said Skylar.

The sorceress looked quite perturbed that they'd foiled her mist. She switched to a new spell, the pure determination on her face giving Zayn a warning as to how much worse this next spell would be, especially since she didn't have to worry about the majority of the gang.

"This is not good," said Skylar.

Zayn fired a few more blasts at her before having an epiphany. "Fire at the shelves near her. Maybe we can knock them onto her."

"Good idea!"

They sent a never-ending cascade of blasts at the industrial shelves, but the metal was sturdy and their hits did little at first. But once the first leg buckled slightly, the other legs quickly followed.

As soon as the massive shelves groaned and pitched over, Zayn realized his error. The first one falling would take out the next like a row of dominos.

"Get off! Get off!" yelled Zayn as he leapt to the shelf behind him.

Deep in her spell, the sorceress was unaware of the falling metal until the upper contents spilled off, burying her in equipment. Her screams were swallowed by the metal grinding and glass shattering inside the boxes.

Skylar made it to the next row over before Zayn, who had two more shelves to navigate before he'd be in the clear.

"Jump now!" she screamed.

He leapt, long before he was ready. He thought he was well short, until she stretched out her hand and caught him. She pulled him onto the shelf.

"That was too close," he said when the noise settled.

"Vin! Portia!" cried Skylar.

They scurried down to the concrete and picked through the broken boxes and shattered glass. They found Vin beneath a pile of empty boxes, unhurt. Portia was not far from him. She'd luckily landed on a gang member, breaking her fall from twenty feet up.

A few shakes woke them. Skylar then went in search of

the old lady.

Skylar proclaimed, "She's dead," after moving aside a box.

From where he was standing, Zayn could see a metal strut had impaled her.

When the door burst open, Zayn fired a force bolt, only to see it knocked away by Instructor Allgood with his staff. He face was etched with deep disappointment. It only got worse when next through the door was Priyanka Sai.

Chapter Thirty-Nine
The Spire, April 2014
Feeling like a leaf waiting for a strong wind

The fifth year that had retrieved Zayn from the seedy motel said nothing of where they were going or what was going to happen when he got there. That they weren't headed to the Hold did not bode well, Zayn thought.

He'd spent the last few days lying on his bed, thinking about what they might do. He mulled running, leaving the Halls and Varna forever, but he knew that was a temporary solution at best. So he'd waited, waited and paced, paced and slept, until at last he was summoned and he was taken to the Spire.

The ride up the elevator took forever. The fifth year hadn't even pressed a button. They just got in, and it started going up. When the door opened, the fifth year made no motion to get out. He didn't make eye contact either, which seemed like the least favorable sign possible, as if Zayn were about to be executed.

Unexpectedly, Zayn stepped into a lush garden. Plants reached to the barely visible ceiling, some with purple-green leaves he'd never seen before. An insect with gossamer wings and a fat, black body whizzed past, followed by two more making strange sounds he'd never heard from an insect. Somewhere beyond the first layer of foliage there was water running, enough that he could imagine a small stream.

Cautiously, Zayn pushed through the leaves on the path that led from the elevator, wondering if he was walking into an elaborate punishment, but he pushed those thoughts away. If they'd been planning on killing him, they wouldn't have bothered bringing him to the Spire.

"Over here."

Priyanka Sai stood on a balcony visible at the end of a path. He joined her, almost expecting the view not to be the city, but found they were high in the Spire, at a point higher than the other buildings in the city. The view faced east towards the second ward and the ocean. Evening approached, and the Glitterdome had taken to its namesake.

"Do you like my office?" she asked.

He checked behind him, motioning towards the plants. "This is an office? I thought it was another realm."

"Most of the plants come from another place, one I like to visit from time to time. But I don't get away enough, so I had some of it brought here," she said.

"What's it called?"

The hint of a smile shadowed the corner of her lips. "Harmony."

"It sounds like it's a beautiful place," he said.

"And deadly." She looked at him like a woodcutter examining the blade on their axe. "Do you know why I asked you here?"

"Hopefully not to throw me off," said Zayn, leaning over the edge. "I wonder how long it would take to hit the ground."

Her dark eyes glittered with amusement. "You *are* charming."

"I hear a 'but' in that statement," said Zayn.

She turned and faced him, moving with the grace and economy usually seen in formal martial arts displays.

"You're not intimidated by my presence," she said, tilting her head. "I have been called Lady Death, or the Mistress of Knives. Does this not bother you?"

"If you were going to kill me, you would have done so already, and I don't believe that's your way. Plus, I've lived my whole life under the Lady of Varna. I guess I'm used to living with the idea of dying."

"What do you think of the Lady?"

The question gave him pause. He knew his patron and the Lady were allies somehow and he also knew that he had to be completely honest, leaving his possible answers fraught with danger.

"I have no love for the Lady."

Priyanka remained stone-faced, giving him no hint as to how his answer was received. His pulse quickened. Zayn worked to steady his breathing, but he knew the stakes had only gotten higher.

"Then why did you not return home when you were given the opportunity?" she asked harshly. "If you complete your five years here, you will become one of her Watchers, serve her until the end of her long days."

"We don't always get what we want," said Zayn.

"That's not an answer," said Priyanka.

"For my family," Zayn said quickly. "To keep them safe."

Priyanka's lips twitched with anger. "Then why not let your cousin take the burden alone? He could help your family from his position. Keelan could give your family many advantages. He *wants* to be a Watcher."

"I..."

She leaned into his face. "Don't lie to me. I know you

used Roy Clovis to hold your spot and then had the Goon pass your name to Carron Allgood when Roy fell out."

"How did you know?"

"Did you think we would not wonder why the Goon would offer up his prized pupil to the Academy?" she said.

Zayn looked away, hoping he could salvage this mess. "I told him I would only stay a year, to learn Academy tricks so I might use them in Varna. But not long enough that the Lady would want to claim me. We thought a year was a safe number."

"But yet when you were given the opportunity to leave..."

"I changed my mind," said Zayn.

"I told you not to lie to me," said Priyanka. "Or you *will* get to learn how long it takes to hit the ground. Now tell me the truth."

His insides twisted. She wasn't messing around. She could toss him over before he could lift a finger.

He was also keenly aware that she might be trying to wring the truth out of him because she was the Lady's friend. If he told her what his true intentions were, then he'd go over the side just the same as if he'd lied to her. He had no doubt that she could detect his lies, either through enchantment, or pure acumen.

"I came for Keelan," said Zayn, continuing quickly as her eyes narrowed. "At first. I wanted to watch him, make sure he wasn't going to give in to his worst impulses, maybe get him kicked out if I saw things going the wrong way. But over time I realized I liked it here, and then I met the people in the ninth ward. Uncle Larice. Mrs. Kettle. Katie. And when things started happening, I wanted to help them."

"Is that what you think we do here? Help them?" asked Priyanka.

"I don't know if it's what *you* do here, but it's what I wanted to do. I wanted to help them and I wanted to stop that drug," said Zayn, letting anger thread into his voice.

She looked at him for a long time before answering. Her lips were flat and unreadable. "Thank you for finally being honest. What do you want to do now? Stay in the Academy? Go back to Varna?"

"The Academy," said Zayn, "though I realize that eventually I'll be back in Varna."

"And the Goon? He won't be happy," said Priyanka sharply.

Zayn shrugged. "He won't have a choice. The Lady trumps him."

Priyanka nodded sagely. "Will you be happy?"

"For now," he replied.

"Then I guess I won't be throwing you off my balcony today," said Priyanka, raising an eyebrow coyly. "You may stay in the Academy."

"May I ask why? You should have every reason to kick me out."

She put a hand on his shoulder and though he was taller than her, she seemed to tower over him. "And lose a mage with as much potential as you have?"

"But you'll lose me to the Lady at the end of my schooling," he said.

"Then I'll get as much as I can out of you before that time. You aren't the first Varna student with promise that's come through my doors," she said.

"What do you think of the Lady?" asked Zayn softly as if he might sneak the question past her defenses.

She frowned. "You haven't earned that answer yet. Ask me in a few years and I might tell you. Might."

"May I ask what happened afterwards at the warehouse? Did you find who Sandy was working with?" asked Zayn.

She seemed like she wasn't going to respond at first, but then she nodded. "If she had partners, they were silent ones. She kept few correspondences. Nothing that suggested a larger conspiracy."

"What about the boxes? I saw they had addresses," he said. "And there was liquid in some of them."

"Very few, and none survived the fall. The boxes came from various universities and research labs, usually a biology department or company. She was probably using them to unwittingly acquire whatever she used to make the drug. There were no notes, no information on the recipe. For now we assume that she took that with her when she died."

"What do I do now?"

She looked out over the city with her chin high, watching the gondolas slide through the sky on invisible wires. "Go back to the Hold and finish the year. Then you can have a nice summer with your family. Enjoy it while you can because you won't have time when you come back next year."

"Yes, Patron Sai," he said, bowing.

"You're learning," she said. "And one more thing."

"What's that?"

"Don't forget you need your named coin from Instructor Allgood. Everything we just discussed is meaningless unless he agrees that you've passed the year, and he won't do that unless you have your coin, which, I might add, will be more difficult since you're the only student left and Carron is not happy with you, so he's going to be extra vigilant."

Chapter Forty
Ninth Ward, May 2014
Respect, man

Zayn approached the bodega with his heart in his throat. The door rattled as it opened, and he turned away in case it was a customer that might have known him. But thankfully, it wasn't a local, and he slipped through the open door.

Uncle Larice looked up from the counter, his wrinkled face breaking into a smile. "You ain't supposed to be here, man. Class is over."

"I couldn't leave without saying goodbye," said Zayn with his hands in his pockets. "And to make sure you'll be okay."

Larice's eyes glittered with thought. "Don't worry about me, man. Your patron hooked me up with a friend of hers from Golden Willow Clinic. My ailments don't bother me no longer."

Zayn let out a heavy sigh. "I'm happy to hear that. I was worried." He checked behind him to make sure no one was coming into the store. "Under different circumstances, I'd invite you back home. I think you and my parents would get along really well."

"I bet they're good people," said Larice. "Like you."

"You don't think what the Academy does is wrong?" asked

Zayn.

"It depends," said Larice. "But I also know there are bad people out there and I don't want to face them without people like you."

Larice put his hand out, and Zayn clasped it. They shook for a good minute before they unclasped.

"Are you outta here? Back to home?" asked Larice.

"No," said Zayn. "I've got more errands today, and then one more thing before I pass my classes. Which reminds me." Zayn put a stack of bills on the counter. "This is to pay for anything that orange tabby steals from your shop. In fact, I'd like you to make friends with him. I think it'll work out for you."

Uncle Larice raised his gnarled eyebrow. His long gray dreads shifted on his shoulders. "You asking me to make friends with that little thief?"

"I am," said Zayn. "Trust me. "

Uncle Larice looked at the stack of bills, shrugged, and shoved them in his pocket. "What do I call the little fella?"

Zayn hadn't thought about it, but an answer popped into his head right away. "Marley."

"Hey, that's a good one," said Larice, nodding with his hand on his chin. "Marley. I think I can do that. And how do I make friends?"

"Give him some chocolate bars. He likes those the best." Zayn checked the time. "There's also enough in there for a nice bottle of wine for Mrs. Kettle. I'd apologize in person but I don't think she ever wants to see me again. I have to get going. If I don't see you, thank you, and respect, man."

"Respect," said Uncle Larice, giving him the peace sign as Zayn walked out the door. When it shut behind him, Zayn felt a tug of lonesomeness. He would miss his Uncle Larice, and Marley, too.

Chapter Forty-One
The Hold, May 2014
Up a creek without his named coin

Zayn was lying on top of the covers in his boxers when his teammates woke him at four in the morning. Portia, Vin, and Skylar were standing over him, anxious and excited looks on their faces.

"I feel like a gazelle who just tripped over his own feet in front of a pack of lions," said Zayn, wiping the sleep out of his eyes.

"It's the last day," said Portia without a trace of the accent she had when she came to the Academy, but then she switched back to her thick Mexican accent for emphasis. "So hurry up, *tonto.*"

"We want to help you," said Vin, a little too eagerly. "This could be like a total heist thing. I've got the perfect costume for you."

There were a few groans at the mention of a heist, but Skylar added with a trace of desperation, "If you don't have your named coin by the end of the day, you can't come back."

Zayn blinked a few times before rolling himself in his blanket like a burrito and turning away from them. "Don't worry, guys. I got this. But I'd like to get some sleep. It's been hell catching up on everything I missed."

Someone shook him. It felt like Skylar's manicured hands, but he wasn't sure since he was so tired since he'd been up all night

"But the named coin! You haven't done anything about it," said Skylar.

He held one solitary finger in the air and wagged it. "That is untrue. I've been very busy."

"Doing everything but getting the coin," said Vin. "You could have literally skipped every class, and as long as you get the coin, you're good."

"But I needed to learn," said Zayn from his cocoon. "I missed so much this year."

There was a heavy knock on the door. Zayn stayed in his covers while someone answered it.

"It's your cousin," said Vin.

"Not you too," said Zayn, peeking from his lair.

"Zayn. You need to get up. We're going to help you," he said.

Zayn sighed. "For one, you can't help me. Them's the rules. And two, I've got this. I've just been busy. I promise you."

Vin kicked the bed. "Get up. We're not letting you get kicked out."

"You four are more persistent than a dog after peanut butter," said Zayn, sitting up and letting the covers slip to the floor.

"What's this?" asked Portia, poking a bag under the bed with her boot.

"Nothing of consequence," said Zayn with a smirk.

Portia put her hands on her hips. "You *are* planning something."

Zayn let a smile color the edges of his lips.

"Why didn't you tell us?" asked Skylar. "We're your teammates."

Zayn slapped away Keelan's hand as he was trying to peek into the bag. "Trust me, you don't want to get in there."

"What is it?" asked Vin, eyes glittering with excitement. "A bag of vipers? A ferocious badger that you're going to throw into Allgood's face while rushing into the room and taking the coin?"

Zayn yawned, stretching his arms. "None of those things. Really, you should trust me."

"Trust you!" said Portia, laughing as she pushed him over. "I suspect that if we keep trusting you, we're going to end up either buried in treasure and glory or dead."

"Probably both," said Keelan. "You wouldn't believe the things he got us into when we were kids."

"If the first year in the Academy is any indication, then I don't envy your childhood. You're lucky to be alive," said Vin, the corners of his lips curled upward.

"So when are you going to tell us what the plan is?" asked Skylar.

Zayn chuckled. "I was really hoping to get some breakfast and a cup of coffee, but I don't think you're going to let me do that. Shall we go get my coin?"

"Go get my coin?" asked Skylar incredulously. "He says it like he's going shopping."

Vin crossed his arms. "You realize that Instructor Allgood has been camped in his room, vigilantly monitoring the box of coins the last few days. If you get your coin, this will be the first time a student got one in the last month of the year, and he's not about to let that happen."

"I hope he gets used to disappointment," said Zayn, tugging on a black shirt and jeans.

He didn't bother grabbing his shoes, but he did snatch a paint marker and a vial of glitter from his desk, along with the bag from under his bed. The others followed behind like children after the Pied Piper. When they cut through the cafeteria, those present left their plates of scrambled eggs and hash browns to join the procession.

The instructor's door was closed. Zayn set the bag behind him, uncapped the first paint marker, and started drawing a circle of runes.

While he worked, his classmates stood back with their arms crossed and discussed what his strategy to get the named coin might be. There was enough murmuring and noise that Instructor Allgood appeared when he was almost finished with the circle.

"I see you've finally decided to make your move," said Instructor Allgood. "But you're too late, and summoning a demon won't help you here."

"You're right about that," said Zayn without looking up at the instructor as he patiently finished the final rune.

Instructor Allgood grumbled. "What you don't understand is that the trick to getting the coin is to do it early. No one has ever gotten their coin from me in the last month. It's my opinion that procrastinators shouldn't be rewarded. This Academy requires a willingness to take chances, leap before you know if you'll be able to land. Waiting until the last moment is tactically stupid. You've allowed your enemy to define the battlefield. Now you have to come through me to get it."

By this time, the whole group of first years were in the room, along with a couple of fifth years that had been in the Hold at the time. Bets were being passed around the room furiously. To his chagrin, his teammates and cousin were betting heavily on him.

Instructor Allgood stepped right up to the circle and cracked his knuckles. "So what's it going to be? Are you going to try and defeat me in combat? I won't even use my staff."

Zayn ignored the instructor and started chanting from the kneeling position in a loud voice as if he were a worshiper at prayer. Mellifluous nonsense words flowed from his lips as he raised and lowered his arms to give his faux spell some gravity. In general, the more complex a spell, the more spectacular the result. Based on his gyrations, everyone except the instructor backed away. No one wanted to get caught in a harmful spell.

Instructor Allgood, however, stared at Zayn as if he had a horn on his head. His gaze moved back and forth from him to the circle, his forehead growing increasingly knotted with the thought that he should recognize what was happening.

At the apex of his chanting, Zayn unstoppered the bottle of glitter and threw it in the air. A whiff of baby powder and stale beer hit Zayn's nose. Instructor Allgood's annoyance turned to disgust—glitter was the STD of craft supplies, and only used in the most frivolous spells.

"What in the hell are you doing?" asked Instructor Allgood.

When Zayn climbed to his feet, the instructor backed away as if he expected a trick. Instead, Zayn calmly moved the grocery bag into the circle.

Zayn sensed the geist enter the dojo before he saw it. There were cries of surprise from his classmates as if they'd been goosed.

A pink shapeless presence rushed into the dojo, bringing with it a wet sex smell. It swirled around Zayn, running spectral fingers across his skin.

Instructor Allgood didn't know what to make of the sex-geist. Either he'd never seen one before or didn't recognize it.

The pink shape folded around the runed circle, but it couldn't find a way in. It peeled away, presenting itself before

Zayn.

"If you do what I asked, then you'll get what I promised you," said Zayn.

Both the geist and Instructor Allgood understood at the same time, but the spectral creature was faster. It'd been snatching dildos and condoms from people for decades, perhaps, so the instructor was no match for a being he couldn't grab as it rushed into the room and liberated the named coin from the box.

It was back and offering the coin to Zayn before Instructor Allgood could stumble back out bewildered. Zayn yanked the bag out of the circle and gave it to the sex-geist, who promptly dropped the coin in his hand before zipping from the room in a whirl of pink smoke.

The stunned silence lasted for two whole heartbeats before the room erupted in laughter and cheers. As his teammates gathered around him, Instructor Allgood stomped back into his room and slammed the door hard enough to shake the walls.

Amid the back-patting, Skylar asked, "What was all that chanting and what was in the bag? I swear I still don't understand what just happened."

"I made up the chanting. I was just doing it to confuse Allgood until the geist could arrive. It was summoned by the glitter I got from a strip joint in the twelfth ward," said Zayn.

"And the bag?"

"I bought their old outfits and some other stuff left in the bar by distracted customers. They were happy to let it go, though based on their looks when they gave me the bag, they probably think I'm a giant pervert. I didn't look because I didn't want to know."

Vin hooked his arm around Zayn's shoulders. "I'm sorry I doubted you. But now that we're flush with winnings, we need to take you out to celebrate!"

"But this time," said Skylar, "no exploding surfer dudes."

"I'm coming along," said Keelan. "I haven't gotten to take my favorite cousin out since we've been in town."

"Don't lie to me, I know Imani is your favorite," said Zayn, laughing.

"Let's go to the wardrobe closet," said Skylar, pulling on Zayn's arm.

"But it's still morning," said Zayn. "I was hoping to get some sleep. I was up all night."

"At a strip joint," said Keelan, "so you'll get no sympathy from us."

"I was working," complained Zayn.

"You can sleep on the train ride back to Varna," said Vin, grabbing his legs while the others picked him up by the midsection. Within moments, they were victoriously carrying him from the room.

Chapter Forty-Two
Varna, May 2014
The cousins return for a party in their honor

There was something comforting about sitting in the courtyard of the Stack, beneath the sheets of red and yellow cloth, as dusk settled. A warm buzz filled Zayn as if he were a pure note struck and his family completed the harmony. Imani was chasing Keelan with a stick in her hand, making "pew, pew" noises, while his dad directed the twins as they hung crisscrossing holiday lights above the tables. Neveah's melodious singing wafted in from the kitchen along with the smells of jambalaya, while Sela and Aunt Lydia were chatting quietly at the end of the table. Lydia was wearing her prosthetic arm, and the hard lines that normally etched her face were missing.

"You're rather quiet down there," said Maceo from the top of a ladder, holding up a string of lights while the twins wrangled another strand across the courtyard.

"Content," replied Zayn, noticing the hints of gray in his father's Afro. "You never realize how good you have it until you're away for a while."

"It's always your choice to be happy or not, no one else's," said Maceo.

"I know, Dad, I know," said Zayn, taking a sip from his lemonade. "Anything happen while I was gone?"

While Maceo threaded the lights through the other wires and sheets, he said, "They circle and circle the Lady like matter around a black hole. Bo Clovis is sheriff now. He's been working towards that for a long time. I do hope he understands what he's signed up for. There were, of course, the usual marriages and births, I cannot keep up with them, so you'll have to ask your Aunt Lydia if you want to know more on that. Doc broke his leg at the junkyard. I've been over there a time or two to help him out. And this might be of interest to you—some say the Goon has been falling out of favor with the Lady."

While his parents never forbade him from working with the Goon, they frequently made pronouncements about the Goon's troubles—a gentle reminder about the company he kept. Before he'd left, they'd been under the assumption that he had severed ties with the Goon, but that had been a fiction the pair of them had dreamt up. As he'd told Priyanka, the plan was for Zayn to complete his first year and then leave the Academy. And that had been the plan, for the Goon. But that's not what Zayn had intended. He hated having to lie to his family, but he hoped if things went wrong, that the fiction would protect them.

"Everyone eventually disappoints her," said Zayn, rattling the ice in his glass.

When dinner was ready, the family descended on the courtyard like an avalanche. Plates clinked, dishes passed from hand to hand, conversations ebbed and flowed like the tides. The twins had taken spots near Zayn and peppered him with questions about the Hundred Halls.

Due to his mother's raised eyebrow, he tried to wring the color from the city and defuse his siblings' interest in the university, but it was hard, when the place reeked of magic and wonder.

Towards the end of the meal, while enjoying a bowl of ginger mango sorbet, Izzy tugged his sleeve. The blue-haired Izzy handed him a crumpled plastic baggie. A stab of recognition went through his gut.

"This fell out of your pocket," said Izzy, nose wrinkled.

Zayn felt relief when he realized the baggie was empty. "Thanks, Izzy."

"Why do you have a baggie with that basketball symbol?" asked Izzy, then added when Zayn hesitated, "The one from the famous player."

"What?"

The word stumbled out of his mouth. He felt dizzy.

"The basketball symbol," said Izzy, pointing to the upside-down Y.

Zayn looked at it a second time, seeing the person flying through the air with a basketball. It wasn't exactly the same logo, but it'd clearly been derived from it. His brain had been telling him it was an upside-down Y before, but now he couldn't see anything but the basketball version.

"Is something wrong?" asked Sela, stopping the conversation at the whole table. Everyone turned to look at Zayn.

"No. Nothing," said Zayn, hiding his discomfort behind a smile. "Was reminded of a school problem that I got wrong, and just figured out the answer. That it took so long made me feel stupid."

Keelan gave him a funny look, but Zayn shook him off.

"Well, you should put your brain away for a little while," said his mother. "You can solve the world's problems when you go back next year."

"Yes, ma'am."

Conversation resumed its normal hum, leaving Zayn a contemplative moment. He caught Keelan watching him, so he smiled and raised a lemonade glass towards his cousin in salute. Keelan received it with a nod.

After dinner, Zayn worked the sink, hand washing the pots, plates, and silverware while Neveah sat on the counter. Her bead-ended dreads were bound in a red handkerchief.

"You okay?" asked Neveah as she swung her feet.

"Yeah, I survived my first year at the Hundred Halls," said Zayn. "Not every student gets to say that."

"I don't mean that," said Neveah. "You seem different since you've been back."

"I am different," said Zayn. "But also, I'm not. I'm still the same older brother who can braid your hair better than Mom."

Neveah narrowed her gaze. "You've always been at the center of a million plots, but it seems different now, like the stakes are raised."

"That's what happens," said Zayn with an offhanded shrug.

"I don't want you to get hurt," said Neveah.

Zayn sighed and nodded. Then he put his shoulder into the wire brush to get the gunk off the edge of the pot, grunting as he scrubbed. "I don't want to get hurt either."

Neveah lowered her voice. "How's Keelan?"

Zayn paused mid-scrub. He looked back to see her face etched with worry. They shared concern for their cousin, and Zayn hadn't told Neveah even half of the things that had happened when they were growing up.

"He's doing fine," said Zayn. "I think the Halls have been good for him."

Neveah screwed up her mouth, so Zayn added, "Really. I mean it."

"Good," said Neveah. "This family could use a break or

two."

"It's good to see Mom and Aunt Lydia together," said Zayn, nodding back towards the courtyard, which prompted Neveah to jump off the counter.

"Oh shit, I told them I'd bring them coffee," said Neveah, grabbing the pot from the coffee maker, and hurrying into the courtyard after sticking her tongue out.

Aunt Lydia and Keelan stayed until late in the night when the full moon had arced across the sky, spilling silver light on the tips of the trees. After they left, Zayn helped his father unplug the holiday lights. Then he headed for the iron steps that led up to his part of the Stack.

Sela caught him before he went into his room. She gave him a long hug and a kiss on the forehead, which had to be delivered with her standing on her tippy-toes. She smelled like lavender.

"I'm so glad you're back, alive and well," said his mother, eyes rounded.

"Me too."

She poked him in the chest with a stern finger. "I know it is your wont to get into schemes, but for my sake this summer, please take a break. No plots, and please, stay away from the Goon."

"I will," he said, kissing her on the forehead. "Good night."

Back in his room, he tugged the cord above his bed to turn out the light. He'd forgotten how loud the insects were in Varna, but at least he didn't have to listen to Vin's snoring. It was good to be home, even if it wasn't really that place anymore.

Zayn waited for an hour before getting back up. Rather than use the stairs, he pulled himself out the window, relying on his imbuement to provide the finger strength necessary to make the hand-over-hand climb down the support wire. When he landed in the dew-soaked grass, he took one look at the Stack before taking off down the gravel road towards the Goon's place.

Chapter Forty-Three
Varna, May 2014
Making right with the Goon

The Goon's place was a mini-compound in the middle of the woods that surrounded Varna. It was ringed with tall fences topped with curly barbed wire and shock-me runes. Cameras covered every inch of the lawn, which was carefully manicured so no one could approach the house without triggering the motion detectors.

When Zayn first came to the compound, he'd been terrified by the layers of protections, thinking the place impregnable. And for the majority of the population, it was. After only a year at the Academy, Zayn saw fifteen different ways he could get into the house without triggering a single alarm.

But thankfully, he didn't have to circumvent the Goon's protections. He rang the buzzer at the gate, making sure to stare into the camera.

He waited for a couple of minutes, longer than was usual, which started to worry Zayn. But then the gate shuddered into motion, opening wide enough for Zayn to slip through. He made his way up the long drive to the single-story ranch. It didn't look like much from the outside, but the Goon had built down rather than up. There were two more floors beneath the main one.

The Goon appeared in the doorway, straw hat tilted back on his nearly bald head. He had big bags under his eyes and a hand on a pistol at his side.

"Is that you, Zayn?"

Zayn stumbled in his stride. "Of course it's me. What's wrong? You look like you haven't been sleeping."

The Goon rubbed his eyes with his palm, glanced around, then waved Zayn into the house. His dad had said the Goon was in trouble with the Lady, but he hadn't thought it had gotten this bad.

As soon as Zayn stepped inside, the Goon latched the door and locked it. Zayn was about to tell him that those simple protections would be no match for one of her Academy-trained Watchers, but he didn't want to rattle him further.

"What happened to the plan?" asked the Goon, turning on Zayn as soon as he was finished locking the door. He had a firm grip on his pistol in the holster and the other around the amulet under his shirt.

"There were complications," said Zayn, walking past the Goon as if there were no problems. "Besides, I think I should stay longer. I'm learning a lot."

"I needed you back here," said the Goon, jaw clenching and unclenching. "My standing with the Lady has moved from difficult to a moth in a shredder. I haven't left the compound in weeks."

"If she sends the Watchers in after you, there's nothing I can do," said Zayn.

"Then why the hell did you go to the Halls? I need protection," said the Goon as he paced, keeping his hand on the amulet.

"You're still not telling me what's going on. And I never

went there for protection. I went to the Halls so we could run bigger scams," said Zayn.

"Well, you should have," said the Goon.

"Easy, man," said Zayn, holding his hands out. "I'm your friend. I'm on your side."

"Are you?" asked the Goon angrily.

"I nearly died at the Academy, like multiple times, so I could come back here and support you. And now you're freaking out, not telling me anything about anything, and worried that the Lady is out for you. What happened?" asked Zayn.

The Goon's expression broke, and Zayn thought for a moment he might cry. "I'm sorry, Zayn. You're right. But I haven't slept in days. I'm just a little paranoid, I guess. I thought you might have betrayed me."

The Goon took his hand off the amulet, which allowed Zayn to relax. He knew a spell that would hide him from the amulet, but he wasn't sure if the Goon could detect it, so he had to do it the hard way, the same as he'd done with Mean Clovis.

"Want me to grab you a drink?" asked Zayn. "I know where you keep the good stuff."

The Goon took his hand off the pistol, slipped the straw hat from his head, and waved air over it with the hat. "I'll get it. Do you want one?"

"Not too much. I'm still a lightweight," said Zayn. "And where are Jordan and Barkley? I was expecting a greeting."

"Down below sleeping. Aren't there spells for hangovers?" asked the Goon as he left the room.

It was strange that the hounds weren't upstairs. Normally the dogs kept the same hours as the Goon, though he guessed they were getting older and might need more sleep.

Zayn yelled down the hallway. "They're sometimes worse

than the cure."

The kitchen was on the other side of the ranch, which would give Zayn a few moments to snoop around. He darted into the game room where the basketball arcade games were located. As soon as he saw the logo, he knew the symbol had been derived from it. But that didn't mean the Goon was behind the Alpha drug. He needed more proof.

He stuck his head into the gun shop. There was nothing there that suggested the Goon had been manufacturing drugs. He really needed to get into the lower levels. But there was no time for that.

Zayn opened the cabinets beneath the counter where the reloading press was located. He was about to close it when he noticed something in back.

It felt like the Goon was going to walk back in at any moment. He couldn't have taken that long to pour a couple of glasses of whiskey, and Zayn didn't have a good reason why he was snooping through his cabinets.

He reached into the back of the cabinet and pulled out a stack of baggies, bound with a rubber band. They had the upside-down Y symbol printed on them.

As soon as the Goon's link to the drug was confirmed, Zayn realized what the yellowish liquid was that had been in the glassware in the warehouse. The Lady's poison. It was the same stuff they had to take at the Ceremony. Everyone knew if you were going to leave Varna for an extended period, you could get some poison from the Goon for a short trip. It was assumed that the Goon had permission from the Lady. But maybe he'd found another use for it.

"Where'd you go?" asked the Goon from the next room, startling Zayn, who dropped the baggies on the floor and kicked them under the center table with his boot.

The Goon strolled in with a glass in each hand, amber

liquid swirling around fat ice cubes. His forehead hunched with concern.

"What are you doing in here?" asked the Goon.

"Killing time," said Zayn, putting a smile on while he hoped he'd kicked the baggies to a place the Goon couldn't see. "It feels like it's different in here, but I can't figure out why."

Zayn glanced around at the walls, trying to keep the Goon from looking down.

The Goon gave a long pause, then his forehead relaxed and he nodded towards the wall. "Painted it light yellow, rather than that ugly gray. Read it was a soothing color. Helps me shoot better since I'm more relaxed."

"Good call," said Zayn, reaching out to take the smaller glass of whiskey.

They clinked them together.

The Goon said, "To a successful first year in the Hundred Halls."

"To bigger and better schemes," said Zayn.

He threw back a mouthful of the whiskey, trying not to spit it back out when the burn hit his throat.

The Goon chuckled while he wiped his mouth with the back of his sleeve.

"Whew, that burned," said Zayn, then glanced at the clock on the wall. "You know, I'm tired. I kept regular hours at the Halls, so I'm pretty wiped. I just came by to check in with you, let you know I'm back. Had to sneak out, as usual."

"When you come back for good, you're going to have to let them know," said Goon, clearly disappointed.

"They know," said Zayn, "and I will. It's about time."

Zayn moved towards the passage that led to the front door. The Goon made a noise that made Zayn pause mid-stride.

"I thought you wanted to know what happened with the Lady," said the Goon.

"Oh, yeah, I did, but like I said, I'm tired," said Zayn, letting his mouth arch into a fake yawn.

"That ain't like you," said the Goon. "What's going on? Why *did* you come over here?"

"It's official," said Zayn. "You and me *both* need sleep. You, clearly more than me. Look, I'll be back tomorrow. We can talk more about it. We got a whole summer to make plans, and whatever happened with the Lady, we can fix that together."

The Goon stared back. "Maybe you're right. Maybe I'll get some sleep. You want me to drive you back?"

"Nah, I'll be good," said Zayn, shoving his hands in his pockets.

His chest started to relax as he got closer to the door, especially when he heard the Goon rattling the ice in his glass. At the moment his hand touched the door, a fateful click sounded behind him.

A gun was being pointed at him.

"Don't you waggle a finger or I'll put a hole the size of Kansas in your chest," growled a voice he'd never expected to hear again. "Now turn around."

He was face-to-face with Levi, the shape-shifter he thought of as Patchy that had evaded him at the warehouse. Hearing the noises, the Goon came into the room and immediately pulled his gun, also pointing it at Zayn.

"What's going on?" asked the Goon.

"This is the bastard that ruined our operation in Invictus," said Levi. "So where can we take him so I can put a bullet in his head?"

Chapter Forty-Four
Varna, May 2014
An unexpected visitor

The Goon seemed to process this new information with exceeding calm, as if he didn't believe it. The gun, however, stayed trained on Zayn.

"Him? You know him? Zayn?" asked the Goon.

Levi nodded feverishly. "Him and a bunch of mages showed up to the warehouse, killed Sandy, ruined the whole operation."

The Goon pushed his straw hat back. "But he was in the Academy, studying to be an assassin. I helped him get into the Halls. He works for me."

"I...I...I didn't know that," said Levi, suddenly nervous. "But it was him. I robbed a bodega, and he was working there. He had a Jamaican accent then. Worked for this old Jamaican guy."

"That true?" asked the Goon.

"The bodega, yeah, I worked there. It was part of my training," said Zayn, trying to find the right amount of indignation. "Why is he here? And why is he pointing a gun at me? I don't know anything about a warehouse, but he killed my girlfriend, strangled her. I chased him off a roof, don't know how he survived."

The Goon pointed his gun at Levi. "This true? You kill his girlfriend?"

"No, I mean, yes. I didn't know it was his girlfriend. She stole some Alpha from us. I had to show her. I had to," whined Levi. "But it was him in the warehouse. I know it. Him and his mage buddies. Academy, I guess. They came in and wrecked the place."

The Goon looked back and forth between them. He placed his hand on the amulet, and came away as if he'd been burned.

"Put the gun down, Levi," said the Goon. "At least until I figure this out. I don't know who's lying to me, but one of you is. Remember, I know people at the Academy, so if you were involved, Zayn, come clean right now."

"I'm sorry," said Zayn. "I didn't know it was your warehouse. I was just after revenge."

"Damn, Zayn. Damn it all to hell," said the Goon as he threw his straw hat against the wall. He pointed the gun back at Zayn. "You might not have meant to do that, but that screwed me. I needed the money from that batch to keep things hush-hush. But now I got nothing, and the bill is coming due."

Levi lifted his gun. He had a sickening smile on his face. Zayn imagined it was the same look Levi had when he was strangling Katie.

"I don't understand," said Zayn. "What was that drug? Does it have something to do with the Lady?"

Zayn knew the answer before Goon replied, but he didn't want to give away that he'd been in the warehouse to stop the drug rather than for revenge. Revenge was something the Goon might understand.

"I used the poison, along with a few other special ingredients"—the Goon smiled at Levi—"to whip it up. It's taken me damn near twenty years to figure it out, and it still ain't all the way right."

"It has something to do with magic?" asked Zayn.

"Thereabouts," said the Goon. "Why do you think everyone from Varna who has a lick of magic can use it without going mad? It's because we've been sucking down her poison in small doses since we were born. We've been inoculated. Like the smallpox."

"You've been paying off Watchers to collect more for you," said Zayn. "First for trials, then for production. That's what those boxes were so many years ago when I first started working for you. You were routing the supplies around the country, to people like Sandy, getting them back from the Watchers who you turned, without the Lady finding out. That's why you're so paranoid—you knew that if she ever found out, it would be bad. Really bad."

"I always knew you were the smart one," said the Goon with a trace of sadness. "Unfortunately, I will no longer be able to use your services. One, on account of your interference creating this difficult situation for me, and two, I need someone to blame it on."

"Can I shoot him now? Or do we have to find a place he won't make a mess?" said Levi, quivering with excitement.

"Shut up, Levi. We're not shooting him now. I might need him alive, just long enough to convince the Lady that him and his family—who everyone knows has no love for the Lady—that they were behind the scheme," said the Goon.

Zayn knew in his gut that the Goon could do such a thing. There were always potions and spells to bend someone to your will, and the Goon had the resources. And it wouldn't be hard for the Lady and her Watchers to believe whatever the Goon conjured up because of what happened with his dad and Uncle Jesse.

"I'm worth way more to you alive," said Zayn. "We can fix this with the Lady. I swear I can think of something."

The Goon nodded with a resolution that made Zayn's stomach turn over. "No, I'm sorry. I cannot see another way around this. I can't come up with the money in time, so I'm going to need a scapegoat."

"But if they already know you're the one behind the drug, how is that going to help you?" asked Zayn.

"Because they don't know it's me," said the Goon. "They just know someone has been buying it up, and that that someone hasn't paid their debts. My spies in the Lady's court have told me that the problem has grown large enough they've paid a Hall mage to track me down. So, like I said, it's a matter of time. Which means I need to get scheming, and I can't do that if I'm worried about you."

He reached into a pocket and pulled out what looked like a bottle of pepper spray. He flipped the lid off with a thumb.

"I'm sorry, Zayn. You were a good kid. I'll try and make this as painless as possible."

Zayn flooded his imbuement with faez in an attempt to sprint past them, but the Goon sprayed him in the face with a sweet liquid that turned the lights out. Zayn took two steps and crashed into the couch headfirst.

Chapter Forty-Five
Varna, July 2007
The price we pay for family

Zayn ran through the woods like the world was on fire, branches whipping his arms and legs, but he didn't slow down. He ran for a quarter mile before he stopped behind an oak tree, staring through the trees to see if they'd followed him.

He could barely contain his breath; it came in great heaves. He wiped the sweat dripping from his forehead. His shirt was soaked through, but that was the Alabama summer. With a black walnut in hand, Zayn kept watch for the other kids. Him and Keelan had made a surprise attack, but when reinforcements had come, Zayn knew it was time to beat feet.

But as he stared back through the dense trees, he couldn't hear or see anyone.

"Shit, Zayn. You ran right out of the game," he said, laughing.

He'd run so far the screams of kids throwing black walnuts had been swallowed by the forest. For all he knew, the game could have ended, or moved further east.

He took the culvert that went behind the Castlewood trailer park. While he'd been running, the skies had taken on a gloomy cast. Zayn smelled a storm, but he relished it rather than feared it. He could use a bath.

He realized the storm had ended the game, so he cut back through the park towards Keelan's trailer. His cousin was probably already there, sitting at the counter with a giant glass of lemonade so sour it'd curl hair.

Booming thunder right over the trailer park startled Zayn, followed by a torrential downpour. Raindrops the size of robin eggs drilled into the gravel, throwing milky mud against his ankles.

He was about to cut around the corner, when he realized a black SUV sat out front.

As Zayn ducked behind the trailer a scream sounded from inside, loud enough to overcome the pounding of rain. Zayn pulled himself up to the window.

Aunt Lydia had her arms pinned to her side by a Watcher while the Speaker with her cobra-like blonde coif held a long fingernail to her throat like a weapon.

"Tell us what your husband did," said the Speaker, "and I will show mercy."

Through tear-soaked rage, Lydia shouted back, "I don't know anything, and if I did I wouldn't tell you."

"Now, dearie, that wasn't a very smart thing to say," said the Speaker. "Tell us what Jesse did. Tell us, girl. The alternatives are much worse."

"I told you," said Lydia, quivering as if her soul had been struck with a tuning fork, "I don't know. He's been out for weeks. He said he was working for *you all*, but I guess that ain't been true."

The Speaker lunged towards Aunt Lydia like a snake striking. Zayn couldn't see what she did, but his aunt screamed so loud he wasn't sure how she wasn't dead already.

But whatever the Speaker had done subsided quickly,

and Lydia was left heaving and crying. Every inch of Zayn shook with impotent rage. Tears streaked down his cheeks as he watched the Speaker step close to his aunt.

"Tell me, Lydia. Tell me something. I believe you that he didn't tell you nothing, but I know you're a smart girl. Give me a boon to take back to the Lady. She's quite cross right now. It would be a salve to her injuries to have some knowledge of how it was done. Do you ken anything? Something you might have noticed or heard? Did he keep company with anyone else? A neighbor? Your sister or her husband?"

Zayn's heart caught in his throat. He'd seen his dad and Uncle Jesse at the junkyard with Doc. He thought they'd been planning new additions to the Stack, but this new revelation left him shaking. He nearly burst away from the trailer to get back home and warn his family—not that it would do them a lick of good—but he stayed, only because his muscles refused to move on their own.

Aunt Lydia opened her mouth once, twice, three times, before finally speaking with a resolute sadness. "Nobody. I ain't seen him talk with nobody. Like I said, I thought he was working for you, working for the Lady. I thought we were moving up in the world. If he was doing something wrong, I don't know what it is, but I am terribly sorry."

"I believe you, girl, I do," said the Speaker as she patted her arm. "But I gotta take something, just the same. Hold her."

To his aunt's credit, she didn't scream or fight. She stood like a statue, staring mutely back at the Speaker as she weaved complex shapes in the air. The scent of faez was rich in the air as it mixed with the storm's musk.

Zayn didn't know what to expect when the Speaker struck his aunt with her hand, but the blow severed her aunt's arm cleanly, like popping a doll's arm out of its socket. Aunt Lydia collapsed to the floor of the trailer, not a sound.

The shock forced an exhalation from Zayn's lips. The Watcher's head bobbed up. Zayn dropped from the edge and went running, through the park and down the culvert, wading through the calf-high water surging from the storm.

He ran until he couldn't see through the tears. When he stopped, the world closed around him as if he'd been cinched up in a sack of verdant leaves. Amid the trees, the storm sounded like it was happening somewhere else. The slow patter on the canopy washed away the world.

He wasn't paying attention when someone reached out and grabbed him. Zayn nearly struck his attacker, until he realized it was Keelan.

"Where you been, cuz?" asked Keelan, then noticing his face, "What happened?"

The words tumbled from his lips in a flood. When he got to the part about Lydia's arm, Keelan made a move towards the trailer park, but Zayn stopped him.

"They might still be there," he said.

"But they took her arm! I've got to get to her," said Keelan.

"If they wanted her dead, there's nothing you or I could have done," said Zayn. "The spell the Speaker used made it so they took it cleanly, like it'd never been connected at all."

"Why? Why would they do that?"

"Something that happened with your dad," said Zayn, pacing because he couldn't hold it in much longer. "It sounds bad. Really bad."

"And your dad," said Keelan, face twisted in rage. "They're always conspiring, like thieves at a lock."

"They weren't looking for him, only Jesse. Something he did, or tried to do," said Zayn.

Keelan collapsed onto the forest floor, head in hands.

"Why! Why did we have to be born in Varna? Why couldn't

it have been anywhere else? This place is killing us." Keelan looked up, and his eyes were bloodshot. "This town is gonna kill us one day. We can't escape. Why did we have to be born here? Why did we have to be born at all?"

"We don't have to stay," said Zayn.

"What are we going to do then? We can't leave, and *she'll* kill our families if we ever do anything," said Keelan, his voice choked with anguish.

It built in Zayn like a volcano. His face was hot, and steam rose from his head in the cool rain. He felt an unspeakable emotion well up, pushing against every cell, a pressure that threatened to burst him into ether.

When Zayn finally spoke, he felt something cleave in him, like the weak and useless parts had slid away. "I'm going to kill her."

"You? The Lady?" asked Keelan, part laughing, his muscles shaking with anger.

Zayn shook his head as he wiped away tears with his thumb, ignoring the rain dripping on his face.

"Yes, I swear it."

"But you can't," said Keelan. "And even if you could, everyone in Varna would die. You're talking crazy."

"I'm not," said Zayn, feeling more clearheaded than he'd ever been in his life. He felt like he was standing on a mountain so tall he was nearly in space and the universe was made visible in its completeness.

"How? You're just a kid. We're just kids," said Keelan.

"I don't know how. Today, anyway. But I'll keep my eye out, keep watch, look for opportunity," said Zayn, tugging at his chest as if he thought he might have a heart attack. He wanted to dunk himself in an ice-cold river. His skin was on fire.

"Opportunity for what?" asked Keelan.

"I wouldn't need too many things," said Zayn, seeing the path in his mind like a river with tributaries rushing in and combining with the head waters until they were a great foamy flood. "I would need to make myself valuable to her so she would trust me. Then I would need a weapon, I guess. Something to get through all the magics and protection. And something to protect myself from her and the Watchers, and a way to sneak up close without her seeing me."

"Even if you could get those things, which you can't," said Keelan, "you're forgetting the most important thing."

"What's that?"

"Not killing the whole town when she's dead," said Keelan.

"I can figure that out later," said Zayn. "One thing at a time."

Keelan, who looked like he didn't quite believe him, said, "You're talking five increasingly impossible things. I appreciate what you're saying, Zayn. I really do. But you'd only get us all killed."

"I might," said Zayn as soft as butterflies' wings. "But is what we're doing right now really living?"

Keelan shot him a look of accusation as he climbed to his feet. "We should go tell your parents. They'll know what to do. Maybe they know what's happened to my dad. They'll have a real plan, not some crazy talk like you. You couldn't even do the first thing, let alone the others. Five crazy impossible things."

As Keelan marched off, tear soaked and weary, Zayn looked back towards the center of town and spoke to himself.

"They're not impossible. And I only have to do the first one for now. I just need to do something valuable for the Lady or one of her friends, maybe find something for her, or eliminate one of her enemies. If I did that, then one thing would be done, and if I can get the first done, why not the rest?"

Chapter Forty-Six
Varna, May 2014
Learning the answer to a question

The promise that he'd made himself so many years ago resurfaced with his consciousness, along with the realization that he was trapped.

The Goon had kept mages as prisoners before. Zayn could tell because his fingers had been individually bound to the wall with clamps so he couldn't move them the width of a single hair. Clamps held his wrists, arms, thighs, ankles, and midsection. A ball gag had been placed in his mouth.

None of this was visible, as the room had no light. Zayn strained against the clamps, finding a secondary reason he would not be escaping. Each binding had a sharp point in the arc—possibly a screw set into the metal—so if he pushed against it, the tip would pierce his skin. It was an excruciating predicament.

Adding to his discomfort was a migraine the size of Kansas. Knockout potions were notorious for post-waking headaches. Zayn could barely string two thoughts together without stabs of pain rushing through his brain.

But despite the circumstances, he found himself in a good

mood. He recalled his vow from so many years ago, when Aunt Lydia lost her arm. If he could only get out of the bindings and the room without tearing his flesh apart, and expose the Goon's machinations to the Lady, he could finally achieve his first goal.

He'd been working towards this moment since that day. All those years of running the Goon's errands were paying off, though not in the way he'd expected. He'd thought by getting in good with the Goon, that would translate to the Lady, but now he saw that he'd picked the wrong horse. But he could amend that mistake. No one in Varna would miss the Goon when he was gone.

First out, he thought to himself.

He thought about the spells he knew that could free him—the Academy placed a premium on teaching methods of escape—but he needed both hands to remove the gag from his mouth and then for the spell. Clearly the Goon had done his homework.

Zayn reached to the imbuement and was rewarded with a surge of energy. He wanted to rip himself from the wall in one rage-filled effort, but that would shred his skin and he'd probably bleed out before he could reach the Goon.

Left or right? he thought.

He decided on the right, since he was better with his left hand.

Zayn focused his energy into his right hand. He knew he had to break free the first time, because the damage to his hand would only make it worse on subsequent attempts.

With a grunt, Zayn pulled his hand and arm from the wall. He strained, the razor-sharp screws pressing into his flesh, tearing skin straight to the bone. But the clamps weren't budging. He feared the Goon had reinforced them with runes, because of course he would know about the Academy imbuements. Zayn almost gave up, but he knew if he did, he wouldn't get out, so he kept going.

A muffled cry erupted from behind the gag as he yanked his arm from the wall. When it came free, he blacked out from the pain.

As soon as consciousness returned, the agony of his fingers, wrists, and biceps torn to shreds pounded him. His hand was wet with blood. The screw in the wrist had torn too deeply. He would bleed out if he couldn't get free enough to stop the bleeding.

Using his right hand, Zayn grabbed the clamp around his midsection and yanked. Pulling it away from the wall was easier than he thought. This gave him enough reach to get to his left arm, and it was free within another half minute.

The first thing he did was wrap his shirt around his wrist to stem the bleeding. The spells he knew wouldn't fix a wound that deep, and Zayn was afraid the Goon had magic detectors in the room.

Then he removed the gag from his mouth. It tasted like petroleum, so he spit a few times to clear it away.

To his surprise, the door was unlocked. He found himself in an unfamiliar hallway with framed pictures of basketball stars. In his years of working for the Goon, he'd never been allowed downstairs, so he didn't know the way out.

He went looking for an exit, freezing when he heard a low growl from behind him.

Zayn turned in time for Jordan and Barkley, the Goon's bluetick hounds, to tackle him to the floor and lick his face and wounds.

"Hey, you two," whispered Zayn. "I appreciate the greeting, but I need you to be quiet."

Jordan looked up at him with his black eyes and gave a whine of understanding. The hounds sensed that something was wrong.

He led them back to a room at the end of the hall where they'd been sleeping. His stomach turned when he saw the stainless steel medical table and rows of sharp instruments. The table had leather clamps to keep someone tied to the table. The floor was concrete, and there was a drain in the corner along with a hose for washing fluids away.

Before he closed the door on the hounds, Zayn grabbed a scalpel. He found the stairs going up.

He didn't know how long he'd been out, but it appeared it was still nighttime. It sounded like the Goon and Levi were gathering supplies. He couldn't tell for sure where they were, so he stayed in the stairwell.

Zayn assumed they had guns and while he was quick with a spell, a bullet was faster. He was going to have to do this the slow and silent way.

Thankful that the Goon had built his house like a bunker, using concrete and reinforced flooring, Zayn confidently moved through the living room without fear of a squeaky board. He considered sneaking out the front door, but the Goon had cameras and would likely see him in the yard. Then he'd hunt him down with weapons before he could make it back to the Stack.

He found the workshop empty. There were no guns lying around, so Zayn slipped behind the curtain over the firing range. He waited with the scalpel in hand like a trap-door spider ready to lunge out.

"We'll hit the trailer first," said the Goon in another room. "Need to make sure we've got the other boy before we hit the Stack. He's the one we have to worry about now."

"We gonna take him captive like the others?" asked Levi from what sounded like the living room. He could hear gear being stacked in a pile.

"No," said the Goon. "I don't want to take chances with him. With a year of Academy training those boys are dangerous enough, and Keelan's not going to hesitate to fight back. We're going to burn the trailer down with the both of them in it. I'll flood it with knockout gas first."

Zayn squeezed the blade of the scalpel harder. He wanted to plunge it into the Goon's eye.

"What was that?" Levi called out.

"You hear something?"

"Something in the back of the house, sounded like something got knocked over," said Levi.

"You check it out," said the Goon. "I'm gonna make sure Zayn's where I left him."

Zayn froze. No one knew he was here, which meant if someone was sneaking into the compound, it was probably the Watchers. This complicated things as it would have been better if he'd stayed captured below. Maybe he could sneak out in the chaos, though that was doubtful given the Watchers were all Academy trained and enhanced by whatever magics the Lady employed.

He peeked from behind the curtain at the same time he heard a shout from below.

"He's gone! Search the compound, shoot on sight," echoed the Goon's voice from below.

From the living room, Zayn heard something being picked up. He slipped behind the curtain as Levi came into the room. Zayn listened for the sound of Levi's steps to near the gun range.

Levi stopped about five feet from the curtain, to his right, so Zayn couldn't reach directly out.

Zayn took a steadying breath and prepared to burst through the curtain. Before he could make his move, a gun went off. In the small space, the shot startled Zayn into indecision. Levi was running out of the room as Zayn slipped from behind the curtain.

Two more gunshots went off in the next room over. Zayn rushed to the corner. If he was caught across the room, they could fire on him with impunity.

When he peeked around the corner, he was shocked to see Keelan standing in the hallway.

Zayn waved at him, but Keelan ignored him and kept creeping towards the stairs that went below.

"Keelan," hissed Zayn, trying to stop him from running right into the Goon.

When he heard Levi coming around from the back, trapping Keelan, Zayn ran back around and into the living room.

Levi saw him first. The blast ripped a hole in the wall, right where Zayn had been standing before he dove. From the kneeling position, Zayn fired a force bolt that glanced off Levi, knocking his arm into the air.

Zayn rushed Levi before he could get his gun back down, stabbing him right in the neck and driving him back against the wall. Levi went limp in his arms, his eyes rolling back in his head as he dropped the gun.

The bloody scalpel slipped out of Zayn's hand as he stared at the motionless body. He'd killed a man. Every bit of him screamed that Levi had deserved it. He'd strangled Katie in her flat, an experience so horrifying it'd scarred her spirit.

His heart thumped in his ears. His face went numb. Priyanka had warned them on their first day that eventually they would have to kill someone. He hadn't expected it to happen in his first year. What right did he have to take someone else's life? Even if it was someone horrible.

"Don't you move," said the Goon from the hallway between the stairs and the arcade room. He'd lost his straw hat. His gun was pointed at Zayn as his eyes flitted to the fallen Levi.

"I never really did like him," said the Goon.

"He killed my friend," said Zayn.

"And you got your revenge. At least you got that much before your end." The Goon turned his head and shouted. "I got your cousin dead to rights. Come out, Keelan, or I'll put a bullet in his brain."

Zayn couldn't hear Keelan, but he knew he had to be creeping around somewhere near.

"You know I really never liked you," said Zayn, hoping to distract the Goon. "I always planned on betraying you to the Lady."

Minus his straw hat, the Goon looked like he was in his eighties.

"I suspected as much," said the Goon. "I should have known when you betrayed me the first chance you got and killed you right there. Your body would be rotting in the city landfill and I wouldn't be in this mess."

"Even if that had happened, you'd still screw up eventually and the Lady would come for you. Sooner or later," said Zayn.

"You sound like you like her," said the Goon, chuckling.

"Not in the least bit. Her day will come," said Zayn.

"But not by you," replied the Goon. "Come out, Keelan. You got five seconds before I ace your cousin. One. Two. Three. Four."

As the Goon's lips started to form the last number, Keelan rushed up the stairs. The Goon spun, firing point-blank into his chest. There was no way he'd survive.

As the Goon's bullet ripped through his cousin, Zayn fired a force bolt into his back, knocking him forward.

With a cry on his lips, Zayn leapt up to finish off the Goon, when he realized Keelan was no longer on the stairs. His surprise was doubled when his cousin burst from the arcade room and jammed a bowie knife into the Goon's chest, pinning him to the floor.

Then standing over him, Keelan spit on the Goon's face as he rasped, blood bubbling from his lips. Keelan had used an illusion to fool the Goon.

"I thought you were dead," said Zayn.

"You should have told me," said Keelan, eyes dark with killing.

"Told you what?"

"That you weren't really working for the Goon," said Keelan.

"I did, sort of, years ago," said Zayn.

Keelan shook his head. "I guess I didn't believe you."

"Thanks for having my back. You followed me when I left the Stack," said Zayn.

"You move like an elephant carrying a carnival," said Keelan with a wry smile. "What now?"

"We call the sheriff. Let the Lady and her ilk sort this out," said Zayn.

Keelan had a strange look in his eyes, but he nodded. Zayn called 911. It took a half hour before all the cars showed up.

Sheriff Clovis was the first to arrive since he lived the closest. He ducked through the front door with a look of disappointment on his face when he saw them sitting on the couch.

"What have you two gotten yourselves into?" said the sheriff.

After a deputy wrapped a bandage around Zayn's wounds, he patiently explained what had happened, including the drug and its connection to the Lady. The sheriff asked a few questions, but otherwise nodded along.

"You should have called me first," said the sheriff.

"They would have killed him before you got here," said Keelan, nodding towards Zayn.

The sheriff shook his head and paced away. "While I appreciate you boys knocking the shine from his treachery, I'm sure the Lady would have preferred to kill him herself, at her leisure. Who was the one to do the deed? She'll want to personally thank you."

"It was me," said Keelan, before Zayn could say otherwise.

"That true?" asked the sheriff.

Zayn nodded, though he wasn't happy about the credit going to Keelan. He needed it to get close to the Lady. "Yes."

The sheriff had a deputy take them back to the Stack, which came as the sun crested the horizon. They were subjected to another round of questioning from his parents, to whom they gave the minimum of answers to keep them from knowing too much.

When they finally let him retire to his room, despite the bone-weary exhaustion, Zayn lay awake for hours because every time he tried to close his eyes, he saw Levi's look of shock as the scalpel went into his neck.

Chapter Forty-Seven
Varna, June 2014
Visiting an empty grave

Zayn had never been bothered by walking through the Varna Cemetery, but as he made his way across the manicured lawns, he kept expecting a hand to grab his ankle in retribution for what he'd done. It didn't matter that Levi wasn't from Varna, and it was unlikely his death had created a ghost, but Zayn felt uneasy just the same.

It was as if he'd crossed a line that allowed the dead to reach him. He'd always wondered why killers often confessed their crimes, even when they'd gotten away cleanly, but knowing that Levi—however flawed a person he was—no longer existed because of him weighed him with guilt.

He found Keelan by his father's grave, hands in his pockets, shoulders hunched. Zayn cleared his throat as he approached to let his cousin know he was there. Keelan hastily wiped his eyes before Zayn made it to the grave.

Zayn took one look at his cousin and knew what he was thinking.

"This is the first time you've come here, isn't it?" asked Zayn.

Keelan squirmed as if someone were squeezing him tight.

"I couldn't forgive him before," said Keelan.

"And you can now?" asked Zayn.

"I don't know. I don't know if I'm ever going to be capable of that, after what he did," said Keelan.

His cousin had spent many sleepovers angry about how his dad had abandoned him by getting killed.

"Did the Lady tell you something about him?" asked Zayn.

Keelan flinched when he looked him in the eyes. "I didn't meet her. Just the Speaker. We had lunch. With tea and cake afterwards."

"Talk about anything?" asked Zayn.

Keelan shrugged. "Nothing in particular, though it felt like it was an interview, a strange one at that."

Zayn's insides twisted with regret. It was supposed to be him that curried the Lady's favor, not his cousin. Zayn hoped it worked out.

"Why are you here?"

Keelan swallowed hard. "You know why."

Zayn looked at his own sneakers. "I didn't expect to feel so guilty about killing someone that probably deserved it."

"I didn't know the Goon, but I knew he didn't like me," said Keelan. "Still, I didn't like killing him. It didn't feel like it was my right."

Zayn felt better that his cousin had remorse for the killing. When they arrived at the Halls, he'd worried that Keelan's past was his future. But it was clear he could change, they both could.

"I don't think we should ever get used to it," said Zayn. "Even if it's our job. Even if it's the right thing to do."

Keelan gave him a look that made him feel naive. His eyebrow arched questioningly.

"I don't regret joining the Halls, if that's what you're

implying," said Zayn.

Keelan put a reassuring hand on Zayn's shoulder. "It's cool, cuz. 'Cause we made it. We survived our first year. I heard it's the hardest one."

"Yeah," said Zayn. "The hardest one. That sounds good."

His cousin chuckled under his breath. "Yeah, I don't believe it either. But that's okay as long as we're in the Academy together."

As Zayn stood with his cousin at his uncle's grave, contemplating the events of the last year, he found a strange optimism buoying him. He knew it was more than likely that one or the both of them wouldn't survive their five years at the Academy, and he knew that even if they did, they'd be faced with servitude to the Lady for the rest of their days. Despite the overwhelming odds that everything would end in tragedy, Zayn knew that to resist at all was worth whatever price he would have to pay, and if there was even a chance, however remote, that he could end the Lady's hold on Varna, he would take it.

"I know the answer now," said Zayn, all of a sudden.

Keelan tilted his head. "To what?"

"Priyanka's question."

Keelan paused for a moment before he repeated what she'd said. "What will you do when you have to kill?"

Zayn left Keelan by his father's grave.

§ § §

Read the next book in the The Reluctant Assassin Series

THE SORCEROUS SPY

October 2018

Also by Thomas K. Carpenter

HUNDRED HALLS UNIVERSE

THE HUNDRED HALLS
Trials of Magic
Web of Lies
Alchemy of Souls
Gathering of Shadows

City of Sorcery

THE RELUCTANT ASSASSIN
The Reluctant Assassin
The Sorcerous Spy
The Veiled Diplomat
Agent Unraveled
The Webs That Bind

OTHER SERIES

ALEXANDRIAN SAGA
Fires of Alexandria
Heirs of Alexandria
Legacy of Alexandria
Warmachines of Alexandria
Empire of Alexandria
Voyage of Alexandria
Goddess of Alexandria

GAMERS TRILOGY
GAMERS
FRAGS
CODERS

Special Thanks

As always, Rachel, the love of my life (I can't believe we've been married twenty-one years, what fun!) is my first reader and content editor. If my stories have any heart in them, or the right amount of clever plotting, it's because of her. Tamara Blain, my line and copyeditor, makes my prose sing and keeps me from embarrassing myself from hilarious wrong word choices. Ravven makes the best covers: I've lost count how many people have been introduced to my fiction because of her art.

This series wouldn't be the same, nor as successful, without the advice and friendship of my fellow writers: Annie Bellet, Marina J. Lostetter, Anthea Lawson, Tina Smith, Andrea Stewart, Megan O'Keefe, and Karen Rocknik. And most importantly, we survived the Murder Cabin, though we never did figure out what was behind that secret door.

No book survives first contact with a beta reader, and this fabulous group helped me make sure that *The Reluctant Assassin* was the best possible story it could be. So thank you: Tina Rak, Patty Eversole, Carole Carpenter, Kurt Pankau, Christie Cassina, Jason Holschen, Brian Botkin, Kathryn Zychinski, Sam Wade, and Jan Carpenter. And last, but not least, the excellent members of the Vanguard— my advanced reader team—who catch those last gremlins in the manuscript, members like Jess Churchill, Lana Turner, Alyssa Washburn, Paula J. Fletcher, Elaine Stoker, Thad Moody, Andie Alessandra Cáomhanach, and Laura Coffing. And to most of all, my readers, who I get to share my stories with. Thank you. Thank you, all.

ABOUT THE AUTHOR

Thomas K. Carpenter resides near St. Louis with his wife Rachel and their two children. When he's not busy writing his next book, he's playing soccer in the yard with his kids or getting beat by his wife at cards. He keeps a regular blog at www.thomaskcarpenter.com and you can follow him on twitter @thomaskcarpente. If you want to learn when his next novel will be hitting the shelves and get free stories and occasional other goodies, please sign up for his mailing list by going to: http://tinyurl.com/thomaskcarpenter. Your email address will never be shared and you can unsubscribe at any time.

Made in United States
Orlando, FL
25 July 2024

49535026R00186